continued . . .

"Another rousing success. . . . Knight brilliantly continues world building on a monumental scale, while adding complexity to the personality of his multifaceted main character, Major David Valentine. . . . E. E. Knight is uncompromising in detail and continues to present a picture of a world that is both believable [and] frighteningly plausible. He molds and develops characters that are sympathetic, layered, and mysteriously familiar. Valentine, the main protagonist, is compelling on so many levels, and has grown steadily from novel to novel. Eight books in and I still want to spend precious time reading about his further adventures."   —BSCreview

Fall with Honor

"The action is riveting as the increasingly complex story line unfolds in a smoothly told yet terrifying look at the future."   —Monsters and Critics

"Action-heavy."   —Publishers Weekly

"Knight is a master of description and tension."
          —Black Gate

Valentine's Resolve

"Knight flavors action with humor in [Valentine's Resolve]. . . . Classic apocalyptic SF on a grand scale is always scary, but Knight makes it terrifically entertaining as well."   —Publishers Weekly

"Another winning installment of horror and breathless battles. . . . Knight has managed to write a book six that keeps fans thirsting for more in the series. . . . [He] maintains a tight point of view, controls scene transitions beautifully, and never wavers in tone. His main character, David Valentine, keeps readers coming back for more."
          —Science Fiction Weekly

Valentine's Exile

"Compelling pulp adventure. . . . The sympathetic hero, fast-paced action, and an intricately detailed milieu set in various well-imagined regions of twenty-first-century North America make for an entertaining read."
          —Publishers Weekly (starred review)

"*Valentine's Exile* isn't an average vampire novel. . . . The vampires and their soul-sucking Lovecraftian masters are like Dr. Moreau on steroids. . . . E. E. Knight is a master of his craft. His prose is controlled but interesting, and his characters are fully formed and come to life. . . . E. E. Knight's work is creative and the voice is his own."
—Science Fiction Weekly

MORE PRAISE FOR THE NOVELS
OF *THE VAMPIRE EARTH*

"I have no doubt that E. E. Knight is going to be a household name in the genre."   —Silver Oak

"A winner. If you're going to read only one more post-apocalyptic novel, make it this one."
—Fred Saberhagen, author of the Berserker series

"Gritty realism, Lovecraftian villains, and boffo action scenes."
—S. M. Stirling, *New York Times* bestselling
author of *The Golden Princess*

"Evocative of Richard Matheson as well as Howard Hawks, Knight's terrifying future world is an epic canvas on which he paints a tale of human courage, heroism, and, yes, even love."
—Jay Bonansinga, *New York Times* bestselling
coauthor of *The Walking Dead: Rise of The Governor*

"Knight is a master of description and tension . . . character-driven speculative fiction adventure at its very best."   —*Black Gate*

"Knight's style made me think that if *The Red Badge of Courage* had been written by H. P. Lovecraft, the result would have been something like this."
—Paul Witcover, author of *Dracula: Asylum*

"An entertaining romp rife with plausible characters; powerful, frightening villains; suspense; romance; and monsters; everything good fantasy and science fiction should have."   —SFFWorld

"I dare you to try to stop reading this exciting tale."
—SF Reviews

"Impressive . . . sure to delight all fans of dark fantasy and hair-raising heroic adventure . . . unique and wonderfully entertaining."   —Rambles

Books by E. E. Knight

The Vampire Earth Series
Way of the Wolf
Choice of the Cat
Tale of the Thunderbolt
Valentine's Rising
Valentine's Exile
Valentine's Resolve
Fall with Honor
Winter Duty
March in Country
Appalachian Overthrow
Baltic Gambit

The Age of Fire Series
Dragon Champion
Dragon Avenger
Dragon Outcast
Dragon Strike
Dragon Rule
Dragon Fate

BALTIC GAMBIT

A NOVEL OF
THE VAMPIRE EARTH

E. E. KNIGHT

A ROC BOOK

ROC
Published by the Penguin Group
Penguin Group (USA) LLC, 375 Hudson Street,
New York, New York 10014

USA | Canada | UK | Ireland | Australia | New Zealand | India | South Africa | China
penguin.com
A Penguin Random House Company

Published by Roc, an imprint of New American Library, a division of Penguin Group (USA) LLC. Previously published in a Roc hardcover edition.

First Roc Mass Market Printing, April 2015

 REGISTERED TRADEMARK—MARCA REGISTRADA

ISBN 978-0-451-41447-2

Printed in the United States of America
10 9 8 7 6 5 4 3 2 1

For Silas,
and all the other little ones who are too young
to even know how brave they really are

The cure for anything is salt water—sweat, tears, or the sea.

—Isak Dinesen

In revenge and in love woman is more barbarous than man.

—Friedrich Nietzsche, *Beyond Good and Evil*
(Apophthegms and Interludes)

CHAPTER ONE

*T*he Hub, April, the fifty-sixth year of the Kurian Order: A new military nerve center is growing in the sleepy old resort town of French Lick, Indiana. The roads have been cleared, the rail line up to Indianapolis reopened, and even the tiny airport has a new wind sock, camouflage hangars, and a generator.

It's a well-chosen spot. Beneath the layers of dirt and rust, the town is something of a gem in a tarnished setting.

French Lick in its Gilded Age heyday saw multiple trains daily from Chicago bringing city folk to its two huge resort hotels in the woods of Southern Indiana. It once was the seat of smoky back rooms where political prospects were reviewed and selected by the parties. Franklin Delano Roosevelt was the last of the breed, chosen in this corner of Indiana in one of the conference rooms of the older of the two vast hotels.

The popularity of the resort waned during the Interstate Age, but the second Gilded Age of the late twentieth century saw the two big old hotels restored to their former glory, especially the cavernous, cream-colored West Baden Springs resort with its huge indoor rotunda. The natural beauty of the Hoosier National Forest had not changed.

French Lick had a role to play in the chaos of 2022. During the last days of the United States government in its brief move to Indianapolis, the Kurian Order and its new adherents maintained a headquarters there, briefly, for the fighting that broke up what was left of U.S. civil authority. After that, the Grog armies moved on west to St. Louis, and the Kurian Order returned to the East to make use of the long-established institutions of government and education near the Atlantic Coast. With no more tourists, French Lick quieted again, save for a small training headquarters eventually established by the Northwest Ordnance, the premier Kurian Zone of the old Rust Belt stretching west from Pittsburgh and Cleveland, through Michigan and Indiana, to the borders of Chicago and the huge patch of still-productive farmland in Central Illinois.

With a thriving new freehold in Kentucky and its attached nub at Evansville threatening the Ordnance, the vast Southern corporate state known as the Georgia Control, and potentially the patchwork of Kurian ganglia on the East Coast, something had to be done.

A third try is inevitable.

"I've heard we Cats have nine lives," Alessa Duvalier said, waiting for the dusk to deepen. "I've never known one to get past the first."

The freckled redhead was talking to herself, as people who spend the better parts of their waking hours outside and alone often do.

It was a way to handle the fear, to vent it like a waiting steam engine releasing pressure. In this particular time and place, any emotion was dangerous, and fear was probably the worst of all. The Reapers would pick up on it as easily as the soldiers would see her setting off Roman candles on the hillside.

She'd learned over the years to cauterize her emotions on the job. No matter what she saw, heard, or guessed was going on around her, she couldn't let it in.

The problem was, it had to go somewhere. Emotion was a funny thing. You could suppress one, but the pressure built up anyway and came out as another, say with hatred converting itself to an inappropriate laugh, or anxiety to a nervous tic. You could get rid of a little by talking it out with yourself, but only a little.

With her, the excess always seemed to pour into her stomach. She had a bad gut, undoubtedly ulcerous, but in her line of work chances were that she wouldn't live to suffer from it in middle age and beyond.

Opening and shutting her hands and flexing her thighs and calves in her belly-down position in a patch of liverwort beneath a thick stand of mountain laurel, she ignored her sour stomach and the occasional vile-tasting burp and contemplated the aging opulence of the resort beneath. Someone had put some serious money into this patch of hilly, heavily wooded nowhere. A local goat rancher had told her that it was the waters—they were once reputed to have healing potential and to be something of a cure-all.

She'd tried it. There were several out-of-the way natural springs in the hills. Apart from a silky tang like Epsom salts, she didn't see what was so special about the water, other than it had made her void her bowels three times in the subsequent twenty-four hours. Her gut felt about the same as it always did, sour with a little stab now and then, as though it was afraid she'd forget about it.

So, the poopy water caused a pair of behemoth hotels to be built. You couldn't fault the setting, a nice stretch of flatter land for golf courses and tennis courts surrounded by higher, but hardly mountainous, hills. It made for pleasant hiking. She sometimes wished she'd lived in an era when the big challenge of your day was a tennis game. Screw the Kurian propaganda spouted by the churches; any culture that can solve so many problems that you have time for the frivolous work of improving your backswing or whatever it is called is admirable.

Naturally cautious, she was ready to bag the idea of stealing into the hotel. Usually, she'd look at a place this big and dance a little jig—the larger the location, the easier it was to find a weak spot to penetrate. This hotel, however, had multiple rings of security—outer patrols on horseback, ATV, and foot accompanied by dogs, then an inner ring on the grounds checking both the outer patrols and a final layer at the entrances. All the lower-floor windows were bricked up with heavy-duty glass blocks. Vehicles were being searched at the main gate at the highway and there were temporary (by the look of the fencing) dog runs between the entrances just in case someone decided to try a climb to the roof or an upper floor.

Short of parachuting in or finding an unguarded secret entrance, she didn't see how she could do it.

Five grueling days ago Evansville's defense and security staff had received a tip through a chain of family relations, it seemed, that something big was up at French Lick.

Hitching a ride with one of the Evansville militia who owned a motorcycle and a sidecar, she and a Wolf named Clay hurried over a mix of defunct roads and smugglers' trails into South-Central Indiana to check out the story. Southern Command's forces at Fort Seng, just across the river from Evansville, went on the alert as she left, and were making preparations for moving a mechanized strike team.

That was the advantage of an independent brigade with an aggressive officer in command. Colonel Lambert got Fort Seng up and moving fast.

After mapping a route and leaving the Wolf with his pack radio back at a base camp on the other side of the old Hoosier National Forest, she penetrated the "base" to see what she could through her old pair of mini-binoculars from the hills.

Something was definitely up. It was at the bigger of the two mammoth resort hotels, a round white thing built around what she guessed was some kind of spectacular dome.

Intelligence did not have a lot of information on French Lick. The round white resort was a recuperative hotel for wounded who needed longer recoveries or adjustments to artificial limbs and so on. The one a little south on the road was allegedly a retirement home for military personnel, run by the New Universal Church. Like most institutions devoted to the elderly, it was a fiction, with the majority of the aged given a few weeks to settle in and relax, with a series of snapshots taken to send to the relatives back home before a death from a food-poisoning incident or a flu outbreak would be regretfully announced—just enough messy detail to let others delude themselves into thinking that the pensioner hadn't had a last dance in the arms of a Reaper.

She'd learned a few things observing the hotel. She got a sense of its rhythms, where people would be, doing what, and when.

At night the huge rotunda of the hotel was lighted up like a Christmas party. Massive amounts of food were brought in, for two hundred people or more. The old hotel hadn't seen that many rooms occupied in eighty years. From what she'd been able to observe, it wasn't the usual Quisling high command work-hard-and-sneak-in-some-play conference, either. The only women she'd seen brought in were in uniform or had the look of professionals and a spouse or two in riding clothes for the hotel barn to the northeast. Back when she was scouting Texas or Kansas or Tennessee, with this many high-ranking Quislings they would have been bringing in sexual entertainment by the busload.

There was a time when her path inside would have been to pose as one of the hookers. She doubted she could turn the trick, so to speak, these days. Too many miles in too much weather without enough food. She wasn't a sleek, youthful Cat anymore; now she was more like a rangy, bug-bitten feral. A man would have to be very, very desperate to risk his job security and his life over an aging specimen such as her. She'd always played down her looks, but now that they'd faded like dried flower petals, she missed them, just a bit.

But what youth and beauty couldn't achieve, age and experience could. The latter were more reliable anyway, and they didn't make her feel like a trollop. Might as well chance getting a little closer.

She wiggled another fifty or sixty feet down the slope just to the northwest of the hotel and paused where she could make out an Ordnance Army sign stenciled in white at the parking lot:

ORD AF 3RD TRAINING BATTALION VS-LSH

She had a better vantage on the parking lot now. Yes, something big must be going on inside. There were mobile communication trucks with strange little antennae that reminded her of the rack on a charcoal grill or xylophones.

There were all sorts of vehicles here parked in the lot or on the grass, even command cars and escort vehicles with markings she didn't recognize. The Ordnance and the Georgia Control were here in force, the pierced crescent of the Moondaggers, but there were a couple of other symbols—a Roman-looking eagle and something that resembled the twisted serpents and staff of the old caduceus, and a pyramid with an eye atop it not that different from the one that appeared on old U.S. currency. She committed them to memory; she could always pick them out of one of the intelligence ledgers later.

The lights inside the hotel flickered and she heard a throaty roar as an up-on-blocks trailer serving as an emergency generator kicked on. They probably had a salvaged generator from a diesel train or two ready to go for just such a contingency.

"Hmmmmmmmm," she said to herself. Indiana's more-promise-than-lick rural electricity must have choked. She reached into one of the capacious pockets of the mottled old duster she wore in the field and extracted a piece of dried meat.

Ruminating, you might call it. She tore off a hunk and chewed vigorously. One had to have a good set of teeth and strong jaws to handle Kentucky jerky. There might be a little beef or pork in there for flavor, but it was undoubtedly legworm flesh, as sure as Spam came in a can with its own opener.

A couple of soldiers in Ordnance uniform trotted out to the generator trailer and climbed inside. She traced the wire running to the hotel's green-painted substation, artfully hidden by shrubbery.

She reached for her sword hilt before knowing why. Peripheral vision had triggered nerve synapses—

Almost seven feet of walking, robed death came out of the hotel's rear entrance and headed for the generator trailer. Even at this distance it was unmistakable. The Reaper paused and slowly surveyed the western hills overlooking the hotel. Duvalier dropped into her usual koan that reduced mental activity to the point where, hopefully, the Reaper wouldn't sense her mental and emotional activity—"lifesign," she'd learned to call it, but God knows what the Kurians thought of it as. She always pictured a dark beach, only the stars above glittering in the milk-warm air, and her sitting on the sand. It was half memory, half fantasy with her ever since she'd spent the night on a beach like that while visiting the Texas coast. All she'd done was mentally edit out all the garbage that the tide had thrown up to litter the beach. Her mental camera concentrated on her toes, then her whole body, and back and back it pulled across the beach, reducing the image of her until she was lost in the gentle surf.

The koan also had the practical effect of relaxing her, so if she had to she could go into action loose, with sure and steady hands.

A Reaper meant a Kurian. With these woods and hills, it had to be nearby. Probably in the hotel—nothing else in the area matched its level of security.

If a Kurian were here overseeing his generals, it was just possible that there would be other Kurians in attendance. Was the alliance already settled, and this conference was just to hammer out the details? Or were they still determining who would do what in joint action against Kentucky in the future? If it were the latter, there might be a party of Kurians keeping an eye, or whatever sensory node the Kurians used to keep from getting consumed by their cousins, on their generals. They'd also want to make sure rival rulers weren't offering deals to the Quislings that might put them at a disadvantage.

That was their weakness. Time would tell if it was fatal. If the Kurians had shown any ability to work together, they would have subjugated humanity as easily as humans controlled life and death in a chicken coop.

That might explain all the security. Even air had some difficulty getting in, judging from the guards on the roof near the rust-streaked, multi-ton HVAC units.

Security might keep her out, or if it didn't keep her out, find her once she made it inside the hotel.

She thought about calling in the cavalry. A single Reaper was a factoid. Intriguing, and further confirmation that something major was in the works here, but she wanted evidence before making a case that the disheveled elegance of the French Lick resort was worth the fight. Maybe they were only deciding on a new communications network or, given the problems with the electricity, establishing a new national grid for the Eastern Kurian Zones. Shooting it up would bring a world of hurt down on the assault force. They'd be lucky to make it back across the Ohio even if they scattered into small parties.

No, she couldn't ask men to die on a hunch.

Full dark came on and the insects filled the night with their signaling. Eating and sex. She knew the Kurians ate. How did they reproduce? Maybe the meeting was just a big insemination (or whatever they did) party to produce a new generation. It would be funny to tell the Bears they had to shoot up an orgy.

The "doughnut" part of the hotel glowed like hot embers.

"Lit up like Christmas," she said, taking a handful of Indiana mud and generously coating her face. They must have no shortage of diesel oil for the generator. The inner ring of security would have their night vision compromised by the hotel's lighting. Dogs wouldn't be fooled, but dogs were at their most useful when they knew what they were looking for. She'd had dogs practically step over her only to whine and lunge at night-feeding rabbits.

She worked her way around to the west entrance, cradling her old, seemingly gnarled sword-stick. The two men at the door looked solemnly alert. A broad patio almost encircled the round part of the hotel. Soldiers were standing and smoking. Perhaps she could try there.

Sliding from patch of growth to pile of broken tile to heap of cleared growth—they had spruced up the hotel for the conference, it seemed—she drew close enough to distinguish the facial hair on the guards.

Fading back into the hillside, step by careful step she headed for the lower lands south of the hotel. The wide road running up to the parking entrance divided the hotel from a rather overgrown garden and some kind of outbuildings that had trees growing out the broken windows. The garden smelled like sweet rot, and she instantly identified the smell of death.

She crossed the road with an easy stride, hoping that she would be seen only at a distance and mistaken for someone with business at the hotel, then quickly took shelter beneath a picturesque bench ringing an oak. None of the men on the porch gave any indication that they'd seen her; their eyes were light-blinded.

A crunching step approached. Heavy boots with

the measured tread of a cop walking his beat. Her back burned with the fear of a Reaper, but she glanced up and saw a mustachioed face. A Reaper could no more grow a beard than achieve an erection. Probably a southerner, then. Ordnance soldiers were almost all clean-shaven.

He glanced at the men on the balcony, unzipped, and urinated on a tree root extending from beneath the bench. He whistled a non-tune as he did so, sounding more like he was trying to entertain a bird than form music. She kept her face buried in the soil, feeling the warm splatter strike her hair.

She heard a sharp intake of breath. She looked up and saw the surprise and embarrassment in his eyes.

"It's all right," she said. "Warmest I've been all night."

Rolling and lashing up, she caught him with the handle of her sword-stick in the solar plexus. His breath came out with a whoosh as muscles involuntarily contracted. So much for a scream for help.

Not wanting blood, she rose and struck again, this time across the back of his neck. That put him on the ground, giving her a moment to unloop the nylon cord around her wrist, slide its falsely decorative beads out of the way, and finish him quietly by strangulation.

Sorry, sport, she thought. *Shit luck for both of us.*

She heard laughter from the balcony.

Some of her clan relished swapping stories of Kurian atrocities. They tried to convince one another that their victims deserved their fate, that justice was being done. She held to no such illusions. The moment he saw her it was her life or his, and she intended to keep on living—at least through the death of another Kurian or two.

If she just left the body there, it would be a fine starting point for trackers.

With an effort, she lifted him into a fireman's carry and tottered across the road, as far outside the paired decorative streetlamps as she could manage. She staggered to the hedges surrounding the outbuilding.

She followed her nose to the death smell. It was strong . . . and she was approaching it from upwind.

She burst through a hedge and almost fell into a long trench. The bottom was lined with bled-out bodies, mostly older specimens. She saw a half-closed stomach scar on one younger specimen—the victim of a botched operation, it seemed. All the bodies near her except the one with the cut above the appendix bore the distinctive tongue marks of a Reaper at the base of the neck or in the upper rib cage.

"Holy mother—," she began, then clamped her hand over her mouth and nose.

She set the body down as quietly as she could.

A growl sounded from the hedge line behind her. She froze, searched out of the corner of her eye.

A dog and a handler stood thirty feet away, peering into the darkness. The dog was alert to her, but the handler couldn't see her in the night shadow.

She flowed down into the body pit at the speed of molasses running on a hot day. The dog whined and pulled.

The bodies were soft and rotting.

The handler raised a flashlight and cast the beam of light carefully into the darkness where she'd been squatting a moment before. She pulled her sword-stick tight into the crook of her arm and covered it with the withered leg of an old man. He had bristly hair.

The beam of light passed over her, resting on her breast for just a moment. In the glare, her own healthy flesh wouldn't be markedly different from the flesh of the bodies.

The dog padded forward, leading the man holding its leash. It sniffed about and snorted in disgust.

The body of the guard she'd dropped drew the handler, following the beam of his flashlight, which had caught the Ordnance insignia, a sort of elongated pentagon—a stylized capital "O."

Slithering with sword-stick cradled, she approached across the bodies. The corpses made noises like sponges.

The handler drew something shiny from his pocket, attached to a short lanyard. A whistle. Its sound could carry a mile or more.

She sprang upward, drawing her blade from the stick. "Help me!"

Arms out and open as though pleading, or rushing to embrace him, she ran forward.

He was having none of it. He put the whistle to his lips—

But no air would enter it. She'd opened his throat at the center of his Adam's apple, the blade slicing as neatly through the nylon cord of the whistle's lanyard as it did the cartilage and tissue of his neck.

He toppled, a confused look frozen on his face.

"Hssssss!" she hissed at the dog. It ran toward the outbuildings, dragging its leash.

Even better, she thought grimly as she hid the bodies under layers of Reaper waste. *One dead or missing man would inspire a careful search. Two would be enough of a mystery that the search would concentrate on the missing men rather than a wiry, scuffed-up redhead.*

She retrieved her pack from her cache on the hillside and put as much timber and earth as she could between herself and the Kurians.

She dug a shallow pit with her folding camp shovel and surrounded it with the flattest rocks she could take from a watercourse. She set her sole tin pot atop it and started boiling the beans she'd been soaking. It wasn't an ideal stove, but just as practical as a campfire, and you could see the flicker of flame only by standing over it.

With a little wild mushroom, her beans, honey, and a piece of bacon for flavor it made a decent stew.

A familiar soft step crept up on her campsite.

"You didn't see the fire, did you?" she asked.

"Smelled your stew," said Clay, the Wolf who'd crossed the Hoosier forest with her two days ago. "Why aren't you camping at our rendezvous?"

"I did check it—through my optics. You must have been away. I didn't remain. Left you a note in the drop that I'd check back for you or another note. If a Reaper grabbed you and started removing digits, there might be a little welcoming party at the spot."

"The idea doesn't seem to bother you that much," Clay said. Poor kid. He'd been a little squirrely ever since they woke snuggled up to each other against the night's spring chill. He'd brushed her breast, pretending it was an accident. When she didn't respond, he didn't press the matter, thank heaven.

Silly. She didn't do recreational sex, not on a job, not with a comrade. She'd fucked and sucked her way into a few headquarters and pass-only Quisling "Green Zones," but that was business, not distraction.

The Wolf was just a kid. But then, most of them looked like kids to her these days. God, she wasn't even that old, just into her thirties.

She liked Wolves. They used their eyes, ears, and noses, and fought only when they had no choice, or a strong advantage. They could run all day on a few mouthfuls of porridge.

Wolves listened to reason. Bears did whatever the fuck would lead to the most blood.

She let the kid finish and light his pipe. He looked like a boy playing with his father's tobacco stand. The pipe had a long plastic stem and the bowl was a rather elegantly carved animal face that she supposed was meant to be a fox; the snout was way too narrow and the ears too wide to be a wolf. The tobacco was rather noxious cheap Kurian Zone ration compared to the rich, aromatic Carolina import that Colonel Lambert, the leader of Southern Command forces in the Kentucky Theater, smoked.

They chatted about what the weather promised over the next few days, and then she broke the news.

"You'll have to run again, I'm afraid, and find Brigade HQ. The hotel is worth hitting with everything we can put onto it."

His eyes flared. Eagerness? The Wolf's buckskin leathers meant he had nothing to prove, at least not to anyone who'd seen his breed cover thirty miles in a day, running and shooting all the way. "Why didn't you tell me earlier?" Clay said.

"If you're going to be running all night, I thought it best that you do it on a full stomach."

"I didn't have to kill an hour smoking. . . ."

"Maybe you didn't, but your digestion did. Take it from me, kid. I've struggled with a sour gut for years. Never eat a big meal unless you can rest for a bit after."

"I could have made the run on an empty stomach," Clay said.

"You never know when you'll need that strength, and you'll be all the faster for it. Get out of here," she said.

"And tell the major to hurry," she called at the retreating back.

Within twenty-four hours they had the Bears in place at Staging Beta, the final campsite, just a two-hour fast-march from the hotel. Lambert and Major Valentine had worked the contingencies ever since she confirmed that there was some important activity at the hotel in French Lick and set Clay running with his pipe still warm in his pocket.

It would be her job to lead them to Staging Omega,

the point where the Bears would make visual contact with the hotel, for the assault.

The column moved well, covering the distance in hard, hour-by-hour hikes with ten-minute rests. Captain Patel's doing, though he wasn't on the op—he'd remained in command back at Fort Seng—his march discipline training showed. They ate nuts and dried fruit as they walked, and took water at the rests.

She guided the Wolves, who chose the trail for the rest of the column. She'd had to give one briefing to the Bears. As much as she liked Wolves, the Bears made her uncomfortable. They sounded ready to kill every soul in the hotel, even the laundry staff and the recuperating soldiers. Most fiddled with their blades, guns, and explosives gear while she talked. They looked as though some sorcerer had taken the word "war" and made from it flesh.

She walked down the line, following Valentine a pace behind and just to his left, suppressing the twitchy anxiety the calculating glances from the Bears brought. Savage fighting dogs watching a meat cart pass would show less naked interest.

Supposedly, all Bears wore the same uniform in the form of a combat vest with a patch sewn over the name on the right breast and black knit stocking caps. Only about half wore even one of the items. Most adorned themselves in a mix of bullet-stopping Kevlar panels and Reaper cloth.

They had a flair for atavism that would have brought disciplinary trial in the old U.S. Army. Reaper teeth, finger bones, ears, jewelry taken off those they killed, all sorts of juju hung off their bodies and weapons. Most were scarred and went out of their way to show off the wounds. Strangest of all was their hair. The fighting men of Southern Command were famous for their beards and mustaches, but the Bears took outlandish grooming to new heights of hair control, tattooing, and other body modifications. Sideburns trimmed like scythes, long ponytails dipped in tar, Mohawks, curiously wrought war picks or other oddball hand-to-hand weapons—the display made her think it was a defiant affront to fate itself, as if the Bears were challenging Death to come and take them, and if Death tried, He might just come off the worse from the encounter.

They tended to operate in small groups, and these groups usually modified their uniform in some small manner to match up with one another. A specific style of boot, a headband, a type of feather, trophies taken off dead Reapers . . . Such atavistic touches added colorful detail to the legend.

Bears growled, quarreled, and shifted from a placid sleepiness to murderous rage—not always at appropriate times in battle. They had a reputation across Southern Command and the United Free Republics as a vicious bunch of brawlers; they were usually garrisoned as far from civilian population as possible, with a few brave souls providing a simulacrum of civilian entertainments outside their bases.

Many of them had up and quit Southern Command, crossed the Mississippi, and followed the numerous supply and communications trails to the newly formed

Kentucky freehold. And not a moment too soon. She'd never heard of Oliver Cromwell, but had she been forced to phrase the sentiment of many in Missouri and Arkansas, she would have used something similar to Cromwell's address to the Rump Parliament: *Depart, I say; and let us have done with you. In the name of God, go!*

The Bears had been trained in reducing lifesign. They didn't care to do it, usually, preferring to let their presence draw the Reapers within swatting range.

On this operation, however, they had to infiltrate. Getting thirty Bears to the spot in the hills she'd chosen.

The Wolves she could rely on. When the balloon went up, they would cut off road traffic. Nothing but an armored column would get through once they set up their machine guns, light mortars, and grenade launchers covering the road.

She led the Wolves and Bears in a staggered double file down the trail she'd picked out, an old fire road that still seemed to see a little traffic, probably as part of Ordnance training. Just behind her the Bear company commander, a Carolinian who went by the name of Gamecock, walked with his communications tech at his heel like a well-trained dog. The pack radio was functional but silent; the Ordnance might be startled by strange radio traffic picked up by listening posts. Gamecock was well named—he had a swagger to him that his fellow Bears liked. Duvalier thought him the most pleasant of his kind she'd ever known; he was mannered and soft-spoken and moderate in his habits, remarkable enough in a soldier with his combat record, damn near miraculous in a Bear.

Radio silence or no, the Bears would blow it. She'd been on three of these combined raids in her early years as a Cat, and every time a couple of torqued-up Bears ended up attacking enemy posts that had nothing to do with the objective, just to get some fighting in. Two scrubs, and on the third time they went ahead with the attack and were burned. After that she started working Oklahoma and Kansas alone.

Fourth time's the charm. Maybe.

"What's that, Miss Duvalier?" Gamecock asked.

Shit, she'd been muttering under her breath again. "About four hours of dark left," she improvised. "We're a little ahead. Maybe call a halt here, while we're still clear of their pickets?"

Gamecock half smiled. "Sure." He turned to his top sergeant. "Pass the word down the line. We'll stop just below the notch, there."

Duvalier gave a coyote yip to signal the wolves ahead and on the flanks, and made a hand gesture for a halt.

Valentine, moving with the middle of the Bear column, came up at the halt to go over her sketched-out map of the hotel and its grounds, and compared it to a couple of photos of French Lick they'd managed to extract from old tourism brochures.

She pulled Val aside after the conference. He was wearing his battle dress of Southern Command uniform and legworm leather. Not anybody's idea of dashing, and between the scar by his eye and his off-kilter jaw not many would consider him classically handsome. His hair, which she always considered his best asset, was still thick and black, with a few flecks of gray at the temples. She had the urge now and then to run her fingers through it, and a few times he'd even accepted a scalp massage.

Once, he'd been on his way to an important staff position in Southern Command, but a general he'd crossed swords with saw to it that a court-martial wrecked him. Even now he was technically only a corporal in the auxiliaries, though everyone under Lambert's command at Fort Seng called him by his old rank of major.

"I'd no idea you'd moved so many men and gear to Beta. I thought it was just a couple of squads of Wolves."

"I had a feeling about this one," Valentine said. "Lambert wanted the Bears out of her hair for a while anyway. They tore up the strip on a rampage."

Major David Valentine had a sixth sense of some kind. She'd seen it in action too many times not to be a believer. When she'd been looking into him before choosing to train him as a Cat (what seemed like a lifetime ago), his comrades in the Wolves had spoken of a "Valentingle" he'd get when Reapers were around. But it went further than that—he could smell both trouble and opportunity in the wind.

"Let's hope they can keep it zipped up for another couple hours," she said.

"Gamecock knows his business. We'll move fast the

last two kilometers. That'll keep their minds on the West Baden."

The Wolves took two sets of prisoners as they approached French Lick: about a dozen civilians who lived at a remote roadside who'd heard there was a bunch of new Reapers in the neighborhood and decided to relocate to some relatives' west of Bloomington, and an Ordnance off-road motorcycle scout training unit that had camped out for the night and hadn't bothered to set a watch on what they'd considered an overnight joyride. The cycles would make a great addition to the motor pool at Fort Seng, and the soldiers could be put to some useful work in Evansville or Western Kentucky.

Walking the motorcycles, guarding the prisoners and civilians to the point where the civilians could not do much harm even if they told the Kurian Order everything they'd seen and heard, and the usual scouting duties of a column moving in enemy territory meant that a quarter of their Wolves weren't in communication with the column. Even the least experienced platoon meant a substantial loss of manpower.

"Only take a couple of guys to guard the bunch and the cycles," Gamecock suggested at the informal council of war at the halt to reorganize.

"All that lifesign bunched up this close?" Captain Patel, in charge of the Wolves, said, leaning on his cane. "Can't risk it. If we have to run back the way we came, they'd slow us up."

Gamecock put a hand on his pistol. A silencer rode in a little pocket attached to the holster.

A glance passed around the group. "No, nobody's shooting anyone captured by Southern Command's uniform," Valentine said. "We can manage without the Wolves. Duvalier, would you mind helping scout the trail? I know you've been busy and on edge for four or five days, but we miss a stillwatch, we're in for it."

Valentine's deference irritated her. Hadn't she proven she was as tough as any? "As long as I can do it alone," she said.

She was moving along the fire trail that ran just below a ridgeline. Even with thin moonlight, the view of the rolling forest was spectacular. The night was alive with birdsong. It comforted her—birds always either went too quiet or shrieked when disturbed, and most birds found Reapers as disturbing as humans did.

The only tracks she'd come across were from motorcycles, probably the group the Wolves had captured.

The linen-tearing sound of gunfire and the heavier chatter of machine guns startled her.

Two figures—no, three—struggled up the hill. She moved down to intercept.

It was Valentine, with a Wolf and one of the Bears. She knew the Wolf, a veteran corporal named Winters. The Bear had a long, narrow face with close-trimmed full beard and curly hair. He reminded her a bit of a poodle.

"Let's move," Valentine said, with his old rank-of-major authority.

David Valentine had a bad leg, ever since a Twisted Cross bullet blew through his thigh, clipping the bone. Duvalier always wondered if there were some remaining fragments hurting a nerve, or if something had been irreparably severed. In any case, he limped, but could still keep up a hard, mile-eating run when he chose. She fell in beside him, and the Bear ran behind, heading northeast. Wolf scouts could be seen intermittently through the thick trees.

"It's a staggered fallback. The Bears counterattacked while the Wolves set up for firing. Then the Bears dropped back behind the Wolves—that's when I grabbed Scour here."

That's how Duvalier learned the name of the Bear.

"You abandoned—"

"We can hit back. Maybe. This many Reapers has to mean Kurians nearby."

"Twisted Cross, maybe," Duvalier said.

"Another possibility."

"Why northeast?" she puffed.

"Higher ground, better signal, closer to the highway leading back up to Bloomington and Indianapolis."

The first warning of the harpy attack was a flutter from the treetops.

A pair of red flares wobbled up into the sky with a hiss from farther up the ridgeline, their parachutes opening roughly above them, probably fired by the harpy handlers. The signal would bring the creatures, who were most likely scattered all over the ridge, into the fight.

"Goddamn them!" Scour shouted. He followed the flare contrails up the hill, unslinging a combat shotgun.

"Stay together!" Valentine ordered, shouldering his short machine pistol and firing a blast at a harpy swinging down on them like a huge spider monkey dressed in a leathery cape. An ugly, pig-nosed, snaggletoothed face snarled at them. Valentine fired another burst and it fell over a thick tree limb like a big chamois hung up to drip dry.

Uselessly, Duvalier thought. *A Bear will do what a Bear does, whether it's shit in the woods or go after some guano-crusted Quislings.*

Valentine's muzzle sparked again and the gun made its brief mechanical buzz.

He knelt to reload, and a harpy dove at him from the night. She stepped quickly to his back, sword low and ready, then swung it up. The harpy banked awkwardly to avoid her, scrabbling with its feet at her face close enough for her to hear the air being cut by its claws, and even more awkwardly crashed, opened from shoulder to bandy hind leg.

"That tree!" she said, pointing with her blood-smeared sword down the slope. The tree was a stunted oak, widespread branches spread low, ideal for eight-year-old kids but impossible for a harpy to flap through.

As they ran Valentine's gun spat again.

"You're hit," Valentine said. "It's not bad."

She didn't feel it. There was a hot, sticky sensation up near her hairline.

The harpy tore a grenade off its waist bandolier. The grenades were fixed so the safety pin came out at the same time it was removed. It threw with its powerful wing-arm, the lever falling off, and the deadly top shape bounced toward them.

Valentine made a move toward the grenade, bending to scoop it like an infielder dealing with a grounder. She was faster and swept his good leg as she threw herself against him. The grenade bounced past and exploded next to the tree trunk. Splinters and shrapnel-torn bark flew off into the darkness.

More flares exploded up the hillside. The harpy that had just thrown the grenade and was grasping another turned its head and took a short, bounding leap into the air, following its nose aloft toward the flares, flapping hard enough to stir the fallen leaves beneath as it gained speed to rise.

When the ringing in their ears subsided and they could hear each other, Valentine said, "Are you trying to kill yourself?"

Irritating in the face of being saved, as usual. "I could ask you the same. Who runs toward a live grenade?" she rasped, applying a field bandage to the claw cut near her hairline.

"The harpies are gone, anyway," she said. "Speaking of which, we have a couple of dead ones lying around. Should I cut a haunch for stew?"

Valentine made a face. He'd rather half starve eating jerked beef and chalky ersatz chocolate out of his ration bag than have some nice fresh meat.

"Suit yourself," she said. She used the razor-edged

butterfly knife to slice off a leg from one of the dead bodies. The corpse twitched a little as she worked.

"I wonder if they're the ones who spotted us?" Valentine asked.

"Nah, some Reaper picked up on the Bears. That's the way it usually goes. They're crap on lifesign discipline, just like every other kind of discipline."

Holding her joint so that it would drain, she followed him on Scour's trail.

They found the Bear at the litter-strewn harpy camp. The handlers were lying under a tree with blankets over them so nothing but their boot tips showed. Half a dozen dead harpies were much less ceremoniously scattered about, with Scour collecting them into a pile. Duvalier was grateful that Scour hadn't done anything more artistic with either set of bodies; she'd seen Bears do everything from sticking heads on treelimb poles to laying them out so they spelled an obscene message.

"There's a big wasp-nest thing in that tree you should take a look at, Mister Valentine," Scour said.

She looked up, saw a shape about the size of a laundry bag. "What the hell is that?" she asked, sidestepping for a better view.

Scour shrugged. "They might have been guarding it."

At first Duvalier thought it was a plastic garbage bag full of laundry stuck in a tree. Then she saw that the material she'd thought was laundry was pale pink projections, like long fingers with five or six joints, gripping the trunk and limbs of the tree.

Perhaps it was two organisms, symbionts, the brain and the hand.

"Looks like that brain's grown itself a set of fingers."

"Wells's two essentials," Valentine said.

"Wells?"

"Something from *War of the Worlds*."

Duvalier knew enough of Valentine's biography. He'd been raised in the basement library of a priest, the closest thing the remote Northern Minnesota community had to a teacher.

"I think—I think that's like their version of one of the old cell phone towers," Duvalier said. "The tissue transmits or boosts or relays whatever link exists between the Kurian and its Reaper."

"Scour, you want to do the honors?" Valentine asked.

The Bear looked up and down the tree, evaluating it. "Sure, Major."

"Let's get that tree down, then."

"Jeez, Val, what did that tree ever do to you?" Duvalier asked, reaching into her pocket and slipping on her cat claws. "I'll do it, seeing as how you two are just too grown up to go up a tree."

She climbed above the mass of flesh, keeping an eye out for harpies. Keeping her legs around the pole and gripping the tree with one set of claws, she drew her sword from the stick and plunged it into the tissue, just where the black, beetlelike shell met the fingers. She thrust up and down, sawing with the blade.

The fingers released and the keg-sized object crashed through the branches below and onto the ground. It waggled to right itself and began to crawl off at a surprising pace, but Valentine and Scour were upon it, Val using the legworm pick he usually carried while in country and Scour wielded a short, iron-headed club like an oversized meat tenderizer. They broke the shell open like a couple of hungry seagulls attacking a dropped crab.

Val thrust the entire head of his pike into the shell and did an impressive imitation of a man scrambling a barrel full of eggs. The fingers made it hop one final time before curling up tight—one caught Scour's foot and he howled.

"That ought to do it," Valentine said, lost in the process of extracting his pick from the mess in the shell.

Duvalier dropped to the ground, drew her butterfly knife and went to work on the clinging fingers. They'd torn through the Bear's boot and reduced his foot to pulp from the heel forward.

It would be a long, painful limp home for the Bear.

"So, are we scrubbed?" Duvalier asked.

"Scour's the handle, Cat," Scour said through gritted teeth.

"Yeah, we're scrubbed," Valentine said. "The Kurians will slip away." Valentine was shaping a branch with a good, solid ninety-degree spur into a crutch for the Bear.

"Why do they want Kentucky so much, Val? You're the big staff college strategist."

"I was court-martialed before I could attend a single class," Valentine said flatly. He'd never been quite the same since, Duvalier noted. He'd risked everything, for so little reward, only to have his own command turn on him to score a few crap political points with some Kansas Quislings who'd undoubtedly done worse than Valentine ever had before they learned to shave. . . .

A good man, more or less ruined by his own people. Who needs Kurians when you have a few enemies in your own high command?

"I know you have all of Seng's old workbooks and so on. I've seen you up late studying. So tell me. They weren't doing much of anything with it before. Raising low-grade meat and hog feed. You can feed a hundred times as many with the Rio Grande valley, and they hardly put up a fight over that. It's not people, either. The legworm clans never offered up lives, and even if you took all of them it wouldn't be much more than a small city's worth."

Valentine handed the crude crutch to Scour. "I used to think it was because Kentucky's a *schwerpunkt*—centrally located. Key ground. You can hit the Ordnance, the East Coast, or Nashville and the Georgia Control using it as a base. But we haven't done any of those things, or begun to lay the foundation for doing them, and with all the spies they probably have crossing the bluegrass, they know it. Has to be something else."

"So they know something about Kentucky we don't."

"That's my conclusion," Valentine said.

"This is all very interesting," she said, "but it's not getting us a step closer to either Kentucky or that hotel."

"You think something's still to be gained?" Scour said.

"Only if we move quickly, while they're excited with the column on the run," Duvalier said.

"I hate running with my tail between my legs," Valentine said.

"We could still get at them. It might be easier than ever now," Duvalier suggested. "They're going to have every man they can trust with a gun after our column, either on them or moving to cut them off from the Ohio. It's a big hotel, there, and I know a way a small team could still get in. We need a couple of Wolves who can drive a truck and a Bear team."

"They wouldn't expect us, not with us on the run," Scour said. "How about the old bringing-in-wounded-prisoners trick?"

"No," Valentine said. "Nothing out of the routine. Ali, you've been watching the hotel. What's possible, keeping in the ordinary?"

"It's a big building," Duvalier said. "Lot of mouths. Lot of laundry and garbage."

Valentine stood silent for a moment. Then his face went poker-hand blank, a sure sign to Duvalier that something was in the offing. "We need a couple of teams of Bears who don't mind getting a little stinky," Valentine said.

"Garbage would be an improvement on some of those guys," Duvalier muttered under her breath, making sure her head was turned away from Scour even so. "Ears like a wolf" was a twenty-first-century aphorism, after all.

✗

By dawn they were in a garbage truck turning off the road and crossing the rail stop that had once, and now again, shuttled passengers to the great resorts.

"Garbage truck" was, of course, a polite term for it. It was, in fact, a much-overhauled farm tractor pulling a big, multiwheeled flatbed that had been converted into a sort of a vast wagon. The workers could drop any of the sides or the back to shovel on or shovel off garbage. Or just tip it over.

Duvalier rode high on the back, balancing on one corner with the aid of a little loop of knotted line, wearing what the Bears called her "scalp." One of the garbage workers had been a stocky female with short brown hair hanging out of her hat. Duvalier decided she must have long ago given up on the appearance of her hair, or it would have been in some kind of protective bandanna under her cap. As it was, she knife-cut it off the prisoner when the Wolves presented the garbage haulers and taped it in her hair after the clothing strip. She didn't quite fill the bulky woman's overall, but a towel doubled and draped across her shoulders gave her the appearance of more heft. Her garrison belt with its assorted components filled out the waistline nicely.

As for the men in the farm tractor, it had a cracked-up vintage windshield polarized against the glare of the sun. Between the tinting, ample dirt, tiny cracks, and accumulations of grease that might have something to do with the loads it hauled, it was a wonder Valentine and the other Bear in the cab could see to drive, never mind being recognized.

Two Bear teams, twenty Bears in all, rode in the garbage. They'd rigged camouflage netting above themselves and tossed a few of the larger, lighter pieces of garbage onto the netting, allowing for a more comfortable, but still smelly, ride underneath. Most of them sat or knelt or squatted on pieces of cardboard or trash can liners.

If they were stopped and searched, the poor bastard Indiana Patrol or Ordnance Guard would be in for a dreadful surprise, she thought. With luck they'd be taken prisoner quietly; they were now near enough for the outer hotel guards to hear shooting.

A rough-looking bunch, the Bears. They'd immigrated to Fort Seng when the fighting dried up around the Ozark Free Republics. Most veteran Bears, she'd been told, grew addicted, in a fashion, to the fighting madness that seized them in action. "Going Red" was one of the many phrases for it.

Their attire could be called a uniform only in the sense that it had the classic insignia pinned on it. And a name badge somewhere on the left breast. Otherwise, it was a mass of Reaper cloth, bulletproof armoring, legworm leather (popular thanks to its availability in Kentucky and the fact that it combined the ruggedness of leather with a breathable, insulative quality like layers of denim and athletic gear), regular fatigues, and in a few cases, painted plate steel or Kevlar. Some wore heavy helms with combat masks that made them look like samurai or old comic book superheroes; others liked to fight in nothing but a headband and tinted safety glasses. Their weapons were equally varied: short machine guns handy for room entry, combat rifles, sniper gear, grenade launchers, and fully automatic shotguns, plus sidearms and blades that gave them a piratical aspect.

One thing they all had on this job was demolition gear, satchel charges, bags of grenades, and incendiary devices. The Bears had learned through long experience that slippery Kurians tended to retreat up or down, and the best way to deal with that was just to blow the hell out of their refuge—soft-skinned, boneless Kurians were notoriously sensitive to explosive fragments and concussions.

Duvalier double-checked the connections on her headset. She heard a low crackle in her ear. The short-range communicator was working.

"We're counting on you," Valentine said. "Two beeps for go ahead."

They had light headset field radios captured from the Ordnance. They'd been modified by the electronics guys to send beeps using the Ordnance's own communications gear. The beeps were so brief and used the edge of some "wavelength" that the Ordnance network ignored it as static, but a rewired sender-receiver could get Morse code out of the beeps. They worked through most of Northern Kentucky, and here in the sprawling Hoosier forest, the network sent and received perfectly.

He winked at her from his scarred eye. "Thirty minutes. It's less than a mile cross-country." He handed her a little earpiece with a button on it attached to a transmitter about the size of a pack of cigarettes. She stuffed it into the pocket of her duster and instinctively checked the edge on her sword-stick. It drew blood.

"See you at the gate," she said, giving him a bloody thumbs-up.

Valentine had a reputation as a sniffer of trouble, and his confidence warmed hers. She'd had a feeling of dread the past few days, but it was gone now. Perhaps the Kurians attending this conference had fled. Now she just felt like a hunter who knows where the game is waiting.

They idled the garbage tractor and opened the hood. Valentine hung a flashlight so it shone into the engine, making his face less recognizable by contrast just in case a passing patrol was familiar with the garbage detail. She checked her "beeper."

The slight discomfort in her finger helped her subsume her consciousness, entering that mental state that reduced the lifesign Reapers read. She was certain they'd have a Reaper or two watching.

That was the dangerous part. They didn't need a clear line of sight to "see" you, so they could be lurking in a hollowed-out tree or thick patch of thorn and kudzu.

She followed a game trail. While you could reduce your lifesign by subsuming consciousness, you couldn't eliminate it entirely, since each of the billions of cells in your body emitted its own fractional amount. Even from a hundred yards or so she might hope to pass as a deer, if she moved in a deerlike fashion, a few steps at a time. But night was fleeing, and she needed to hurry.

So she trotted, hoping that she might pass as an escaped dog or coyote. By pausing every now and then to circle a tree, she hoped to add to the illusion. There was no need to lift a leg.

She slowly ascended the hill line opposite the hotel. When she could see the crest, she stopped and made a careful examination with her eyes, allowing them to rest on every tree stump.

The shock of recognition hit her square in the back before her brain fully caught up. There was a Reaper on watch looking east, sure enough. From its point on the hill it could watch the main east-west highway running north of the hotel, as well as the off-road approaches from the east. Just about where she expected it.

As a hunter, you want to know your game.

The Reaper stood still, only its heavy cloak moving slightly in the breeze. At the moment it was looking west. Its head moved slightly at each slow respiration. Perhaps the beast part of it was exhausted and sleeping standing up, or the Kurian animating it was engaged with another Reaper. A few Southern Command personnel were missing, she understood; it was possible that one was being questioned, or worse, by a different Reaper.

She moved crossways on the hill and restarted her ascent.

This was the hard part of quieting your mind. She was getting into the range where the Reaper didn't even have to see her to know she was there.

When she spotted its head again she let herself relax into lifesign-reducing consciousness. The big problem with this discipline is you never knew how well you were doing it. It wasn't like a flashlight where you could measure the candlepower or distance of the beam. You just had to go through your concentration exercises and hope. Not even hope—hope was an emotion that might alert it as much as fear or lust.

From close up, it appeared to be only half awake.

Reapers had physical needs like everyone else. It had probably been up all night chasing down Southern Command's column, and been recalled so a fresher avatar could take over. No Kurian ever had enough Reapers for all its duties: protection, food gathering, surveillance, and interacting with the Quislings. This one was operating on a "reduced power" mode; if it saw unusual traffic on the road it would probably rouse its master, who would in turn bring the Reaper back to full activity.

She suspected she could sneak up behind it easily enough and cut its head off. But its brief pain and death would alert the Kurian that there was someone in the neighborhood with the skill to take out one of his drones.

Instead she reached into her satchel and brought out a heavy fragmentation grenade and a loop of wire. With utmost care she crept to the rocky outcropping beneath the Reaper and slipped the wire around its ankle. A free piece of light cording (she always carried forty or fifty feet of thin cording that was practically weightless but strong enough to bind a prisoner or serve as a bootlace or hold a bundle together for transport) was tied to the pin in the grenade. She fixed the cording to a stout branch.

Ever so slowly she tied off the grenade up tight against its boot.

As soon as it took a step, the pin would pull. It would drag the grenade while the fuse burned—with a little luck it might even notice something bouncing around by its ankle and reach down to see what was the matter and have the grenade go off in its face. A Reaper with a foot blown off would be slowed considerably until it could bolt on (or whatever they did in the Reaper repair shops) an artificial replacement.

With that done, she descended the hill at an angle that put the most rock, trees, and earth between herself and the Reaper, making a beeline for the little strip of town opposite the old resort grounds.

She tried quieting her mind again, but it was difficult with the excitement of action near. The sentry Reaper meant there was at least one Kurian in the neighborhood. Was it at the hotel? If she was very, very lucky she might find out. Killing a Kurian would be the best way to kick off the action of her third summer in Kentucky.

At the sentry station, two guards stood on duty at the gates. A culvert running between the hotel grounds and the road smelled faintly of sewage. She'd heard that the mineral springs at French Lick had an odor that attracted wildlife for the salts or whatever, but this was definitely human waste being dumped out of a latrine into the nearest standing water.

She used it to approach the sentries. They were both

keeping well away from the bog. They stood behind one of the gate's thick posts out of the indifferent wind. Next to them a wooden beam painted optic orange served as a polite warning to stop.

She considered just walking up to them and using her claws. With her arms inside her oversized duster, they wouldn't know she had her claws on.

The three curved metal blades were something of a joke to most Cats. She'd been made fun of in her earlier days with the Cats for carrying around that extra, easily identifiable metal. They weren't as effective at killing as a single good knife, and were just about useless on something as tough as a Reaper.

She argued back that they were more than weapons. They were great tools for quickly scaling a tree, any kind of wooden-sided construct like a barn, or an old-fashioned wooden utility pole. They could even be used to go up aluminum or vinyl exteriors if you didn't mind the noise. And a kill by cat claws could be mistaken for an animal attack or a Reaper under the right circumstances, leading to confusion among the enemy.

What she didn't say was that she just felt safer with nasty sharp hooks extending from her fists.

But after closer examination, she decided that the best approach was through an overgrown ditch that ran between the ancient railroad line bordering the hotel grounds and the road. There weren't any dogs on patrol or at the gate. She could wiggle up like a salamander and not be seen until she was too close for them to do much about it.

Crossing the highway would be difficult in the light, but not impossible. There was a dip in the road a few hundred yards north of the sentry gate, and she used it to make the crossing with a quick belly crawl.

Once across she observed from the brush. They didn't see her, or they would have whipped out binoculars. Unless they were very experienced counterinsurgents, that is, quietly relaying her presence up to the hotel while appearing not to notice.

She dropped into the chill water and mud of the ditch, and began her wet wriggle toward the gate, hugging her sword-stick to her side so as to disturb as little vegetation as possible.

Her cat claws and several knives accompanied her, including a skinner and a tough all-purpose bayonet with a wire cutter, but the one she rarely touched was a well-balanced thrower. She extracted it from its neck sheath (easily reached while absently scratching your head or when ordered to put your hands up and behind your head).

She wanted to get right into action if it looked promising. She hated waiting. She'd wasted too many opportunities, letting a good moment pass in the hope of a perfect one. According to the Cat who had trained her, she should wait until one guard went off to take a leak, or was occupied in some bit of phone business, before disposing of the other. But Val and the Bears were waiting, the guards were bored at their post, and one of them had his back to her.

No sense waiting.

The thrower made hardly a whisper as it cut through the air and disappeared up to the hilt in the sentry's back.

His companion gave the stricken guard a quizzical look—he didn't scream put probably had an odd expression.

She followed the knife up the bank, sword blade ready and point down behind her, a classic samurai carry, though she hadn't been given the lineage of her killing technique. Just as the sentry with the thrower in his back sagged, she struck the astonished guard.

Making sure of both of them with her razor-edged sword tip, she pulled the bodies into the wet ditch, minus one overcoat and hat. From the hotel she could pass as one of the sentries.

The sentry-box phone remained silent. She gave it thirty seconds to be sure. The thrill of remaining alive while two enemies bled warm into the cold of the ditch was exhilarating. Valentine sometimes remarked on her eyes after a kill. She'd known too many Quislings to feel sorry for these two. Valentine sometimes grew melancholy after action, as if he'd prefer to be the one dead on the ground while the harvesters of humanity triumphed. Moody bastard.

She suppressed a giggle and tried to regain the pose expected of a Cat of her years and lives.

She sent the two-beeps signal. Three beeps replied—message received. Now she just had to wait for the Bear-filled garbage truck to reach the gate. She cleaned her blades as she waited, hoping some other vehicle wouldn't arrive first. How quickly could she kill a driver and his passengers, if any?

The garbage tractor puttered south down the highway, two tires of the trailer crunching vegetation on the verge, giving nonexistent faster traffic room to pass.

It pulled into the hotel driveway. The circular white behemoth waited a little way up the hill, perhaps a quarter mile away.

"There's a lot of trash up there needs burning," Duvalier said.

"Our specialty," said the Bear at the wheel. After all these years, Valentine still didn't much like to drive. Valentine's hands were running up and down his gear, a familiar sign that he had the nerves. He calmed down in action, always did.

"Coming along?" Valentine asked.

"Mass mayhem's not my style," she said. "I'll hunt around outside, see what I come up with. Something valuable might come out one of the fire exits."

Valentine nodded. He gave her one last, long look that she felt somewhere between her hip points. "We'll leave in a hurry. We won't have time to look for you," he said.

She touched her fingers to her stolen cap in a wretched excuse for a salute. "Just take care of yourself, since I'll be too busy for the next couple of days to do it."

She gave the trailer two hard knocks with the wooden sword sheath as it reeked past. The Bears answered with the classic shave-and-a-haircut tattoo, reversing the usual order of things.

That's what the Bears lived for, reversing the usual predator-prey structure of the Kurian Order.

Once they were halfway to the hotel, she grabbed one of the sentry's battle rifles and a bandolier of magazines and followed cover north. She was no sniper, but with enough trigger pulls she could put some quality shit on target, as her shooting instructor used to say.

She'd gone only a hundred yards or so when the crack of grenades exploding on that big veranda opened the action. Firing began, quick bursts that made her think the Bears were already slaughtering their way inside. With blood on the walls they'd be half mad with the fighting already.

She watched the hotel over the rifle sights for a few minutes. A man jumped out a third-story window, but lay on the ground clutching his shin. He was too far away to finish off without the luckiest of shots. She decided not to reveal her position just yet, in case there was someone up in the main parking lot on the hill above with a rifle and a view.

The shooting quieted; what little noise she could hear from the hotel now was probably grenade blasts. The question was, how much killing would they be able to accomplish before having to organize their getaway?

With the Bears raising hell and bringing down thunder, she decided that she would just be in the way of all the bullets.

She heard another faint explosion from off to the east. Had the Reaper sentinel triggered her grenade?

She tried to put herself in the minds of the startled Quislings in the hotel. They were staff types; they wouldn't make a fight of it. There'd probably be a mad rush to the hotel parking lot, but to make the road you had to drive past the hotel, right under the guns of anyone standing on the porch. No, a clever Quisling would make a different escape.

The hotel stables had several tough four-wheel drives and at least one motorcycle, plus the horses. A good rider on a fresh, strong horse could even outrun the Wolves in the thick timber of the Hoosier forest. The stables were out of sight of the hotel with a wooded hill and a gravel golf-course-type path between the two. They could get themselves organized away from the shooting. . . .

When she reached the stables, it turned out that she was the only one who'd thought of it as a likely escape route, at least so far. The stables seemed quiet and deserted, except for the sounds of the horses and the methodical movement of a couple of them grazing in the field. A couple of fresh hay bales had been tipped off a cart without being cut open, a sign that whoever was feeding the horses had found something more important to do in a hurry.

She stepped out onto the path and started for the stables. Better hiding spots for ambushing escaping Quislings could be found there, and she would have a few hundred yards' worth of better view of anyone coming from the hotel.

Once at the stables, she set to work disabling the vehicles. She didn't have time for permanent wreckage, but she could slow them up by a couple of hours by destroying tires and electrical systems. She started with the biggest truck, a double-rear-axle job with a horse trailer attached. It wasn't until she'd punctured the tires that it occurred to her that it might be a good escape vehicle for the Bears, since it had Ordnance markings and you could fit both Bear teams in the trailer.

She sighed. *Too used to working alone.*

Footsteps behind.

A kid in jeans and a white T-shirt with food stains came tearing around the truck, running for his life. She couldn't check the swing of her sword but she did alter its course, giving him a slight haircut and an abrasion as the flat of the blade skipped across his head. The boy fell at her feet with a cry as if she had killed him. He smelled like fryer grease and onions. He probably worked in the resort kitchen.

She readied her sword again and kicked him hard in the ribs. He yelped, but his appearance didn't blur or alter. He wasn't a Kurian escaping in disguise.

"What's your name?" she asked.

The boy was silent for a moment. Then he said, "Tyler."

"Get across the highway, Tyler," she said, pointing. "The shooting won't last much longer."

"They're killing the patients, too!" the boy sobbed.

"All the more reason for you to run. Now get!" She nudged him with the toe of her boot and he took off.

She wasn't surprised. The Bears, with their blood up, would go through the place like a buzz saw. While they probably wouldn't shoot wounded in their beds, she could see them blasting anything in Ordnance colors.

The hotel served as a convalescent home for Ordnance wounded and they wouldn't be able to tell who was who when shooting down a hallway. It was a healthy environment for physical rehabilitation. That's probably why they kept a few horses around—gentle exercise.

Valentine would be upset. He put more stock into the niceties than she did. She thought it was odd that you could do anything you liked to a man on a battlefield, but the instant he was in a hospital he was off-limits, until he got well enough to go back out onto the battlefield to get blown up again.

Speaking of blowing things up, since she had some time she rigged a couple of the trucks with her remaining grenades. It took her just a few minutes to booby-trap two of the bigger trucks.

Thankfully, boot heels on gravel could be heard some ways off. A fat man in a colonel's uniform came puffing toward the stables. He moved quietly and gracefully for his rotundity, on little feet that bounced him along like a dancer. His face was a greasy sheen of sweat and his oversized mouth split his face in two, with wide-set pop eyes giving him a froglike visage. Along with the flab around his belly, he carried a big boxy briefcase full of maps and a smaller, expensive-looking leather satchel with papers and a power cord peeping out.

She hunkered down behind an official-looking open-topped four-wheel drive, but the fat colonel surprised her. He hung his overcoat on a gas pump for the utility vehicles, then headed straight for the motorcycle and set about attaching his cases, the map case in the back and the leather briefcase to the handlebars.

Well, if a speedy getaway is what you're after, you can't beat a motorcycle. The colonel looked more like he enjoyed a few brandies and pastries in a comfortable chair than a motorcycle saddle, but you never really know.

She carefully worked her way toward him.

His getaway seemed well planned, but his fingers kept failing him with the various latches and nets on the motorcycle for military gear. She felt almost sorry for him, struggling to tie off an elastic cord that had its usual hook missing. She reversed her throwing dagger and sent it sailing at his head, hilt first.

It struck him on the back of the head with a satisfying *rap!* but did not lay him out senseless. Nor did his appearance blur, so he wasn't a Kurian in an unusually imaginative disguise.

Instinctively, he turned around to see who'd thrown the rock or whatever had hit him, and he locked eyes with Duvalier.

"Oh shit," he said. His face went white. He looked like he was about to faint.

She really should kill him. He was a colonel, and by the look of the fabric and cut of the uniform, someone well cared for by the Kurian Order.

But there was something about his rotund shape and pop eyes that made him a figure more to be laughed at than hated. She was picturing him lying on a lily pad with legs comfortably crossed and fingers clasped. Where did that image come from? Maybe that was how he survived in the snake pit of Quisling rivalries, by making those who might be enemies discount him on appearances. If he'd only make a move to a weapon . . .

Let this cog in the Great Machine live, Kansas girl, she thought. She drew her sword. "You're not on the Control's list. You have five seconds to disappear."

He hesitated for half a second, a full ten percent of his allotted time.

Valentine had once moved an ornery mule by doing a spastic dance. She lifted her sword above her head and stamped forward, raising a thin ripple of stable-yard chaff with her boot. He took the hint and ran off in his light-stepping manner, leaving the map case and the briefcase half connected to the motorbike.

Good thing, too, or she would have had to run him down and probably kill him. Perhaps her spycraft on this operation wouldn't be a complete waste. She was rather proud of herself for working in the mention of the Georgia Control, the biggest and best-organized Kurian Zone in the eastern half of the old United States. A little extra confusion about who did all the killing wouldn't hurt.

She carefully looked his luggage over for hidden triggers or other gadgets that might destroy the contents—and her—and decided they were safe to touch. Still, it took a conscious effort of will to pick them up and tuck them under her arm. They were heavy enough, loaded with paper. She hoped she wouldn't have to lug this crap back across the Ohio on foot. That would be just her luck.

Of course, the solution was munching alfalfa all around her. Now that she had time to think about it, a horse was the best way to make her getaway—especially if she took off in a direction a fleeing Quisling might take. If she headed north, she'd be in very tall timber in no time.

While a vehicle missing from the motor pool would attract attention to her escape, there was always the possibility of a horse not being noticed, or disappearing from its paddock out of fright over the noises echoing around the hill from the hotel. She might make a clean getaway, with no one looking for horse tracks until all the survivors had been interviewed.

A few minutes in the stables led her to choose a hardy-looking small thoroughbred gelding. She had a good deal of distance-riding experience and he seemed suitable. Though no one would call her a born horsewoman, she'd found that smaller horses often had more endurance in them than the big, impressive ones. He seemed like he had a nice temperament, too. He gave her a friendly rub as she hooked a lead line to him.

It occurred to her that she hadn't heard anything from the hotel in a while. Half the Ordnance in Indiana would be converging on the hotel now—and, not incidentally, giving up on the pursuit of the Fort Seng column retreating toward the Ohio.

As she saddled the horse and tied on some bags of grain, she heard a few explosions—possibly booby traps left behind by the Bears to strike the unwary.

She carefully bagged the captured papers and maps from the colonel's motorcycle and hurriedly set them on the back of the horse. She threw the colonel's overcoat over her duster and put a rag in his hat to make it fit her head. In one of the overcoat pockets she found a very nice pair of sunglasses with real glass lenses. They were a little large for her head but she could bend the bows a little. From a distance, she might be mistaken for an Ordnance scout or courier.

She found a patch of springtime mud and made a generous application of it to her face. Between that and the colonel's sunglasses, and with the overcoat buttoned high, she was barely recognizable as a woman.

Satisfied, she walked the horse out of the stables. She probably should have ridden him a little before loading him; it would be a tedious process to saddle another one if he turned out to have a bad hoof, but he seemed fit enough. She turned due north and pointed his nose at the heart of the Hoosier forest.

There was one highway to cross and she'd be safely out of the French Lick area. She paused the horse on the edge of the highway to listen, then kicked him across.

He wanted to trot alongside the road; she could tell. It was probably what he did out riding with the convalescents. She found a walking trail and turned his nose up in.

A muddy, cloaked figure appeared in front of her. Dead gray leaf fragments clung to it like camouflage. Reaper! How did they do it?

Her hand reached for her sword-stick.

The Reaper held up an arm. She noted there was nothing but a tarred stump where its foot had been. Her friend from the hilltop.

"colonel?" it asked. *"why are you not on a motorcycle?"*

Duvalier never minded a case of mistaken identity. The more confusion, the better for her, usually. "Change of plan. What are your orders?"

"i am told to help a colonel escaping on a motorcycle." It must not be in direct contact with its Kurian at the moment. Conversing with a Reaper as if it came naturally was no easy matter. She gulped down her fear. "You don't look like you can run."

That was a puzzler for the thing. The answer required it to think about its own physical condition. *"it is difficult. i fall frequently."* The mud, leaves, and burrs in its cloak attested to the truth of the statement.

How would that colonel talk? Would he be ingratiating? Haughty? "I might be pursued. They might even be in Ordnance uniforms. Scare them off, and if they don't scare, take one prisoner. We need prisoners."

"prisoners," it repeated.

"Were you told who I was?" She didn't like the idea of leaving a Reaper who had seen her alive, but then it clearly wasn't in contact with its Kurian. How much would its memory retain when it reestablished contact? Well, the briefer she made this encounter, the better. She went into a fake coughing fit that would let her use a raspy voice less likely to be remembered.

"chief of staff, force integration," the Reaper said.

"Then you know why it's vital that I get back to Columbus," she rasped back. The last was a guess—Columbus was the general headquarters of the Ordnance. She departed swiftly. No sense in lingering to possibly make a mistake.

Half a mile later she realized she was ravenously

hungry. The lifestyle of a Cat in the KZ did not lead to frequent chances to sit down to eat. Ration-type foods were hard on her always troublesome stomach.

She took the easy way out. She walked the horse for an hour to rest it, extracted a big bandage from her first-aid kit, and took out her sharp skinning knife.

At a pause to let the horse drink, she nicked open a cut inside its leg. The horse cried out and jumped sideways and it took her a moment to calm it. She let the blood run from the cut into her ration cup until she had about a pint, then put a dressing on it.

The warm blood made a satisfying, easily digested meal. Its saltiness soothed her muscles, full of old aches from the past few days' exertions and new ones from the riding.

Though Alessa Duvalier would never make the claim, anyone who knew her record would consider her the best Cat between the Appalachians and the Rockies. She was certainly one of the oldest still active. It was the most natural thing in the world for a predatory Cat to enjoy the taste of blood now and then.

CHAPTER TWO

The Southern Command Headquarters at Fort Seng: The former great house of the Audubon National Forest quietly chatters with activity. A command is often a reflection of its commander, and quiet, ceaseless professionalism characterizes both the colonel and her headquarters.

Fort Seng still sits near the banks of the Ohio—in fact there are guns commanding the Evansville riverfront—but its administrative area has grown. Fort Seng and the independent brigade there—heavily reinforced by hundreds of Wolves and Bears who'd grown sick of the defensive crouch the rest of Southern Command had adopted—are now the military nerve center of multiple substations, each increasingly capable and independent as the months progress. Perhaps a third of the soldiers of Fort Seng are dispersed to these stations, conducting training to better integrate the whole.

Other communities have grown up around the fort, as it is increasingly called in Western Kentucky and Southeastern Indiana. Some are opportunists, if not outright parasites, like the bars, cleaners, entertainment dens, and eateries rising just outside the base entrance off of old Federal Highway

41 the way mollusks show up around a bayside canning plant sluice.

To the southwest, the Xeno "Gray One" Grogs are scattered according to their tribal system between the banks of the Ohio with the old Shawnee National Forest and its wilder Grogs. The Baron—as he is still known—is holding his military alliance together and his beloved Grogs seem just as happy to fight under Southern Command and Kentucky's flags as under the Kurian Order, and perhaps more content when at home in their charcoal-dusted huts, thanks to the milder weather. To the east, the Golden Ones brought out of Iowa the previous year are setting up communities in the arc between the Ohio and old Interstate 69 leading to Owensboro. They are making themselves useful at the huge electrical plant feeding the region and in the coal-rich mines, as well as building their preferred sod-roofed homes out of the plentiful limestone.

The fort itself is much expanded, with "Wolf Country" to the south and the "Bear Dens" running up toward the Ohio River. Fort Seng has won itself a reputation as a daring, fighting command, attracting men and women who want to be where the action is, where the war against the Kurians is still on the march.

With power up and running, Evansville has dozens of small manufacturing concerns, all using the new Kentucky Free Zone coal-backed "Black Dollars." Rumor has it that a substantial amount of gold that was once housed at Fort Knox but hidden during the Overthrow after the defeat in Indianapolis is in the hands of the Kentucky government, some say hidden at Lincoln's boyhood home, or Mammoth Cave, or sitting quietly beneath bourbon at a distillery, or buried under the finish line at a Lexington racecourse. Speculation about legendary gold aside, there is a confidence that Kentucky is increasingly established as a permanent freehold. Young people with a desire for a change of occupation or society leave the legworm clans for peaceful Evansville or the more contentious Lexington to start their lives. There are opportunities for both, and even the sleepy riverside city of Owensboro is now a trading hotbed for Grog crafts and constructs. Some of the more high-minded have established a human-Grog school in Owensboro where adults learn about one another and the young play and sing one another's songs.

Eastern Kentucky is even attracting the interest of a few writers and academics interested in the structure of a post-Kurian world, should such a dream ever come to be. Besides the newsworthiness of a new freehold east of the Mississippi, there has never been a military organization or political state quite like this one, built on the legworm clans who depend on a Xeno species for their life and mobility, and the cooperation between humans and two sentient Grog species.

So after a violent birth and a period of uncertain flux, the Kentucky Free Zone is ready to take its place among the nations of the earth. Interestingly, it was almost left out of the great Baltic Conference, added as an afterthought when a Baltic League radio broadcast mentioned the hodgepodge of Grog tribes and humans cooperating in the fight against the Kurians. One of the organizers contacted Southern Command and suggested that they bring a delegation from the new freehold, and the rest would shortly become history.

X

Duvalier's exhaustion after the long escape from the Hoosier National Forest required an epic session in the headquarters tub.

The slate-tiled bathroom, a lavish holdover from the days when the headquarters at Fort Seng was a powerful Quisling family's mansion, was bigger than her meager lodging in the stable. Formerly a spa-retreat for the lady of the house, now it was women-only, just adjacent to Colonel Lambert's sleeping quarters and private office, in her little aerie at one end of the headquarters upstairs. Another officer might have kept the sanctuary with its tub jets private, but Lambert opened it to any female on base and installed a reservation roster allowing up to an hour of private bathing. As there were just a few short of thirty wearing the Southern Command uniform, plus a couple of auxiliaries such as herself, most opted to use it as an occasional treat. Lambert herself used it once a week, very early Sunday morning before her usual appearance at the interfaith services.

Duvalier, just before departing for the Hoosier Forest, had requested a slot for three nights of the week she judged likeliest for her return from Indiana and had wound up with the third.

Southern Command's male soldiers weren't up to the standards of gallantry of previous centuries, but they accepted the idea that the women on base deserved a lavish bathing retreat and set about putting the former luxuries back in order. They'd installed stained glass on the windows and returned a cedar-lined mini-sauna to functionality. They'd also recovered a huge wardrobe from somewhere and filled it with the thickest towels and robes to be found in the Evansville area.

Not for the last time, Duvalier was grateful that she operated with southerners.

In Duvalier's experience, most COs and their senior staff bring a certain flavor to their commands, like a chef influences the food in a restaurant. With Valentine signing off on the design and facilities at Fort Seng, you could be sure hygiene would rank high on the priority list. It wasn't just this tub room. They'd sunk fresh wells into the limestone-filtered water table, run fresh pipe to all corners of the camp, and put in heaters so anyone could have a hot shower or do laundry whenever time permitted. The camp had a laundry worthy of a base three times its size—either Valentine was planning for the future or he really liked clean sheets—and a couple of barbers and a family of cobblers were allowed to build and live on base. They were also piping waste out these days, to the fort's own sun-drenched rock bed, where it was circulated through an old irrigation sprinkler over three layers of gravel before draining into some swampy ground, and eventually, she supposed, into the Ohio. You could trust that the drinking water wouldn't be tainted with sewage when Valentine had a say about the plumbing.

So after selecting a robe and towel, she relaxed in the deep, old-fashioned soaking tub. It had jets and a little dial for the control of the flow, but the tinkerers hadn't found the needed parts to get them working again. She'd lathered herself with a bar of "French-milled" (whatever that meant) soap she'd swiped from

Valentine and given her dreadfully gnarled (at least to her eye) feet a good scrub.

Valentine was no sybarite, but he was fastidious about his hygiene. He had a connection who had a connection in the Quisling luxuries trade and always had a few concealed bars of buttery soap that instantly worked up into a lavender-scented foamy lather. Funny aroma for a guy as no-nonsense masculine as David, but she'd shared space with enough men to know they all had some habit that indulged their feminine side whether they admitted it or not.

Lambert interrupted her as she was dressing, after inquiring whether it was okay for her to enter. She'd even given a regulation-sounding knock, neither too soft nor too demanding. Duvalier always suspected that if you unscrewed Lambert's skull under her symmetrical bob you'd see circuits and gears whirling away, waiting for the latest instructions from Southern Command. She threw on the clean, long, men's garrison shirt she'd brought to wear after the bath and checked to make sure she'd left everything in reasonable shape for the next user.

Whoops. She'd forgotten to hang up the foot-scrubbing brush after rinsing. She rectified that and tightened the closure on her robe.

"All yours," she said, exiting.

Colonel Lambert looked her usual razor-cut self, polished and not a hair out of place.

"Stop by my office later, if you aren't exhausted. I'll be up for a couple hours yet. Not official. Not an order, therefore. More social than anything."

Social? There were rumors about Lambert, but they

mostly circulated around the more feminine, pinup-candidate camp females. Duvalier discounted them; she couldn't believe Lambert had any needs that couldn't be met by a well-arranged, color-coded three-ring binder. Once she'd even thought the colonel and Valentine had been a couple, at some time over their long history, which dated back to the officer training school he'd attended on his way to his lieutenant's commission, but now that she'd seen more of Lambert since her brief tenure running Southern Command's Special Operations, she doubted it.

Funny, though, that two promising officers of Southern Command both ended up serving in the same Kentucky backwater. Together they'd turned it into a whole new front of the war.

In the old rough-and-ready days when she was informally serving with Valentine's Razorbacks in Texas, Duvalier plopped down in his bed when he wasn't using it. Even in those days, when she was a good deal younger and of fresher skin, the men didn't call her "Valentine's woman" or anything like that. She was more like a mascot to the regiment, and like a brigade hound—or cat—she was expected to sleep in the CO's quarters.

Colonel Lambert was a little more strict about such matters, so she carved a little niche for herself among the rafters of the stables. The Quisling aristocrat had built quite an outbuilding, with a limestone foundation capped by heavy beams. Along with a few horse stalls, there were little apartments sharing kitchen and bath facilities, presumably for servants, guests, security staff, grounds- or gamekeepers, and such who might need to be active over twenty-four hours, and therefore were kept outside the main house so their routines wouldn't bother the family.

In the stables she joined quite a collection of Fort Seng's "odd men out"—including the basset-faced former New Universal churchman, Brother Mark, a former Wolf and Kurian agent named Frat, and now Blake, Valentine's adopted Reaper "son," who slept in a storage basement. Despite not having even seen his tenth year yet, Blake was already Valentine's height and stringy as angel hair pasta.

She didn't like the little apartments. She'd shared too many kitchens and washrooms in her years. So, using a little plywood and salvaged foam, she rigged herself a space in the rafters above the horses. There was no obvious way up, which she liked—she climbed atop a stall divider, then used an old stirrup she'd nailed into an inconspicuous corner to swing herself up into the rafters. There were a lot of flies, and spiders after the flies, but she preferred insects and a bat or two to the rodents of a hayloft or feed stack. The fort's horses just below were even better than dogs at raising an alarm against prowling Reapers. Fortunately they'd grown used to Blake, and perhaps something about his mixing with humans and using their soap for his skin and clothes gave him a more familiar smell.

She was right under a skylight, too, so on impossibly hot summer nights she could escape to the roof and sleep in the open air. Gamecock, the Bear commander who'd made a couple of good-natured passes at her, joked that she was going to roll off one night and suggested that she tie a safety line around her waist. He'd even help with the knot. . . .

She liked to take a little food and a big glass of milk up on the roof and watch the goings-on in the main house. She wasn't exactly prying—she just had spent so much time as an observer, watching the action through a window and trying to piece together what was happening.

She cleaned herself up, then popped her head through the skylight. Sure enough, Lambert was still in her office, tunic off and hung on a hook in the wall. Knowing Lambert, Duvalier figured she probably ran a hot iron over the tunic quickly before hanging it up, just in case. She threw on fresh underwear and a shirt and strolled over to the headquarters for the promised chat. There were rumors that Lambert was expanding her staff to help cover the greater number of sub-posts reporting to Fort Seng. She hoped she wouldn't be asked to serve at headquarters rather than in the field. Headquarters meant people, and people meant annoyance. She'd rather be in the boonies working alone.

The colonel had a private office, too. It had probably once been a dressing room or something in the lavish house. There was a tall window and a mirrored wall opposite the desk. A carpenter had put up organization shelves and bins for a collection of pre-2022 reference books. The mirror had delicate etching in it, curlicues of burnished, softened black running around the edges. The other wall, opposite the mirror, had a large map of Eastern North America on a pinboard to better hold the myriad of colored pins designating known concentrations of Kurian Zone forces.

Lambert was studying a map. "Just a sec," she said, making a note. When she finished, she returned the pencil neatly to a small tray—she had two, one for pens and one for pencils of various colors—and looked at the rather ragged Cat sitting across the desk from her.

"I like the new towels in the bathroom," Duvalier said, by way of starting a friendly chat.

"There's an amazing little market that's sprung up on the Evansville riverbank. All sorts of people with little barges of goods. One of the staff, Barranco, enjoys visiting it and found them for us. Dirt cheap.

"We've been tearing through the documents you brought out of the conference. It's interesting stuff, all about defensive arrangements should the Kentucky Free Zone make a move north, east, or south. They seem to think the next most likely target is Memphis, in cooperation with Southern Command."

"Is it?" Duvalier asked.

"It might be if I were our esteemed commander in chief, General Martinez. As I'm not, it's anyone's guess. The Kentuckians have had enough fighting these past couple of years; they're just trying to organize what they've won, and Southern Command seems to have fallen into a military funk. Right now they're fighting over force drawdowns more than they're fighting the Kurians."

Duvalier didn't really follow politics, but the Free Republics must be pretty sure of themselves if they were returning troops to civilian life.

"What did you need?"

"I'd like to hear again how you came across these."

Duvalier retold the story. She was pretty sure she'd put it in her report, but she hated paperwork, and the events at the stables didn't have much to do with the operation against the hotel one way or another.

"Okay, we can be pretty sure they aren't deliberate misinformation, then. Your colonel was well away from the fighting."

"And trying to get farther," Duvalier said.

"There is one interesting tidbit in there. You know there's a big all-freehold conference coming up this summer."

"Ummmm, no."

"It's sort of an open secret. They have one every four or five years. It's mentioned in the colonel's notes on the meeting. They spent a long session on what was expected from the Resistance this year, and among the details was a mention of the conference and that they were expecting a report shortly after it finishes. Do you know what that implies?"

This was a field closer to her interests. "That they have a reliable source that will tell them what happened at this big meeting. Or that they've managed to insert one or more agents to attend the conference personally and gather information."

"Yes," Lambert said. "I'm wondering if the colonel didn't screw up and make a physical note of something that was classified. I did some quiet checking, and it appears that no one is aware of this little fact. It seems a little vague to make a big deal about it with the conference people, but if I can open a line of communication to the Baltic League I'll tip their security people that their conference might be penetrated. I also need to send a copy of the evidence by courier, and I was hoping you'd take the trip, since you found it."

"To the Baltic? I wouldn't begin to know how to get there. I'd have to read a map to even find it."

"Oh, no, I wouldn't expect you to get there on your own. The Kentucky delegation consists of exactly one representative tagging along with Southern Command. Since the invite allows up to five, we thought we could add you on for the trip. You'd be a passenger the whole way."

"Not interested," she said.

"Might make a nice break. Really, you just have to have a quiet word with the head of security at the conference, show the evidence, and you're done. You can enjoy yourself the rest of the time."

"Send some kid on the errand. Send Clay—he deserves a treat after running his ass off. Some vodka and a bedspring bounce with a Swedish gal sounds about right."

"Val's been in to see me a couple of times, Smoke," Lambert said. Usually only fellow Cats would call her by her old code name, but Lambert had been her CO back when they both were on the other side of the Mississippi and Lambert was overseeing special operations outside of the usual Southern Command areas. Duvalier decided she was using it here to make the conversation less formal, old soldier to old soldier. "About you."

Now, why would she name Valentine? Strange for such a squared-away officer. She wasn't surprised that Valentine had been quietly nudging the colonel about her, but why give him away? To irritate her into something? Did she know she was touching a sore but private spot? "Asking permission for my hand in marriage?"

Lambert looked puzzled at the jibe. "No. Actually, he's worried about your health. He thinks you need a long rest."

Always thinks he knows me better than anyone. "Don't we all?" Duvalier said.

"I can't exactly order you to stand down. Cats aren't like Wolves and Bears—you're neither fish nor fowl, not combat or support. I'm specifically required to aid you logistically and with combat support at discretion, so you've got the upper hand with me. By the book, as the Fort Commander I can order you to keep out of certain buildings, or turn in your weapons, or see the doctor, or keep off the friggin' grass. As Zone Commander, Southern Command, I can ask a Cat to do something, and if I really press my authority, I can issue a written set of orders limiting your interaction with the locals or sending you packing out of the Kentucky area of operations entirely. I can court-martial you for a crime. What I can't do is order you to put your feet up for a couple of weeks. Only a doctor can do that. I think."

Duvalier was a little shocked. That last sentence indicated Lambert was unsure about some element of regulations.

"I'd say Major Valentine needs the rest more than I do," she said. "He does three or four ops for every time I go out."

"Those are mostly patrols and training runs. You put in serious time in the KZ. You're due for a vacation from all that."

"Still, he looks ragged as hell lately. He's been killing himself getting everyone organized. No one's ever tried to integrate Grogs and Bear teams before. It's not working real well. I can't decide if it'll be a heart attack or a nervous breakdown."

Lambert smiled. "You exaggerated. I'm a pretty good judge of human machinery and, without the hyperbole, I'm of a like opinion. I'm going to see if I can't get both of you away from the bullets for a while. You both deserve a holiday." She reached out and patted Duvalier on the hand.

Duvalier was shocked at the physical contact. It felt as unnatural from Lambert as a blow job scene in one of those Jane Austen naturals that Val secretly read.

"What we're about to discuss is classified at the highest level. So, usual discretion."

"I've never had trouble keeping secrets. I bet I'm better than you at it."

Colonel Lambert gave her a look that was at once both friendly and a glare. "Don't be so sure.

"But back to my way to kill three Reapers with one stake. There's an all-freehold conference to take place in a couple months. I can't tell you where—nobody's told me that yet, even—other than that it's on the other side of the Atlantic, in one of the Baltic League freeholds. Kentucky, as the newest freehold east of the Mississippi, is invited to attend, of course. The problem is the Kentucky delegation doesn't have the ability to travel thousands of miles across the ocean, so they asked if they could travel with Southern Command's group. Southern Command and the Ozark Free Republic agreed, which I find curious because we've always been the proverbial redheaded (beg your pardon) stepchild. There's to be one delegate per freehold, and the delegate is allowed to bring up to two assistants and two security guards for travel. I intend to have you and Valentine as the security. Think you could convince him to join you? The trip won't be easy, but it shouldn't be dangerous beyond the typical risks of long-distance travel. Might be a pleasant change of scenery."

She sighed. As if she had any leverage over Val. But she could offer some insight. "He won't accept. He's convinced the Georgia Control is going to hit us with everything they have, and soon."

"Well, the Georgia Control seems to have gone quiet. In fact, it's been the most peaceful summer worldwide in the history of the Resistance. What do you think of that?"

"Maybe the Kurians are having a conference, too, to figure out what to do with us. Why a security detail?"

"It's a long trip. Southern Command has made arrangements through the Resistance network for transport up to Halifax. You'll take a boat over."

"Arrangements—Halifax? That's way at the eastern tip of Canada, right? Just getting there would be the farthest I've ever been, anywhere."

"You'll still have a long way to go after that. That's why

I like you and Valentine for the job. Hopefully you'll spend most of your time sleeping in transport. The conference itself has its own security, so once you're there you should—should—be able to relax."

"You've no idea where it is?"

"It's certainly going to be one of the north-shore Baltic league states. Norway, Sweden, or Finland, probably toward the north. Kurians shy away from cold climates."

"Except in summer, and it'll be summer by the time we get there, I'll bet."

"Maybe you'll see the midnight sun. That would interfere with the Kurians, too. They'd lose all kinds of distance on their Reapers."

"They don't need Reapers to kill a bunch of people. They have Grogs, a big bomb, commandos. . . ."

"They've never managed to hit a conference before. Anyway, that note indicates that the agent or agents is just going to gather information. That's probably more useful to them than killing a bunch of overfed delegates."

She was almost looking forward to it. Of course, the last time she'd been promised a long, easy trip, she'd wound up sweltering on the Gulf Coast posing as Valentine's wife, and had returned home in the middle of Solon's takeover of the old Ozark Free Territory. Valentine had been briefed with her and received the same assurances. He wouldn't care to hear them again. "One problem, though. Valentine. He'd never agree to go. So unless you give Ahn-Kha and me orders to tie him up, stick him in a diplomatic bag, and label it

'Kentucky Delegation,' your security detail won't have a full complement."

She returned to her little garret platform and watched the sky. It was a partly clouded night without enough ambient light to really make out the clouds, so the night sky seemed like a jigsaw puzzle with two thirds of the pieces missing.

Did she need a rest? Maybe. She wondered how her stomach would handle an ocean trip. It used to be she had good days and bad days with her digestion; now they were mostly bad days. Valentine suggested milk and yogurt, and even brought her yogurt back from a dairy in Evansville that he bused over to for his own purposes—Val was a big milk drinker and liked it as straight from the cow as possible, whereas most of the time Fort Seng made do with reconstituted powdered milk that was hard to distinguish from a piece of chalk dissolved in a glass of water.

It would be nice to be tasked with something that didn't involve penetrating a Kurian Zone and taking out some manner of well-guarded target. The delegates would have plenty to eat and drink—what did they live on up there? Vodka, herring, and reindeer meat, she suspected. If it was to the north. Maybe it was, who knows, Malta in the Mediterranean. She'd once read a book on Malta and all the sieges it had survived—everyone from Greeks to Turks to Germans. Sun would be better than glaciers.

Transport. Her feet could use a rest, too. The idea of not walking or bumping along on horseback appealed.

She wondered if they could shoehorn Ahn-Kha into the trip. Kentucky was more than just people now; there were a couple of thousand Golden Ones and a few hundred Gray Ones camped out south and west of Fort Seng. The Golden Ones had already scouted out a limestone quarry for building dwellings that would be more substantial than tents. His reassuring, muscular bulk sometimes prevented problems with local roughnecks from even starting. And he'd be warm at fifty thousand feet, or if the weather turned on them at the North Pole, or wherever over there they were heading.

Her closest thing to a partner, in war and in her personal life, slumbered in his loosened uniform. Only his soft, moccasin-like legworm-leather boots with their crepe-rubber soles were off.

He had a sparse little room. He had a few books, most of them histories. Valentine was a Civil War buff and swapped books with other enthusiasts. His little collection of toiletries, the expensive soap that he always managed to acquire one way or another, was arranged on a small shelf by the door, with his towel and washcloth both hanging on hooks. A wardrobe held spare and dress uniforms and a smattering of civilian stuff, and some overalls he wore when quartering logs with axe and wedge and sledge and splitting maul.

He kept himself exercised that way when at Fort Seng. Something of the old hot desire she used to feel for him could still rekindle when she watched him quartering wood. He worked relentlessly, back muscles writhing like coiling snakes as he placed his logs. Then he let the axe slide through his fingers until he swung it effortlessly around, letting the weight of the blade build momentum through the swing until it struck with a resounding *thwack!* that echoed off the barn and south hill.

Wood cutting was a metaphor for how he approached most jobs. He broke any task up into smaller pieces, then struck hard at each little piece of it. She heard him give a talk about strategy on the campaign in Texas to his Razorbacks once, where he predicted that the Kurian rule in Texas would be quartered and split into kindling.

She'd recruited David Valentine after his name had been passed to her by the Lifeweavers. She read his confidential file—it was easy enough to swipe, since in those days Southern Command's headquarters had very little security in the personnel department—and she'd become intrigued by him after reading a lengthy report he'd written about his experiences in Wisconsin and Chicago. Chicago was not mission-related; he'd gone there chasing after a girl named Molly Carlson who'd helped him when he was slowed by a wounded comrade.

The old-fashioned gallantry of the gambit impressed her, though she wondered if he could make a good Cat. To operate in the Kurian Zone, you had to have no more regard for those rounded up for the Reapers than you would for a livestock car full of pigs rattling toward the slaughterhouse. She had been a Cat for five years at that time—she started very young, still in her teens—and had seen his type. They usually ended up doing something courageous, suicidal, and ultimately useless.

One odd thing about his file also intrigued her, and

years later she still had no idea of the real answer. His mother's name was missing. Not missing, as in never entered, but missing, as in someone had gone in with a razor blade and cut the name out of the permanent record, then made a fresh copy so that a quick glance made it look blank.

Valentine had told her, openly enough, that his mother was a beautiful Sioux originally from the Canadian side of Lake Superior, and his father a Pan-American mutt from the San Francisco area. Easy to believe, given his features, bronze skin, and thick black hair—now with a contrasting brush of gray at the temples and an off-color strand or two up top. He didn't seem to think his mother any big secret, so why did someone at Southern Command want it that way?

Still, the men liked him. In the field he was a fighter; back at the fort he spent most of his time trying to make their conditions more livable. She liked him. She wouldn't mind travelling with him again on what was basically courier duty. Maybe they'd get some of their old closeness back that they'd had down south when he was posing as a Quisling marine. She found herself more than half looking forward to the trip.

Like anything, planning helped. She thought for an hour or so; then, when she'd decided how to approach him with the job, she finally had a clear enough mind for sleep.

She found him with a corporal, laying out training gear for an excursion. Looked to her like it might be a scavenger hunt—there were plenty of bags, cutters, and tools. Even an automobile battery with a current rig that could be used to test everything from an electronic fuel injection system to an old phone.

"We're taking a trip, Val," she said. Who could say no to orders?

He sighed and set down his clipboard. "We are? Where?"

"Lambert is sending me along with the delegation to the all-freehold conference or assembly or whatever they're calling it. I need you."

"I'm needed here."

"Hate to pull rank on you, Val, but officially you're just an auxiliary corporal on the Fort Seng roster. As a serving Cat, I'm nominally a captain. The major thing is just a courtesy."

"So are the captain's bars, when it comes down to it," Valentine said, yawning. "I bet you don't even have a set."

"I do, but they're from a member of the Iowa Guard who really should have known better than to stop and question hitchhikers. Look like ours, though."

"Let's see them," Valentine said. "Otherwise the order's not official."

"I keep them up my ass for emergencies. You want to get a spoon?"

Valentine grimaced. "That's not regulation. Order's still invalid."

"Now you sound like Lambert. She can't give an order unless her butt is clenched to regulation tension. Listen, Val, you've been bitching at me for a couple years now that I need a break. Maybe we both do. Don't you want to dine on caviar and champagne for a couple weeks? Have a month of travel with someone else worrying about all the arrangements?"

"There's no such thing as a joyride these days," Valentine said. "This will probably be just as exhausting as an operation. If we get stranded over there, God knows how we'll ever get back."

"We can get in a refugee pipeline, worst-case scenario," she said. "C'mon, man, it'll be fun. I have a good feeling in my stomach about this. Caviar and champagne sound pretty good compared to the summer's legworm barbecues."

She could see Valentine melt a little at her mention of her stomach. He was always worried about the state of her digestion. "Who's promising caviar and champagne?"

"Stands to reason. If a bunch of suit-and-ties from here to New Zealand are getting together for a gabfest, there's going to be plenty of top-shelf food and booze. You know politicians."

Valentine retied his hair. It was a time-buying move he liked to do when thinking something over. "There are one or two I like. Sime, for instance. The operator. He's a snake—smooth, quiet, and poisonous. I'm damn glad he's on our side."

Might as well drop bait here, she thought. The conversational waters seemed promising. "Well, I have another worry. Remember how we hit that conference in French Lick."

"Poorly," he said. She assumed he meant the first attempt at an assault, rather than his memory.

"I think we went too large. We should have just gone in with twenty Bears," Duvalier said. "Spilled milk gone under the bridge, Val. Suppose the Kurians catch wind of this and try the same thing."

"It's more their style to try to give everyone a disease or poison the water."

"All the more reason to drink champagne," she said. "I think we should go up there and do a little informal security work."

Valentine looked in the direction of the colonel's office. "Lambert's been burned so many times with ops blowing up on her, I'm surprised she's even sending anyone."

"She told me Kentucky wants to be represented, too. They're as good as any other freehold. The Southern Command delegation is letting us tag along."

"Hmmm. Ahn-Kha's been dealing with a delegation from the Kentucky government for the past few days. I thought they were touring the Grog settlements, but maybe they're the delegates and they're getting some kind of handle on the numbers and strength of our new allies. Who are the Southern Command delegates?" Valentine asked.

"Good question. I don't know. Your old friend General Martinez, maybe?"

"I don't see him leaving his commander-in-chief chair for a long, cold trip. He'll send a mini-me, though. I'd hope they'd have enough brains to send Sime; he's plainspoken and experienced at these conferences. He had a tough job to do at the establishment of the Kentucky Alliance."

"Well, do you want to give it a shot?" she asked.

"I'll let you know in a day or two," Valentine said.

Blake, the young Reaper, was hunting rats in the barn. He squatted, as motionless as a waiting spider, and then when some sound or movement attracted his hyperalert senses, he pounced, as swiftly as a striking cobra.

Big as he was, he was unsettlingly fast, even to Duvalier, who had seen plenty of Reapers in action. Perhaps the lack of a link to an animating Kurian allowed his reflexes to reach their full potential.

However physically developed he was, his emotions were still those of a young child. When he missed the rat, he kicked straw about and let out a terrifying, high-pitched howl that set all the horses to stamping.

"Boy," Narcisse said from her walker, roused by the noise. The ancient Jamaican—and something more— who'd been Blake's caretaker since he was a few months old let her voice do most of the chasing these days. She had a way with him. "You calm down. Horses and folks tryin' to sleep, see?"

He finally ran down a rat and drained it with a single crunch.

Of course a rat wasn't enough to sate a growing Reaper. Blake had a primitive digestive system that couldn't even handle cooked meat. He thrived on blood and could make do with animal fats, though if he had too much fat in the diet he became lethargic and craved salt water, which made him sicker. Every time an animal was slaughtered, a few gallons of blood went right to Blake and any spare was frozen for future use—though he much preferred the fresh, since sometimes the frozen separated while they were warming it up again.

Sometimes Duvalier cursed the fit of sympathy that had made Valentine keep the thing in the first place. She often thought he should have quietly throttled it shortly after it was born, or left it to starve or die of exposure. There was just so little known about Reapers—that a Kurian could conceivably detect him and somehow take control of him didn't seem out of the realm of possibility to her. Half of Fort Seng felt the way she did; the rest went out of their way to be kind to Blake.

Word came that the delegation to the all-freehold conference would be arriving by airplane—or rather airplanes. General Martinez himself, who'd never visited Southern Command's allies in the new Kentucky Freehold or the Southern Command's brigade supporting them, would make a short inspection visit before seeing the delegation off as it departed from Southern Command's most easterly outpost.

Higher-ups meant there would be an all-officer scramble to make sure the brigade was presentable. With all the Grog, Wolf, and Bear teams at Fort Seng, things were bound to look a little shaggy, especially to someone with a reputation for tunic-button counting like General Martinez.

Duvalier decided to bury herself in the kitchens for the visit. She could lay out rat traps or make sure scrap food got to the camp pigpen or clean the coolers and refrigeration equipment and avoid the inevitable inspection-and-dinner that she could already hear coming like a distant thunderstorm. She checked the assignment list—one clipboard at headquarters was mandatory, the other volunteer; Lambert and her exec must have been up all night typing it out. She noticed that she just had one simple mandatory assignment—a water filtration equipment check. Easy enough. She'd just have to take a few test tubes of Fort Seng water to the camp's medical office and see that the results were properly recorded and filed and then make sure that the water-purification tablets were stocked up in all the field cases. She noticed that Valentine had volunteered to lead a Wolf team on the farthest-out reconnaissance patrol during the visit.

She knew there was some kind of bad blood there, dating back to the brief Kurian occupation of what was then the Ozark Free Territory. She'd been busy herself, performing in a Little Rock club frequented by the Quisling officers to pick up information and be in a position to kill a few colonels if and when the need arose, and so she didn't know all the circumstances, but the short version was that Valentine suspected Martinez of keeping his forces mostly out of the fight until they tired of hanging out in the mountain brush and were willing to undergo an orderly surrender.

She volunteered for the pens and coops. Animal waste didn't bother her—actually very little bothered her, except being grabbed, poked, or touched. She sometimes wondered at her dislike of contact. After making a to-do list for obvious fixes with the livestock, she looked over some of the maintenance logs and found that there'd been no lead test of the supply—ever, apparently. She set about getting a water-testing kit from the company stores when she saw Lambert passing through headquarters with an unknown woman in Southern Command Guard rig with a captain's bars.

"He'd like to make a short speech to the men, of course," she told Lambert. "Where would you suggest that take place?"

Duvalier made a show of adjusting the strap on the testing kit so she could pause and listen.

Lambert said the athletic field would serve. There was a wooden platform at the center that would allow him to address the whole camp with minimal amplification.

"The major general likes a little more theatricality. I have a banner for the new year's motto: Purpose to Everything." The visitor paused after she repeated the phrase, as though expecting a squeal of excitement from Colonel Lambert. When no such oohing and aahing arose, she cleared her throat and continued. "They'll be expected to repeat it after the major general. Loudly."

Kurian Zone crap, Duvalier thought. *Keep everyone up to date on the latest pap from on high.*

The water checks gave her an excuse to go get some fresh air. She'd read a short book once, George Orwell's *Animal Farm,* that she'd found in an overgrown house where she'd waited out a storm. Someone had stuck a whole bunch of college books in a plastic tub, and the other literature was too long to begin and too heavy to carry around, and she didn't see what good a calculus and a physics book would do her apart from helping her fall asleep. At the end, the mistreated animals that'd revolted against their farmer found themselves led by a group of pigs that were even worse than the old, lazy farmer had been. The pigs grew so used to dealing with men that it was tough for the other animals to tell the difference. She'd felt that a few times during her stint in Southern Command, but attributed it to efficiently run military organizations being much alike, thanks to command-and-control necessity.

Southern Command was in a fight for survival against beings that wanted to harvest humans as food, and the priority of the man in charge of that fight was to make sure everyone knew this year's slogan? Someone's water wasn't hot enough to cook the crayfish, as her uncle used to say.

It irritated her enough that she wanted to talk about it with someone. Narcisse would just laugh it off as meaningless tripe and not worth the emoting. Ahn-Kha was stoic about everything.

She found Valentine with Captain Patel, picking out Wolves and a couple of aspirants for his patrol. The tents and barracks of Wolf country, as it was called at Fort Seng these days, put her a little on edge. The shaggy, rail-thin Wolves always eyed her hungrily. She felt a little like a chicken invited to dinner at the fox den.

Valentine finished his business with Patel and escorted her out. A bag full of variegated human hair stood outside one of the tents, and she heard scissors snipping.

"Colonel Lambert wants hair and beards regulation," Valentine said.

"Even the Bears?" she asked.

"Patel and a couple of his big timber boys are going to find something for the rowdies to do," Valentine said. "Gamecock has the rest finding their A uniforms. Which means no cut-off sleeves, from what I understand. We'll put the Bears in the back."

"The whole camp should find something else to do during the speech. Rah-rah speechifying like that reminds me too much of the KZ. You know he actually has a slogan for the year? 'Purpose to Everything.' I already heard Corporal Manfried in the mess call it 'Porpoise on Biscuit Ring.'"

"Banner?" Valentine said. His face went poker-hand blank, which usually meant he was brewing something up. "Hey, Smoke, old road friend, you wouldn't be interested in volunteering for the stage decor?"

"I might. What do you have in mind?"

"I've heard a lot of speeches from Martinez. I don't want to inflict them on our poor fighting men without an opportunity for real entertainment. . . ."

Maybe it was the slogan-of-the-month. Something sent her back to her childhood once she fell asleep. The Great Machine. She dreamt of it again.

She'd first had the dream as a little girl, growing up in the gentle rolling hills of Eastern Kansas near the edge of the great flat plain of the rest of the state. Even in her little town it was still a vista of vast horizons, fifteen-mile views if you could just get up on a roof or high in a tree—always her favorite spots, in almost any weather. She liked being up out of the view of searching eyes, which always seemed to be attached to gossiping tongues.

At the age of seven or eight (she couldn't be sure which), she began to have dreams of the machine. Maybe they were connected to the visits of Quislings to her mother. They'd started before then, she suspected, but only once she'd been moved into her neat green-and-white-painted little school with the other Quisling kids did she hear about what her mother was undoubtedly using for payment for her access to the best education available, in one of the unofficial schools where she could be taught by someone other than the New Universal Church and its youth organizations.

The dreams were horribly vivid. She was in her home, occupied with some chore, when a rumbling, growing as it approached like an avalanche, drew her to the window. Mechanical spikes like clock towers mixed with talons erupted out of the earth in showers of dirt, puffing out dark gas like a steam engine as they unfolded and expanded, always sending out more points, barbs, hooks, irregular rows and rows of them like the broken saw teeth or the shark jaws she'd seen in New Orleans. Mad lights blinked and searchlights opened and shut, sending patterns of light and dark and color over the landscape.

The house would rock on its foundation and she sought escape to the roof, calling for her mother. Mother tried to follow, but a piece of the machine, like a mechanical tree root with the grasping ability of a hand, reached in the door and yanked her out of her shoes. There was nothing to do but clutch at the empty shoes and try to escape.

Once she was on the roof she could see, like a mountain, a centerpiece of the Great Machine, with an eye atop the pyramidal mechanism like the seal on the old one-dollar bill. All the individual spines were connected to it deep underground. The pieces all hooted and chattered like a conglomeration of television sets, radios, and alarm klaxons. The noise was such that it was a weapon itself; you wanted to squat and put your hands over your ears. She wished some attack aircraft of the Old World would zoom in, shooting nuclear-tipped missiles into that eye, putting out the eye and silencing the cacophony, but the Great Machine couldn't be destroyed. It didn't have a weakness like a dragon's missing scale or a space station exhaust port. No one weapon would wreck it.

In fact, it did a good deal of destruction to itself. In her dreams the Great Machine was a shambles. Spines would collide with other spines, breaking both and sending rusty bits showering to the ground below. She could reach out and tear off pieces of it, the way she removed old aluminum siding from rotting homes in metal drives organized by the Youth Vanguard.

Even as a tweenager she realized that her dreams about the Great Machine were really about the Kurian Order.

In waking life, she knew the Great Machine was a fantasy. It had long ago lost its power to scare her when she was awake the way thinking of it had frightened her as a child. Reason slumbered with the rest of her body, however, so it still had the power to terrify her in her dreams. Sometimes her mother was not pulled into the machine, but embraced it, let pieces of it enter her in an obscene fashion—the Great Machine dream had matured sexually just as she had.

Sometimes the dream ended when it destroyed her house. When it went on, she ran through the streets while clockwork talons waved around and above, bending down to stab at the people on the ground like a heron taking a minnow or a lizard. Some of the people were running away with her, some seemed oblivious to the machine, and others, having been engulfed by it, were having their hands turn into gears, their eyes into lights, and their mouths into speakers.

One thing was certain: the machine would never take her. In the twilight time between wakefulness and sleep, when the world was half dream and half dawn, she thought of how she would always keep a grenade at the ready, just in case a piece of the machine grabbed her. She would blow apart her own components, and hopefully a few of the machine's, to prevent her mouth from adding to the noise or her fingers from becoming the gears bending a new spine toward the ground to impale another victim.

The wonder of it was that the machine had reached for her so many times and missed. She wasn't that good. Either she hadn't yet struck a blow that really hurt the machine—in that case she'd have to redouble her efforts—or the machine itself was something of a lemon.

It was probably some mixture of both. The Kurian Order was like a huge, overweight boxer. It could pummel a heavy bag easily enough; the heavy bag didn't move, and the layers of fat and muscle, combined with its height, made it hard to really hurt it. But if you watched your step and didn't get cornered, avoiding its clumsy, muscle-bound blows was fairly easy.

She'd never told anyone about the dream. Transitory lovers, like that boy from Ohio, had sometimes questioned her about her nightmares, asking if she wanted to be woken up from them. She said no, they were brief, would pass, and she luxuriated in her sleep. Even David, who at times was some combination of partner, husband, and brother, didn't know about the Great Machine. The meaning was so obvious it wasn't worth discussing, especially with a man who now and then woke up sweating and calling to his dead mother, killed by some kind of Kurian Order hit team.

She descended from her aerie early, feeling achy and anxious from the dream. Her muscles had never relaxed properly last night.

They had an old tack room that had been converted to an extra walk-in cooler for the camp by the simple expedient of adding a heavy-duty window air conditioner and extra insulation. She went in and poured some of the camp goat's milk, then shuffled off to the first-floor communal kitchen to find some baking soda to brush her teeth.

Narcisse had just drained a couple of chickens for Blake and was in the process of plucking them. The feathers lay all about her feet. "You had a bad night, girl."

"Bad dreams," she said. "You need help?"

"Oh, I think you have things to do. General Martinez arrives today."

How did she know about that?

She wondered about Narcisse, the old woman Valentine had picked up in the Caribbean on his mission to find Quickwood—a rare hardwood that might have served as the basis for legends about vampires being killed by stakes—and brought north. Physically, the old woman seemed more dead than alive these days. She'd seen a few people in hospitals kept alive by machines, and Narcisse reminded her of them. The same dead-looking skin, withered hands, sunken cheeks. Yet for all the decrepitude of the body, she managed to keep going somehow, some inner animating spirit occasionally showed in her eyes, especially when she was interacting with Blake. And mentally, she was still more insightful about the people in camp than even Brother Mark was.

She washed up in a basin, ate some cold jerked chicken left over from last night, and attended to her very limited duties. Then she joined other idlers in waiting for General Martinez to arrive.

He put on a pretty good show, she had to admit. His red-white-and-blue-painted plane circled low over the camp and made a couple of passes over the highway to make sure it was clear of traffic.

He was a little fleshier in person than in his newspaper photos. She wondered if they were doctored. Still, he had a nice head of hair that was equally impressive whether real or fake—if real, because of its youthful thickness and luster; if fake because of the expensive craftsmanship that must have gone into it.

She noticed there was a woman in uniform taking pictures. She looked tired.

Sime, the United Free Republics politico who handled the Kentucky Alliance, trailed in his wake along with other staff. She'd seen Sime on one or two occasions. He'd been involved in Valentine's troubles with Southern Command in some manner.

Martinez bounced out of the plane and exchanged salutes with Lambert and the other officers there to greet him and pumped the hands of the Evansville and Kentucky civilians with a good deal of enthusiasm. He apparently made a compliment to one of the women; she blushed and rocked on the balls of her feet as they had the photographer take a picture. He did everything but kiss a baby.

He got into a waiting, lightly armored four-by-four and turned up toward Fort Seng, with his official photographer riding precariously in a folding seat attached to the rear bumper. Duvalier was a little surprised at the security vehicle. She didn't think it came from the motor pool. If not, some poor chump had had to drive it through Western Kentucky, wash off the inevitable chaff that accumulated, and have it ready in time for the general's arrival.

She lost interest after he disappeared into the camp. She bought a couple of small soaps and shampoos from one of the traders across the road from Fort Seng. She visited a bakery—it had once been a doughnut cart, but now it actually had a counter, although the counter was festooned with pictures of cute kids at Youth Vanguard day care doing something with flour. There were copies of the New Universal Church's Guidon near the cash box.

Martinez was supposed to have a quiet meeting with Lambert and her staff, then eat lunch with the soldiers, give a short speech, and depart.

General Martinez gave a good speech; she allowed him that. Too bad more weren't there to hear it. Most of the Bears and Wolves had found other things to do. The ones who did show up concentrated on their food.

The slide show was nothing but self-aggrandizement. Photos of Martinez as a youth, doing hardscrabble farm labor, in a poorly-sized uniform for his frame as a new lieutenant, an entire biography. After Consul Solon's occupation of the Ozark Free Territory and eventual defeat, the pictures suddenly became a great deal more professional than friends' snapshots and service journalism. Martinez had evidently recruited a professional or found someone who could do a very professional job making him look good in still life.

The second-to-last slide was just the words PURPOSE TO EVERYTHING. Martinez made a few rah-rah statements, but the audience was just as cold to it as she was.

The final photo received some cheers and whistles. Martinez basked for a moment in the whooping and cheering; then it dawned on him that there was some laughter in the crowd, too. He turned around and

there he was, in a rather grainy press photo of a banquet, asleep at the table with his head lolling back and
collar unbuttoned, tie loosened and hanging like an
overheated dog's tongue. A pair of champagne ice
buckets stood on the table with overturned bottles in
them. In the background, the president of the UFR was
speaking from a podium, though no one seemed to be
paying him much attention. You could practically hear
Martinez snoring in your imagination.

Martinez turned around. His jaw dropped when he
saw the photo.

"A different slide is supposed to go there!" he thun-
dered at the projectionist. "Go back."

The picture returned to the PURPOSE TO EVERYTHING
slide, but the projectionist must have been having
technical difficulties, because it went forward again to
the picture of Martinez snoring at the table. And back.
And forward, while the technician frowned and fur-
rowed his eyebrows and pulled at his chin, peering at
the slide projector. It clicked from the title card to Martinez dead-drunk at a banquet table, and back again,
over and over, to the laughter of the assembly.

The general's face went even darker. Duvalier grew
afraid that he'd stroke out or have a coronary right on
Fort Seng's main stage, so to speak.

"Just unplug it, Corporal!" Martinez bellowed
across the laughing ranks.

One of his aides hurried to intervene. He ran up to
the slide projector and pulled the plug. The screen
went dark instantly. There was still a good deal of
laughter in the audience.

As Martinez left, the aide made an explanation to the men that the slide was a private joke between Martinez and his staff and had accidentally been left in the presentation. "The general has quite a sense of humor about himself," he insisted.

It didn't look like it as Duvalier watched him on his way out of camp back to the red-white-and-blue plane.

General Martinez needed to lash out and Lambert was the nearest target. Duvalier watched him pace back and forth in front of her as he dressed her down.

"So, if I could summarize," Lambert finally said, "somebody knew you were showing up with a slide show, had a slide manufactured, inserted it into the tray that was always in the control of your people, then manipulated the soldier working the slides—one of your staff, I might add—into making your slide projector malfunction in order to humiliate you in front of the troops?"

She had a strange moment when putting her things together in her little space in the barn, that she would never see it again. The premonition bothered her more than she would admit to anyone.

Just in case, she had a few words to Brother Mark about a will. He was used to comforting the fearful, probed her on her concerns, and asked her about the three worst moments of her life and how she got through them. "Now, a long trip to attend some meetings doesn't sound as bad as that," he said, after she told him about the time she'd stomped a Quisling to death as a teen. Her first murder.

With that done, he helped her write down a few things on a standard form and they turned it in to the administrative service together.

"Good choices," he said, as they made their farewells.

He was referring to the disposition of her assets. She had a fair amount of pay stored up, since she was out of the home areas and in the KZ so often she hardly had time to spend it. Much of it had automatically been placed with Southern Command's bond funds. She arranged for a division between Ahn-Kha and Val, the closest she had to family, except for a few thousand dollars to build a kids' park somewhere. Her happiest times as a child had been on a few pieces of playground equipment, and she still liked watching kids climb and slide. She wrapped an old red bra and a phony wedding ring in some tissue paper and labeled the package for Val, a little memento to remember her by.

Feeling somewhat more optimistic and lightened— odd how preparing for the eventuality of your death put a shine on the day—she ate what was for her an enormous meal at the canteen and took a last walk around the camp. The nights were growing warmer and there were a few pickup soccer and volleyball games going. She won five straight games of darts in the base lounge, listening to the Fort Seng guitar band play old rock and roll, and returned to the bugs of her attic vaguely proud that she hadn't given in to her loins when they flared up over a pair of cute sergeants shooting pool with a Bear.

They said bullfighters always wanted sex before a fight, and sometimes in the past she'd given in to lust before an op. But Fort Seng was almost like a big extended family, and there was bound to be gossip—and if she returned, she didn't want to deal with the are-we-or-aren't-we questions.

In any case, this wasn't an op with obvious dangers, like the exploit in the Hoosier National Forest. It was supposed to be a kind of vacation. Still, she worked her blades against a whetstone as a way of preparing herself for sleep. The *rasp-rasp-rasp* soothed and her breathing slowed and deepened, and after returning the blades to their sheaths she dropped right off, to the sound of horses stamping and swishing.

CHAPTER THREE

"*Travel.*" To the early twenty-first-century ear, the word is full of romanticism. Travel means delicious exotic food, sightseeing, meeting interesting people who might turn into friends or lovers, and above all, a pleasant, relaxing break from ordinary life.

To those who live in the post-2022 world of the twenty-first, however, the word has taken on a fearful aspect. Travel means danger, difficulty, and the longer the distance you intend to go, the less likely you will be to reach your intended destination. "Travel's a curse" was a line in a very popular theatrical production set in the nineteenth century, but in the Kurian Order a journey isn't even up to those standards. A trip of any length is closer to the pilgrimages of the Middle Ages, fraught with difficulty, and therefore something engaged in only once or twice in a lifetime.

Still, it is a necessity for certain high Quislings in the Kurian Order. While they have fewer difficulties with finding transport, the fuel to put in it, and a route to their destination, there's still the worry of treachery at one of the stops. Many have been lost to "poaching" or a sudden switch in loyalties between Kurian factions.

While the Resistance has its betrayals, too, they are rare. Travel is more difficult from a logistical point of view, but there are several networks that allow journeys of even extreme distances to be completed. Sponsored and supported by various freeholds worldwide, they run something like the Underground Railroad of the pre–Civil War United States.

There are the Pacific Charters, able to move people and cargoes all about the Pacific Rim, and the Pan-American Viajes Azure has been able to move people from the Tierra del Fuego to Canada.

The Refugee Network is the great chain binding Old World to New in the days of the Kurian Order, mostly taking escapees out of Europe and over to Canada. Canada's vast, often chilly wilderness offers climatic refuge from the Kurians, and while passages are often arranged for those with wealth or needed skills, there is usually room to be found for those just desperate to get away. There are many heartbreaking stories in its history of groups of families arranging for all their children to be sent across the Atlantic under the care of a single adult, with the present generation sacrificing itself so that more of a future may be brought to the Free Territory.

It was the Refugee Network that set up the travel routes from North America to the Baltic. The delegates received travel advice, but were to make it to either Vancouver or Halifax on their own, and from there departures to Europe would be arranged. Southern Command and the Kentucky Freehold both opted for the Halifax route, and as matters turned out, it was simpler for them to travel together.

✗

On the morning of departure, she met Ahn-Kha and
Valentine at the back door to Headquarters, just adjacent
to the HQ parking lot. They wouldn't have to ride the
"bus" (usually an old army truck) into Evansville; thanks
to the official nature of the trip to the airport, they'd get
an honest-to-Martinez staff car.

Ahn-Kha was slumbering atop the duffel bag con-
taining his odds and ends. She could see that Valentine was nervous. He was whittling a stick down to
nothing with a little sheepsfoot blade he carried.

Valentine had something against timber when he
was agitated. She'd seen him sweat out anxiety by reducing timber to kindling more times than she could
count. The sweat equity was usually appreciated by
whoever was feeding him at the moment.

"What's up?" she asked him.

"I'm always nervous before a trip. You know I settle
down once we're on our way."

After all these years, it was odd that he still tried to
bullshit her. Her mother had once told her that men
cover up their feelings more for their wives than they
do for their whores. Maybe that girl he visited in town
knew the real story. "C'mon, Val. You're talking to me
here. I'm not some lieutenant you have to reassure."

He flung the stick into the soft spring ground and the
point dug in, like a dart. "The last time I left on a long
trip, I fathered a baby girl and returned home to find the
Free Territory under Solon's Quislings."

She shrugged. "The Kentuckians were taking care
of themselves before we ever crossed between the Tennessee and the Ohio with the clans. Remember that.

They'll still be here when we get back. As for fathering kids, you could break with tradition and keep it zipped up. You're grouchy when you're celibate, but you get more done."

He laughed and unbent. A little. "Is my reputation that bad?"

"I've never heard any of your women complain. Just jealous fellow officers. They don't have that luscious black hair, either." Actually, he was going a little gray at the temples, but she didn't want to mention it.

"I can't help feeling that this will be the make-or-break summer," he said. "The Georgia Control is building up to something."

"Last I heard, they frittered away six thousand men trying to pacify the Coal Country again, and all they did was see to it that the rebels there are better armed than ever. They'd have to take fifty or a hundred thousand into Kentucky. They don't have it, at least not combat-capable troops, even if they strip their other frontiers."

"I still think it's going to come down to Kentucky and the Georgia Control," Valentine said. "They have all the factories and the foreign connections. All we have is home-field advantage."

"Maybe we'll make some foreign connections at the conference."

"So we become best friends with a resistance faction in the Ukraine. They won't be able to provide much effective support."

"We could give them a handful of Quickwood seeds. Maybe they'll have something similar for us."

"Those went out ages ago. By the time the trees have matured to usable age, they'll have reengineered their Reapers to be less vulnerable."

"David, even if the Georgia Control comes with everything it has, will you being here make a difference? Let's say it's the biggest debacle since Indianapolis—how does you dying or getting captured with the rest change much?"

"I helped them get this started. If there's a finish, I want to be with them."

The car pulled around. Captain Patel was at the wheel, there to see the kid he'd trained as a very young junior lieutenant in the Wolves off on another long op.

"Talking to the women instead of loading your gear, Valentine," Patel said. "You never change. C'mon, kid, I'm not working for tips here."

They woke Ahn-Kha and as they stowed their gear in the back of the camouflage-painted all-wheel drive, she thought of one more thing to tell him: "You did more good by showing up with the Quickwood when you did than you would have if you'd been just another guy runnin' and gunnin' when Solon invaded. Don't forget that."

They covered a vast distance in a gray two-engine plane, the largest aircraft Duvalier had ever ridden in—not that she had much experience in the sky. It was named the Bucking Bronc and had some vividly colored nose art of a brunette with bangs and leg-revealing chaps riding a man in exaggerated cowboy gear. The cowboy seemed vaguely familiar to Duvalier. The pilot, a Texan named Silas A. Montee whose only insignia was a perfectly scratch-free set of golden wings on his chest, told her the cowboy was a film icon from the twentieth century. Montee was by far her favorite of the Southern Command group. Sadly, he would be with them only to Newfoundland, where they'd transfer to a ship with the delegates representing the Green Mountain Boys.

Before they boarded Montee's plane, Patel slipped Valentine a box with something that clattered faintly. She suspected alcohol. The veteran captain had good connections with the Kentucky legworm pack traders, thanks to his endless overnight training hikes with the men.

Ahn-Kha was the official delegate representing Kentucky. He was a last-minute change; the original delegate was to have been the leader of the Gunslinger legworm clan, but when he learned he would have to cross the Atlantic, he judged his chances of ever seeing the back of the clan beasts again to be slim, and withdrew his name.

Ahn-Kha was more than willing to travel once more with Valentine and her. "With the three of us together, let the mountains of Europe tremble."

"We don't know we're going to the mountains," Valentine said.

"Glaciers, then."

"For all we know, the meeting's on a ship anchored in some fjord," Valentine said.

Duvalier wouldn't mind that at all. She'd seen pic-

tures of fjords in old books and would enjoy the opportunity to visit one in person.

Duvalier really wasn't that surprised by the decision to select Ahn-Kha for the honor. He was impressive to look at, and had a reputation that extended
from the Virginia tidewaters to beyond the Mississippi
and Missouri. He was "Golden"—meaning lucky—to
the coal miners of West Virginia and Kentucky, and
there was no question about his loyalties.

The Kentucky Alliance, practical as always, knew
that the Baltic League would not be able to offer any
real help to their allies on the other side of the Atlantic.
Even under a best-case scenario, a trickle of weapons
might make it over, or valuables that could be used to
buy black market items of similar quality, say some of
the production of Atlanta Gunworks that "fell off a
truck" passing through the Cumberland Gap.

What exact powers and instructions he received
from the Kentucky government Duvalier never learned,
but Ahn-Kha described his brief as "to assess the situation and use my best judgment."

Fair enough.

Sime gave a sly smile when they met at the Evansville airfield. "I'll be the voting delegate for the United
Free Republics," he said. "We'll have to check, but you
are probably the first Xeno to attend as a delegate."

"The Lifeweavers always are there, right?" Duvalier
asked him. She was looking forward to a chance to
have a talk with them, if she could ever corner one.
They'd almost vanished from the middle of the United
States. The ones Val had brought out of the Pacific

Northwest were being hidden in a vault somewhere, apparently, and without a few Lifeweavers to guide them in the war against the Kurians, things would continue to go the same piss-poor path they'd been on the last few years.

Sime shrugged. "I would think so. I have never been to one of these, but I've read all the available reports of the previous delegates from Southern Command."

The group from Southern Command was the same size as Kentucky's. Sime's group made the Kentuckians seem like bumpkins. As always, Sime was dressed immaculately in colors flattering to his dark skin. To her he reeked of KZ apparatchik with his finger-bowl manners and careful talk that said very little.

He shook her hand as she climbed into the plane. "Welcome aboard," he said, as though he were personally flying them to Europe. His hand was as strong and hard and cool as tortoiseshell. He didn't seem the type for manual labor, so she wondered where the calluses came from.

With Sime was an executive assistant named Alexander—it seemed to be his first, last, and only name. He gave her a card with an address at a contractor's office in Texarkana that read only "Alexander" with "Capabilities Enhancement" beneath it. Shadowing Sime was a bodyguard named Postle who wore a civilian fishing vest. He must have had either very bad acne or a terrible case of chicken pox as a child, for he was dreadfully pockmarked and scarred. Everyone save Sime called him Pistols, as he wore no fewer than three visible guns and, she suspected, had a couple more concealed. Within two hours of meeting him, she knew that he had fifteen years in Southern Command's Guard and had washed out from Wolf candidacy because of flat feet. The heaviest of the guns, kept on his hip, was "the Judge," which could fire shotgun shells, but he'd fitted it with Reaper-killing distillates of Quickwood, which were, sadly, unobtainable in Kentucky. A stiff leather shoulder holster held "the Jury," which he named because it was a 12 + 1 .45 Colt. Finally, there was "the Executioner," a snub-nosed .357 revolver worn on a belly band rigged for a ten o'clock cross draw. "Killed six Quislings with it without reloading, all shot in the back of the head in graves I made them dig," he said. She was more interested in his utility knife, which had a built-in flashlight and a deadly-looking backstabber that he claimed was an old commando dagger.

Sime's other companion was a woman named Stamp skilled enough with cosmetics and hair coloring that it was hard to determine her age, but Duvalier's best guess was that she was just about ready to turn fifty but able to keep up appearances for ten years younger. Like Sime, she had the air of limo service about her. She didn't seem the personal secretary type; indeed, she spoke to him as if she were giving orders, though Sime had been named publicly as being in charge of the delegation from Southern Command. Duvalier thought she looked like some duchess or baroness from a painting in an art museum save for her modern—and very stylish, from what little she knew of such things—clothes.

Duvalier found that she liked her instinctively. Stamp always knew what to do with her hands. If they weren't doing something, they were casually crossed in her lap. Duvalier disliked fidgety women who were always fretting at hair and attire.

As they found their seats, Postle looked at her small backpack and his mouth dropped open. She wasn't sure if the astonishment was feigned or not. "That's all you're taking, girl? I've never known a woman to travel so light. I think I'm in love here, Sime!" He poked her square in the right breast with two extended fingers. "Just put some meat on those bones and I'll call a preacher."

Ahn-Kha, who was eyeballing the shape of the Bucking Bronc's seats and already shifting his feet in discomfort, flattened his ears against his head. "I do not enjoy heights or constant motion," he grumbled.

"Prone to airsickness, Old Horse?" Valentine asked.

"I hope not," Ahn-Kha said. "It might be best to provide me with a very large bucket."

"I hope Postle didn't offend you," Sime said, picking up Duvalier's bag for her. "He's always in the locker room, so to speak. You'll get used to it, hopefully sooner than I did."

Pistols reached up and rubbed Sime's bald head. "We should all do this for luck on the flight." He sat down next to Duvalier.

"Sergeant Postle, please," Sime said. "You have your seat at the back. Get in it."

"That big Grog's going to need to take up two seats, and I don't want to be anywhere near him if he spews. I'm comfortable right here."

Duvalier just settled deeper into her duster and put a towel behind her neck to make her head more comfortable.

The plane lurched into motion as the ground crew dispersed from the final checks, taking the chock blocks with them. It took up so much runway on takeoff that she had a brief moment of terror when it appeared they were going to run out of runway before getting the tires off the ground. But the plane clawed its way into the sky, picking up altitude and speed.

She felt Pistols's poke in the tit for the first hours of the flight, not that he'd pushed into her flesh so hard, but just from the shock of the greeting.

The plane had one major shortcoming. The heaters for the cabin were either broken or entirely inadequate. She huddled in her duster, hands jammed into pockets, colder than she'd ever been on any stakeout, or at least that's how it seemed to her.

Pistols pressed against her shoulder for much of the flight. In more comfortable surroundings she would have objected, but under the circumstances she was grateful for the shared body warmth. He mistook comfort for interest, and when he purposely moved her hand, pressing it against his half-erect penis down the pant leg nearest her, she got up and changed seats, risking Ahn-Kha's airsickness.

When they made it to the wooded hinterlands of Michigan for the first fuel and maintenance check, she had to use all four limbs just to get out of her seat. The field had a single building about the size of a gas station and a wind sock on a high flagstaff. There were pine trees all around and above them some overgrown power lines. She couldn't even see any roads on her side of the plane.

"That was a weenie-shrinker," Pistols said. He stamped life back into his feet as he reached up for her bag.

"One-hour break, everybody," Sime said. "They'll have coffee and rolls and some kind of protein in the main building of the airport."

"You mean the only building of the airport," Alexander said with an implied sniff. His nose and cheeks were bright red—perhaps he'd been fortifying himself against the cold the old-fashioned way.

"Ten bucks to a quarter it's venison sausage," Valentine said, emerging from the cabin where he'd been helping Montee with the navigation. He'd grown up in the Northwoods a few states over.

"And a warm toilet seat, please, God," Stamp said. Duvalier could sympathize. "I apologize for being crass, everyone, but it's an icebox back there."

Though he treated her dreadfully, she liked Pistols better than Sime, as at least he was authentic and up-front. He was an awful bastard, but you could just climb into the big-girl panties, deal, and move on. Sime was like an overalert dog—she nervously waited for him to reveal his nature and bite. Or piddle.

She didn't like how Sime looked at her. A snake looking at a bird with a broken wing would show more empathy. When you met his gaze, even by accident, he either stared you down, unblinking, until you broke off or he looked at something in the neighborhood of your face, say, your earlobe, and stared through and past it as if you and your earlobe weren't even there.

As for the other two in Sime's party, she was hoping to keep clear of Alexander; about Thérèse Stamp, she hadn't quite made up her mind. Like the others in Sime's contingent, apart from Pistols, she believed she could throw her into a New Universal Church fertility-enhancer cocktail party and not be able to tell Quisling from freeholder.

She didn't mind having another woman along, to tell the truth. Stamp could siphon off some of the male energy.

The Bucking Bronc was a tough little plane. Montee said it was day/night and all-weather, which was good for a flight north of the Great Lakes in April, when the first Midwestern thunderstorms met winter weather still boiling out of Canada and the always unpredictable North Atlantic. The passengers might be bounced around in the rough air like pills in a stunt cyclist's pocket, but the aircraft itself pushed bravely northeast at cruising speed through two fronts' worth of weather.

Valentine liked Montee as well. Val took a couple of turns in the front seat working the controls or helping with the radio getting weather reports from exotically named Canadian operators and stations. Valentine had picked up flying out west somewhere or other. She vaguely knew his father had something to do with aircraft in the pre-Kurian years. After the novelty of being at the altitude the Bucking Bronc could reach wore off, she relaxed and slept pillowed against Ahn-Kha's softly hairy arm, waking to find that someone had tucked a blanket around her.

She didn't speak much with Ahn-Kha or Val, and everyone but Pistols pretended to sleep on the flight.

The cold was dreadful. Even Val, who never complained about weather, admitted that the enforced idleness of the plane seat drove the cold between buttons and gaps, ever inward.

Flying made her wistful for the lost comforts of the old, pre-Kurian world. She'd ruined her feet walking innumerable miles, paralleling old railroad tracks or tree-broken roads. How easy it was to skip from cloud to cloud rather than plod along, down in the thorns and the bugs, desperate for cool, clean drinking water and famished for a good roast potato just dripping with sour cream.

All those wasted days, with nights shivering in some ruin full of bats and raccoons. It's so much nicer up in the clear blue air, watching the patterns clouds made on the ground. No wonder birds sing all the time.

In the air, all your stops were planned days in advance. Hot food, warm rooms, flush toilets with paper. Montee was no dummy. Well, obviously he was no dummy to handle all the math and weather analysis and navigation and mechanical checks. He had brains, and the good sense to put them to use in a comfortable cockpit with a big reclining chair.

On the ground, if you knew the country, you knew which homesteads held people who were friendly to the fight against the Kurians, ready with a cot, meat, and clean bedding for one of the "fighting folks." They sometimes paid a price, too. The Kurian Order paid informants well, and often carried out brutal reprisals. There were sad moments when she walked up a familiar path only to find the house ransacked and empty. You never learned the full story. Sometimes there was a little line of chest-high bullet holes against a basement wall, sometimes not.

The hot anger you felt at the destruction of people who treated you like family kept you going through hunger and illness for another six months or a year.

The problem was this shit epoch she'd been born into. Fifty years earlier and she would have been able to fly anywhere—Paris, the Great Wall of China, the Great Barrier Reef. If she'd been born fifty years in the future, assuming a big chunk of Earth could be cleared of the Kurian Order, they'd be flying all the time again. The knowledge was all there, even now new planes were being built. It was up to her generation to get rid of the Kurians, and do it mostly on foot, while dusty, sweaty, and thirsty.

Sometimes she hated those in the past, who didn't know how good they had it. Even though she was fighting for them, she held a grudge against the future generations, too. She had risked her life fighting across a big piece of the old United States for their sake, after all.

Valentine and Ahn-Kha never groused about these awful years. Hell, Ahn-Kha wasn't even on the right planet; he should have been born light-decades or whatever they were called away.

She'd keep on trudging, of course. And when they finally shot her in some basement, would anyone remember? Yeah, there'd be some statue looking over a park somewhere. "Tomb of the Unnamed Resistance Guerilla," but the name Alessa Duvalier would be nowhere, once the handful of friends she had in the world died.

Well, maybe not. When she returned from this trip, assuming fate gave her that outcome, she should really sit down with that journalist Boelnitz back in Evansville and tell him some of her stories. Maybe she'd make it into an appendix chapter having to do with the Twisted Cross or the Golden Ones or the discovery of what was going on at Xanadu, that Reaper ranch in Ohio.

Montee set the plane down on a blacker-than-black runway with big yellow lettering and numbers in vast blocks. The hieroglyphic numbers and arrows must have meant something to him, because he made several turns on his way to park the plane inside a little hangar at the end of a row of much larger hangars near the terminal.

This was a serious airport. Hangars and multiple areas for the planes, not just a patch of land with some tie-downs near the airstrip.

"Welcome to Canada," Montee said over the intercom. "Ontario, to be exact. You'll be happy to know we're spending the night somewhere warm. We'll be deplaning out of public eye," Montee said, emerging from the cockpit as a little tractor pulled the plane into the hangar. His boots were untied, she noticed. Did he trim his toenails in the air or something? "Fourteen-hour overnight, refueling, and maintenance. The airport has twenty-four-hour food and drink, for those of you who just want to sleep in the seats or the aisle. There's a functioning pre-2022 hotel nearby. This is not my first time at this airport, but I tend to bed down by the plane, so I can't vouch for the cleanliness of the sheets."

"What do we use for money up here?" Stamp asked.

"That's taken care of, courtesy of Southern Command," Alexander said, patting a travel satchel slung over his shoulder. It had a luggage tag that matched his watchband.

They all worked the kinks out of their frozen bodies and deplaned. They were tucked in way at the end of the hangars. A military-looking jet with camouflage and drop tanks for extra fuel was the only other flying occupant in the hangar. Red tool cases on wheels and some machine-shop gear filled one wall. A pair of uniformed men watched them through glass from a little hangar office with doors to both outside and inside the hangar.

"Want to go halvsies on a room, Red?" Pistols asked her.

"Yes, but not with you," she replied.

The airport in Free Canada was the busiest she had ever seen, even accounting for military activity in the better-equipped Kurian Zones. There were twenty or thirty small planes in various degrees of readying for flight, taxiing, landing, and embarking and disembarking passengers.

"That's Canada for you," Montee said. "Lots of remote little hamlets. Only way to get there is by plane, with the roads mostly in disrepair. If the Kurians want to come up from the south, they'll have to cut their way through an awful lot of trees. Fuel's no problem; they've got fracked oil out the wazoo all over the place."

They would have a night's rest at the airport. There was a three-story hotel nearby if they wanted, and there were plenty of homes in the small town that took in "layovers" less expensively. Montee handed out a labeled envelope to each of them with Canadian currency inside. It had pictures of birds and bears and wolves, the wildlife kind.

She ended up getting a room at the pre-2022 hotel with Valentine and Ahn-Kha. It had a whitewashed outside and most of the lights around the entryway doors still worked, bathing the drive up to the hotel doors in warm, welcoming light. The desk staff's English sounded a little strange to them, kind of a Green Mountain Boy nasal twang. It wasn't cheap—or maybe the Canadian paper currency they'd been given didn't count for much in this particular province. Hard to say. They had to pay extra for towels, and declined a soap-and-shampoo purchase three times.

"You're getting the shampoo free with the bar of soap," the desk clerk said.

"Or the bar of soap free with the shampoo, if you

want to look at it that way." The manager laughed, though the humor in his statement was a little hard to detect.

They asked for extra blankets and paid a "laundry fee" for them. For such a classy-looking hotel, the Canucks sure bled you with a thousand fees.

But, it was warm, and it was quiet once night fell and the buzzing of the air traffic lessened to a single night landing after nine. She awoke, feeling very refreshed, to the sound of Valentine in the shower.

"He is getting his towel money back in hot water, I think," Ahn-Kha said. He was in a foul mood; the way the toilet was set next to the bathroom wall made it hard for him to properly use the facilities.

She wasn't looking forward to another long day in the bouncing, cold plane. And in all likelihood she'd get stuck next to Pistols again.

Time to straighten matters out with Postle once and for all. After her morning ablutions she spent a few minutes in the washroom sharpening her cat claws.

She and Ahn-Kha waited while Valentine drank coffee with Sime at the other end of the lobby.

Ahn-Kha was a living anthill, crawling with kids from a fecund family of travellers. They were using his long forearm and back hair to pull themselves up onto his shoulders, where the view was higher than anywhere else in the terminal.

"I told Sime about the possible penetration of the conference," Valentine said.

She felt her cheeks flush with anger. "You what?" It was a stupid thing to say; the reason she'd become infuriated was that she'd heard him properly, after all, but it was practically one of those reflexive responses that came out the way your leg jumps when the doctor taps your knee with a hammer. He ignored the steam and let her cool off, like a picture she'd seen of Hawaiian lava running into the ocean. Behind him, Ahn-Kha bore the pulls and pinches of the kids with a toothless smile and a wince.

"Simmer down. I trust Sime. He's always been straight with me, brutally so, sometimes. He said he'd keep it from his team, for now. He's worked with Postle and Alexander before, but this is his first trip with Stamp."

"Who is she, anyway?"

"Some friend of the president's. She's a money person. A financial backer. Sime said this conference was really supposed to be a sightseeing jaunt, at least for the Southern Command delegation."

Touring. Well, nice work if you can get it. "Did he seem concerned?"

"He said he'd be surprised if the Kurians didn't manage to sneak a spy or two in. He's not that concerned, for two reasons. One is that there's a lot of security, and the location of the conference isn't even going to be announced until thirty-six hours before it is supposed to start, and second, he's there to make sure the UFR and Southern Command commit to zilch."

"I thought it was supposed to be, you know, unification for victory grand strategy session or something."

"That's the impression the invitation gives," Valentine said.

"I wonder why so many freeholds bother going at all," she said. She took out the Canadian currency. "A trip like this can't be easy, or cheap."

"I'm wondering that myself. Appearances, I suppose. Solidarity, maybe. Can't be that fun of a long trip—nobody's getting there by luxury liner," Valentine said. "Sime said something about votes on strategy, and different freeholds agreeing to pressure the Kurians in certain areas. I know Southern Command's gone into a defensive crouch ever since the victories in Texas. My guess is that Sime is going because he's well known outside Arkansas and Texas, and when he says Southern Command won't do any joint operations for the foreseeable future, they'll believe him."

Not for the first time, Duvalier wondered why Lambert had insisted that she make this trip. Ahn-Kha she understood—Valentine without his faithful shaggy friend was a bit of a sourpuss. He was like a big, savage dog who loved you and you alone; you slept better at night knowing he was ready to rip out a few throats in your defense. But what did she bring to the table, other than a joint history? She liked to complain to him on an op; it was nice to have a real set of ears listening and talking back rather than having imaginary conversations with yourself that made you wonder if you were cracking up far from help and safety.

Valentine was always harping about her needing a rest. Maybe he knew this was going to be a big political circle jerk and just saw it as a way to get her out of the bluegrass and the mosquitoes for a nice break with clean bedding. If so, she should just roll with it. Life was handing her a tiny taste of what those Old Worlders enjoyed without much appreciation.

Well, she might as well relax and have a good time, at least until they reached the still-secret destination in the Baltic. *Cocktails and hot towels all around, steward.*

"So, what are we supposed to do?" she asked.

Valentine shrugged, but his eyes remained distant and thoughtful. "We don't have to follow Sime's orders; we're representing Kentucky. I'd still like to find that infiltrator. We can't count on whoever it is to just be there to take notes. I imagine there are a lot of people there the Kurians would like to see captured or eliminated."

"Maybe we should double-check the garbage trucks," she said. She'd seen those dreadful Grog-grown Reapers that had attacked Fort Seng one wild night. What if the Kurians somehow introduced a hundred of them to the conference?

"We should keep that in mind," Valentine said. "I'm sure they wouldn't mind the whole conference being wiped out. I don't know that anyone could do anything about a ballistic missile, but I hope they've planned for anything and everything. I've had some experience with cold-water amphibian Grogs. They could come up out of the Baltic about anywhere."

"They'll be sorry to lose Ahn-Kha here," she said. "He seems like a hit as a tourist attraction."

"I don't think there are any Grogs in Eastern Canada. There are some out west, I believe. That lost tribe of Golden Ones," Valentine said.

"Well, they must not get around much."

"I'll go rescue him," Valentine said.

They returned to the airport to find that one of the engines on the plane was being worked on. It would mean an extra three or four hours on the ground, the pilot predicted.

Sime didn't want them wandering the airport, so he confined them to either the hangar or the hotel they'd already checked out of.

"Not going back there," Valentine said. "They'll charge us for breathing the lobby air."

The soldiers, showing the renowned politeness of the region, were willing to hand over the little hangar office and withdraw to attend to some minor maintenance duties for the hangar's portable work lighting. The office had a little radio tuned to cheerful music coming in across Lake Ontario from the Ordnance. There were but two chairs; neither could be called comfortable, but the space heater made up for the lack of seating with its cozy glow. She and Val and Pistols made themselves as comfortable as possible. The Canadians had a big aluminum thermos of something, but none of them felt like pressing the hospitality that much.

Sime paced the hangar with Alexander, and Stamp went off to the washroom to do her laundry in a sink. Ahn-Kha, who was always interested in something new, made himself useful around the engine as it was being worked on by Montee and the Canadian Provincial Defense air mechanic.

Valentine lost himself in a book for a few minutes, then announced that he'd have to sit too much in the plane. He left to go join Ahn-Kha at the engine, leaving her alone with the bodyguard.

Postle considered not-in-air time as off-duty time, and drank. He wasn't a heavy drinker as most people would call it, more of a steady one, consuming two beers an hour over a span of increasingly frequent bathroom breaks. He seemed the type to relax into a nap before becoming loudly drunk.

The drinking also released a certain amount of libido, she discovered. As they passed each other just outside the office, she leaving for and he returning from the toilet facility, he interposed an arm, blocking her way.

"Do you know what it's like to be with a real man?" he said, the alcohol on his breath setting every nerve in her body on fire with a fight-or-flight reaction. "Someone who can show you what it means to be a real woman?"

"I know at least three women better at making me feel like a woman than any man," she said. It wasn't strictly accurate to throw down the lesbian card, but men like Postle tended to be as sticky as a filled condom if you didn't handle them just right.

"Maybe you haven't met the right man yet. Could be me," he said, tipping his forehead so far forward it almost touched hers.

"I'm sure the right man for me doesn't have breath like an iguana," she said. She had no idea what an iguana's breath was like, in truth, but her imagination was stuck on lizards for some reason.

She slipped her hands into her pockets and into her cat claws in their loose sheaths of chamois that kept them from puncturing or getting caught on the fabric.

"I love a woman who knows how to play the game," Postle said.

"Game? Let's set the rules, then," she said, pulling out her claw-fitted hands. She reached around him with them and hooked him by the buttocks, the sharpened points piercing his denim with ease. A brief, excited *ah-hhh!* turned into a gasp of alarm as he realized that she wasn't using her hands.

She dug the flesh-ripping hooked blades into each cheek near the crack.

"Now, you can either promise to leave my body alone—talk whatever shit you want whenever you want, just don't touch—or I can open you up and let the asshole out, so to speak. If you want to spend the rest of your life with a double-cut gasket and be on a first-name basis with adult diaper washers, just keep rubbing my breast like you think a genie is going to pop out."

"You're drawing blood!" he said.

"I'll bandage you up personally, using plenty of iodine. Do we have an understanding on the hands-off policy?"

"Understood," he said, crinkling his eyes in pain.

She extracted her claws. He didn't seem the type to pull a gun in rage, but she watched him carefully nevertheless.

He stepped back, exploring his pants with a hand. He pulled out a blood-smeared finger.

"You owe me a pair of pants."

"You owe me an ungroped breast," she said. "How about we call it a push?"

Covering the damage with his tactical vest, he headed off to the men's room.

The Canadians announced that they were going to the terminal for lunch, and offered to make purchases for the delayed travellers. She decided to try to bury the hatchet with Pistols and buy him a largish Canadian beer to make amends, and a hot pretzel to go with it. She handed over what she had left of Alexander's distributed currency meant for "food, drink, and necessities" to get them through the night. When they returned, she gave the beer and pretzel to Pistols and sat down with Valentine and Ahn-Ka to eat her own stew.

The meat was tough and a little gamey and seasoned with something that was trying to be oregano. She wondered if she was eating moose or caribou or some other denizen of the Northwoods.

"I thought you didn't like Postle," Valentine said, seeing Pistols lift his bottle to her from across the hangar with a friendly smile.

"I like Postle just fine," she said. "It's his penis I can't seem to get along with. It does too much of his thinking."

With Pistols tamed and everyone else occupied and the office warm, she stretched out on the floor and napped until Valentine woke her (she didn't know it, but after Pistols told of his impromptu blood-draw, everyone was careful not to startle her).

The pilot waved to them from the door. He looked freshly shaven and had a new chart under his arm.

"Last leg. In the air, anyway," Valentine said.

She spent much of the flight looking at Postle, who was shifting uncomfortably in his seat. She honestly hoped the claw pricks weren't becoming infected. She'd probably gone a little overboard in proving her point, but she'd managed to get back on board without so much as a glance from him. Maybe he'd have an entertaining story for the Swedish girls, or the girls wherever they were heading in the Baltic.

She was growing used to the rattling old plane now that their trip in it was just about over. She wished it were flying them all the way overseas; it seemed capable of a transatlantic hop if it could refuel in, say, Iceland, but it seemed there were stealthier arrangements for the other legs of the journey. Well, she wasn't organizing it.

For some reason or other, Valentine liked the man. Probably because he was about as emotional as a reptile. Valentine had a hard time dealing with the messiness that went with any kind of emotional display. Besides, he and Sime had a past, mostly bad. They were like two drunks who'd beaten the snot out of each other in a bar fight and ended up drinking buddies. The combination of their air of cool appraisal and the inability to read their expressions put her on edge. She could never relax around such men.

Pistols, on the other hand, was more her type. Deadly—well, she hoped, for their sake—and direct. Now that his grabby habits were straightened out, that is.

CHAPTER FOUR

H*alifax, April: Part fishing village, part seaport, part land's-end outpost, the city is as tough and crusty as a barnacle. For much the same reason. The cold North Atlantic besieges the port, seemingly trying to force a retreat toward more hospitable ground. But this outer corner of Nova Scotia isn't ready to surrender yet. Centuries of tradition have inured the residents to the weather, and they are rightfully proud of their important role in the struggle against the Kurians. Their port is the main seagoing gateway across the Atlantic that is free of Kurian control—or even occasional disruption. For once, the long, cold winters worked in the city's favor. The Kurians, while they have the technology to survive in any climate, prefer warm ones for safety's sake. They never know when they might be forced from their holes and have to dive into the nearest waterway or drift in high winds to a new refuge. They generally leave the administration of cold climates to their allies.*

From Halifax, shipping and passengers break up into smaller contingents that can be transported by lighter smuggling craft into the Great Lakes or down the eastern seaboard of the United

States. Some trade, mostly furs and precious metals or rare earths scraped from the tundra and cold shores of northern Canada, heads east to Europe as well, mostly in the hands of experienced smugglers.

There's still the fish, as well. The cod fleets are busy, save for the wild winter months, when even their tough boats and legendary seamanship are not equal to the challenge. Some larger ships, mini oceangoing factories, process the cod into frozen strips that serve as cheap, nutritious protein brought by rail and the seasonal roads to the eastern half of Free Canada that runs from the midway point between Toronto and Montreal all the way northeast to the ocean.

One could be forgiven for assuming that the isolation would make for a lifeless city where the residents scuttle from breakfast table to work, work to washing basin at home, and washing basin to curtained bed before beginning the cycle again. Nothing could be further from the truth. The little town is filled with everything from theaters to taverns to, remarkably, a pair of fine-dining restaurants, one complete with potted palms and a black-and-white checkerboard marble floor polished to a brilliant sheen and white-jacketed waiters. The people of Halifax, most of the year trapped beneath iron-gray skies, have found in this wind-and-spray whipped point of the New World cultural resources that a twentieth-century resident wouldn't have imagined.

The cold was dreadful. The wet gave it a penetrative staying power; even after you stepped inside, it took a few minutes to warm up. She hoped the whole trip wouldn't be like this.

They had arrived with six days until their transatlantic ship departed for the Baltic, and had already spent three of them working out the kinks from the long, segment-by-segment flight.

"Easy from here on out," Sime announced upon their bouncy landing into the wind at the Halifax airstrip, with a smile that for once didn't look practiced and professional. Sime was probably sick of riding in a walk-in cooler that was being tossed around like the last tablet in a pillbox on a courier's galloping horse.

Valentine was fond of Sime, and being Valentine, wanted her to like him, too. He was always defending Sime as being "good at his job." She could put up with him for the trip to the conference, but it didn't mean she had to like him. He always evoked memories of the Kansas "quality" of her youth. Their faces and hair were always as polished as their vehicles' dashboards, and to her, just as plasticine. They were all good at their jobs, too.

They were met at the airport by a bearded man in a furry hat that made Duvalier think of Russians. She had no idea what kind of hats Russians wore, honestly, but this one was tallish, with flaps at the sides, and neatly trimmed in gray fur. She'd seen something like it somewhere or other, maybe on a vodka bottle. It looked warm. Indeed, it must have been, because he wore only a goose-down vest over a wool shirt as protection against the North Atlantic wind.

"Welcome to Nova Scotia," he said, with an even

thicker accent than they'd heard in Ontario. "Name's Preffer. I'm with the Refugee Network. I'm arranging your departure for Europe. I have a car waiting to take you to your hotel. We weren't sure about your arrival, so you have a couple days in balmy Halifax before starting your crossing." He cracked his knuckles before shaking their hands.

He bundled them into a delivery van that smelled like kerosene. There were little fold-down seats in the back. It made Duvalier think of the collection vans from the Kurian Zones, save that this one wasn't armored. And there were handles on all the cargo-area doors.

"Sorry about the no-windows thing," Preffer said. "We use this when we need to discreetly shuttle refugees around. Not that you're refugees—no offense."

The town was full of "refugees." Halifax, as it turned out, had families who'd escaped from the Congo delta to the Gulf of Murmansk.

Valentine had talked on the flight about Hong Kong, how it was a poor province of China until some revolution or other. A lot of people fled to Hong Kong because it still had British law, and within a few decades a poor collection of muddy hillside villages became some of the most valuable real estate in the world.

Before she grew bored and more or less quit listening, she had heard Val go on to say that something similar was under way in Halifax. People with the means to escape the European Kurians tended to flee to Southern Argentina or Canada, and Halifax had become what Ellis Island was to an earlier generation of immigrants: a gateway to a New World. Despite the cold North Atlantic climate and the damp chill through most of the year, they stayed and prospered, bringing with them all sorts of intriguing abilities. There were restaurateurs and clothiers, makers of precision instruments and doctors, furriers and perfume manufacturers—Halifax still did a little whaling to help feed its population—making it a more cosmopolitan city than it had ever been, even during the World War booms it had known.

The immigrants had mostly settled in an area of the city known as the Beehive. It covered the old North End of the Halifax peninsula, centered around the old Hydrostone and the memorial to the Halifax explosion in 1917 when an ammunition ship in the harbor exploded, leveling most of the city. The colors, sights, and sounds of the Beehive ran almost around the clock. The locals had covered stretches of the narrow old streets with a sort of plasticized canvas to keep out the rain.

Preffer set them up in four rooms above a twenty-four-hour café. The kitchen had been stripped and turned into a dormitory with sinks for washing and laundry. Everything was double-layered. Double layers of glass to keep out the cold, double layers of door with steel bars over the regular door for security, blinds and curtains on the windows. At least there were no bugs. Duvalier was an expert on critters in cheap lodgings.

"When do we depart for Europe?" Sime asked.

"Your boat is here. She came in a couple days late,

sorry to say, and the crew needs a few days of rest. Soon as the captain gives me the okay, we can ship you out."

"A ship?" Stamp asked, making a face as Pistols removed his boots and socks to air out his toes.

Preffer cracked his knuckles. "Well, not really a ship. But you'll be comfortable enough."

"Must we be isolated until then?" Stamp asked, aiming the question at Sime rather than Preffer.

Sime glanced at Preffer.

"The town is safe enough. Nobody's going to get shanghaied for their aura," he said. "There are a lot of touts soliciting people for labor of one kind or another, long hours at low pay. Pickpockets might get something, but we don't have a lot of violent crime. Don't be loud and drunk; that's a guaranteed night in the cells and while we have good relations with the black-and-blues, they don't have to do us any favors. So please, stay out of trouble."

He extracted a small phone from his pocket and plugged it into the wall. There were two numbers written on it in indelible pen. "Call if you're at a loss about anything. The bigger number is mine. The smaller is the Refugee Network. Only a few people know about your trip, so if you can't reach me and you have to go through them, just tell them you're new arrivals and you're above the Ballyhoo Diner. Someone will get here in minutes."

They could order up food from the café through a dumbwaiter, of all things; Preffer had made some sort of arrangements. There were people going in and out of both front and back at all hours with no small amount of noise.

Valentine and Pistols fell asleep within minutes of deciding on sleeping locations, Sime and his secretary were comparing notes about the journey, and Ahn-Kha was pushing two single mattresses together to make a bed able to accommodate most of him.

The next morning, they ate breakfast over the smell of drying socks.

"I've been cooped up too long," Stamp said as Ahn-Kha loaded the breakfast dishes back into the dumb-waiter. "Alessa, feel like exploring?"

She shrugged. The cold wasn't what she'd call pleasant, but compared to a Wyoming winter it was within an elbow poke of balmy. "It's what I do."

Sime had produced a small radio and everyone was listening to the news from the Baltic English-language station. She buttoned up her duster, picked up the sword-stick, and followed Stamp, who was dressed in her nice camel-colored long coat, out the door.

They explored the Beehive. It was already humming with human, vehicular, muscle-powered, and horse-drawn traffic.

Duvalier noticed there were little decorative bees everywhere. On signposts, in store windows, on the door handles of a few of the more expensive shops. She commented on it and Stamp just shrugged and said, "Let's ask."

In every store where they engaged in casual conversation, they asked about the bees. They received a slightly different answer every time.

No one knew where the bee symbol came from. Some said it was Newfoundland honey, a "free" three-ounce jar of which was given away to every immigrant, thanks to the resources of the Newfoundland Relocation Resource, the entity that helped refugees find a useful life on the island or elsewhere in Canada. Others said it was a manufacturer symbol, that of a large cutlery concern that had set itself up in Halifax, reputedly owned by some French. Others claimed it was the Mormons, whose missions also did a great deal of fine work with the most destitute of the refugees. Or it might have been the Canadian currency, which featured a bee on its hundred-dollar bill. It could be that bees were also relative newcomers to Newfoundland, and had prospered under the altered weather patterns of the Kurian Order.

In any case, bees were a theme of the Beehive. They were pictured in shop windows, decorated lampposts, and glowed golden brown when painted on lampshades. The town certainly buzzed; despite the cold, everyone seemed to be outdoors: talking, standing around with steaming mugs or glasses in their fists, enjoying the night and the camaraderie. There were string quartets playing and accordions, with rival musicians playing spirited dance numbers—Duvalier recognized the "Pennsylvania Polka"—or sadder, wistful songs. She noted that the livelier players had larger audiences and more money thrown into the proffered hat.

And the food! There were street vendors and restaurants, cafés and bakeries, all doing a thriving business, with everything wrapped up in brown paper and string that all seemed to come from the same source. Every three steps a new aroma seemed to strike: coffee, yeast baking, chocolate melting, meat roasting (she had to follow that one; it turned out to be a vast wheel of spiced flesh rotating on a heated spit that a man would shave and then sell with a little red onion and sour cream on a piece of flatbread, her first encounter with a "gyro").

The Old World must have been something like this, she thought.

She mostly watched Stamp shop. A few of the Canadians remarked on her syrup-sweet Southern accent, but not as many as Duvalier would have thought.

When their feet grew sore, they stopped in one of the cafés.

"You haven't bought anything," Stamp stated, as though it were an accusation.

"I don't need anything."

"Oh, sweetie pie, you should treat yourself. I wasn't expecting Canada to have so much. I figured I'd have to wait until we got to Europe. But wouldn't it be nice to have some fresh, stylish clothes for the trip?"

For just a moment, Duvalier was jealous of the world that Stamp inhabited. She had time to think about clothes, how they looked, what others thought about how they looked. It seemed both frivolous and appealing at the same time.

"Listen, Alessa, I have a stash of gold coins. I want to change one of them for the funny-money currency they use around here and spend it shopping and eating. They have cheap seafood everywhere here, and I'm in the mood to stuff myself, enjoy some wine, and pick up something nice." Stamp wore an inviting but practiced smile.

Duvalier wondered briefly what she meant by "pick up something nice."

"Why me? Sime seems more the type for perusing a wine list."

"You seem like you don't know what girl time is. I like exploring. This is the first time I've had an opportunity to travel, and I need a partner in fun. I'd feel a little safer with someone tough around. I don't want one of the guys. I'm not looking for a date or anything like that. Certainly I don't know you, but I feel comfortable around you and, well, I'm sorry to be blunt, but you look like you need it. Don't take that the wrong way."

How many guys have given her the "diamond in the rough" line? Not as many lately. "Honestly, I've never been one for appearances."

"Well, I think you could be really something if you made a little effort. You'd be shocked at how little it takes. C'mon, as a personal favor. I know a lot of people between Austin and Little Rock. I should be able to do you a good turn someday, when you're no longer doing front-line work. Truthies."

"I don't care for the front lines any more than you do," Duvalier said. "I avoid them if at all possible. But what I do, I plan to keep doing until they get me. There are a lot of forgotten bodies out there, people swallowed by the crematoriums after the Reapers have had their fun, who deserve a little payback."

Stamp looked a little ashamed. "I should really do more to support the cause. Maybe I can get a hospital built by one of the foundations. I'm on three boards."

Duvalier found herself smiling back. "Okay, build a hospital and name the operating room after me. Or maybe a mortuary room. Something sharp and bloody would be a nice legacy."

Stamp's smile grew more natural. "There you go, then. Deal."

With the beginnings of a bond formed, Stamp asked her to "truthies" on Valentine. While Duvalier had no end of anecdotes that might be entertaining, she didn't much feel like issuing them in exchange for a few pieces of clothing.

Refreshed, they wandered around the blocks for a few more hours, looking through windows. Off the main streets and in the alleys there were a lot of secondhand-clothing stores, places to get shoes repaired, and on every other corner there was a place to sell valuables. Duvalier looked at the gleaming jewelry behind armored glass and thought about the broken dreams each piece represented.

Of course, she'd never had much in the way of dreams to break to begin with. The only rings she'd ever worn were as fake as a thirty-dollar bill.

The raw spring cold made them hungry again quickly, and as Duvalier's ever-troublesome stomach growled, they looked at menus posted next to doors until she found a seafood place where Stamp liked the look of the "plating." The only kind of plating Duvalier was familiar with involved armor on reconnaissance vehicles, but she figured Stamp was in her element when it came to how the forks should lie on the napkins. She just nodded when Stamp asked her if she wanted to get a bite.

She had a chowder soup and a pan-fried piece of cod covered with little pealike things that Stamp told her were capers. They were nicely salty, without the overtaste of olives, and went with the cod admirably. Stamp drank wine and Duvalier had a cola. It was a real cola, a wonderful combination of fizzy and syrupy with a hint of fruit cocktail—the restaurant's own concoction, which they called an Italian Soda, though the waiter seemed to take it as a personal insult that she wouldn't drink wine with the meal.

After they were fortified by the food, the real shopping began. Duvalier found spending time with Stamp strangely exhausting, like trying to converse in a foreign language. Her one triumph came when she found some "French milled" soaps for Valentine and a boar's-hair brush for Ahn-Kha. Stamp offered to pay, but she still had some of Montee's Canadian currency left, and it was enough to get soap and their biggest brush, anyway.

"You're not getting yourself a little indulgence? Not even chocolates?"

"Gives me the runs," Duvalier said. Which was only sometimes true; the ration chocolate in the Kurian Zone had some strange fat in it that kept her squatting. She'd had real Hershey bars and been fine.

Stamp wasn't quite the sophisticate she claimed to
be. Some of the shop staff corrected her on minor
points: she called any sort of fancy dress "couture" ("if
it's hanging on a rack, it's not couture," sniffed an Italian shopgirl) and she called an alligator purse "patent
leather." Even Duvalier, who wasn't quite clear on what
culottes were, was pretty sure alligator hides weren't
patent.

She did, however, insist on taking Duvalier to a salon
to have her hair and face done. She agreed more enthu-
siastically than she would have believed possible a few
days ago. The trip was seeming less and less of an op
and more like the vacation Colonel Lambert had promised. Stamp was much more in her element there, and
Duvalier had had a theatrical streak and done stage
makeup a few times in her life. She'd had to doll up
enough times that she was comfortable with makeup.
She tried a few different colors and finally went with a
pale violet base and purple highlight to go with the
green in her eyes. It felt oddly relaxing to lie back in a
chair and have someone putter away at her eyes, and
the results were startling, even before they moved on to
finishing touches with the hair. They couldn't do much
with her short-short hair, but they did plaster it down
with something that gave it a nice shine and brightened
the color.

The cosmetologists tut-tutted over her skin. "Do
you live under a sunlamp?" one asked.

"I'm outdoors a lot," Duvalier said.

"Take care, duckies," the beauticians said as they
left. Stamp gave a wink and a wave.

Stamp wanted more wine, and Duvalier hoped she wouldn't have to carry her home. Rain and wind came in from the sea with the evening, ruining their makeup and hair in a few minutes of chill exposure.

"Short hair has its advantages," Stamp said as they surveyed the ruins in the shelter of a doorway.

"I'm pretty tired. Time to call it a day?" Duvalier asked.

"I was going to save this for later, but you might as well have it now," Stamp said, handing over a little gift bag.

In it was a selection of makeups, lip glosses, and some kind of little pearly drops you were supposed to break open and rub around your eyes and forehead to get rid of wrinkles.

Duvalier snorted. "I feel like I owe you an apology for wasting your money."

"Plenty more money where that came from."

"From where does the family fortune spring?" Duvalier asked.

"UFR contracts, mostly. Roads, bridges, power lines. We do a little of everything. We've been busy with the respite buildup. War's such a dead end."

They left the hotel for Halifax's harbor side on a chill morning, before dawn on the first day of May, piled into that same plumbing supply van with the fold-down seats.

Everyone, even so-phlegmatic-it-was-hard-to-tell-he-was-alive Sime, had enjoyed Halifax. Duvalier now found the cold ocean air refreshing. Valentine had told her what the west coast of Lake Superior was like in winter—cold and damp that sank in deep and was tough to get rid of quickly, even in the warmest room—and she'd been expecting something like that. This was more like wet and windy fall weather, which she always enjoyed, provided she didn't have to walk far in it.

They were waiting for their ride to the docks, having received a message that their stopover in Halifax was coming to an end the following morning. Everyone was back in their travel clothes, toiletries and freshly washed laundry all packed away. Stamp had on a blue-and-white-striped shirt under a navy-colored blazer, with a cute white hat. Valentine had muttered that she looked like a Cracker Jack sailor as they shared a last round of coffee from the café below.

"No, that just won't do," Stamp said, looking at Duvalier.

"What won't do?" she asked.

"You're about to take your first cross-Atlantic voyage. You can't board looking like a stowaway rat," Stamp said.

"I believe this is your first cross-Atlantic voyage, too, Thérèse," Sime said. "While you certainly look nautical, I doubt it'll be a yacht parade."

"I'm going on board looking right," she replied. "Whaddya think?" she asked, performing a clumsy pirouette for Duvalier.

"Anchors aweigh," she said.

Duvalier submitted to having her makeup put on. Stamp loaned her a nautical-looking cable sweater. Fortunately, Stamp's shopping mania on Duvalier's behalf hadn't gone so far as to include a new wardrobe, so she was able to slouch around in her duster and the borrowed sweater. She wondered how her tired old Evanshikers—rubber-soled ankle boots from a cottage industry in Evansville that turned worn-out tires into new footwear tread—would handle seawater.

Preffer nursed the old van through the tight streets, going gently through the turns and taking it easy on the brakes. If there was a Kurian spy keeping tabs on the activities of the Refugee Network, his job was made a lot easier.

"Do you have any idea of the cabin arrangements?" Stamp asked Sime once they were loaded in the back.

"No, the Baltic League organized the rest of the trip through the Refugee Network," Sime said. "I just had orders to get to Halifax by a certain date."

"Hmmm. Let's hope we're not sharing."

"I'm sorry to hear that," Ahn-Kha said. "I put in a request to bunk with you. We settled it while you were napping off the wine yesterday. I hope I get you. You're so clean and quiet. But I must warn you, when I get seasick, I become very gassy."

"What?" Stamp asked, shocked.

"A joke," Ahn-Kha said. "I suspect we'll be down in a hold somewhere for at least part of the trip. We'll be lucky if we're just sharing with each other and not the ship's rats."

"He's contrary from not being able to stretch out in bed," Valentine said. "I'm looking forward to it. The only blue water I've ever been on was the Caribbean. The North Atlantic will probably be a little more exciting."

"I prefer my jokes starting with animals walking into a saloon," Stamp said.

Sime wanted their departure quiet and discreet. Their transport couldn't have been more humble.

The *Out for Lunch* was a disappointment to Stamp. Her pleasure-cruise outfit seemed clownish when set in front of a rust-sided fishing boat that had a definite odor of fish to it.

It was a wide-bodied boat with high sides, with roughly the proportions and lines of an oversized row-boat, except for the big control house amidships. Masts with yardarms for nets and the placement or extraction of fishing gear stood to either side just behind the control house. Much of the woodwork on deck looked newly replaced, and the control house had a fresh coat of paint. It seemed the captain-owner maintained the boat by working on whatever was the most pressing need in the winter off-season.

Instead of a steward ready to hand them welcome-aboard beverages, they were greeted by a line of men in yellow plasticized overalls and thick rubber boots. Most of them had scruffy beards, but they smiled in greeting regularly enough.

You also had to walk down from the high pier to get

into the boat. Stamp made the descent tentatively, as though aware that the next leg of the voyage wasn't the sort of conveyance she was used to.

"Gew, what are we going to do with him?" one of the crew asked as they sized up Ahn-Kha. "Hope this'un likes fish."

"As a matter of fact, I do," Ahn-Kha rumbled. "I can catch my own on a long line."

Appearances aside, once the captain took them below, Duvalier was impressed. It was a ship designed to smuggle people. The fishermen on board could create, with their ice machine and a realistic, permanent board of fish heads and tails (mostly haddock and cod), false fronts to the fish bins below that could conceal two people in each bay.

They were little compartments, about the size of a large closet. Duvalier thought them perfectly sized—indeed, cozy—but Ahn-Kha could barely squeeze into one of them, folded up like a card table. Because you did not stretch out your full length in a hammock, you could sleep comfortably—if you weren't a Golden One, that is. There were little grates between the compartments, allowing you to converse in the manner of a Catholic confessional.

Their passengers did not have to spend the whole voyage in hiding, of course. During the day they could move about the ship—there was a small galley and recreation area with a little locker full of books in various languages, plus the control room for the captain.

Captain Ableyard of the *Out for Lunch* was a very

young man with sandy hair and permanently wind-burned skin. Duvalier doubted he could be much into his mid-twenties.

"Been at sea since I was twelve, apprenticed to a tuna fisherman," Ableyard said. "I know, the boat has a day-sailor's name. Most working boats have women's names, a mother or a wife or a daughter. Old Captain Spangler had a real odd sense of humor—never really fit in with the other captains and men. He was the one who converted it into a refugee boat. Honestly, he didn't care much about fishing. I like to bring in a commercial-sized catch, in case I'm searched."

"It's a new experience to have people outbound," Ableyard said. "We're usually picking up midocean."

She learned a little about the refugee extraction system from Europe. The European fishing boats would take a few out and pass them off to fishing boats of another nation, Ireland or Iceland most frequently. They in turn would pass them to the Canadians.

"There used to be a great line through the Azores to Florida or the Caribbean or South America, but the Kurians occupied the Azores and cut that off. Everyone always asks me what good I think I'm doing, bringing them over in threes and fours a few times a year. They wouldn't ask if they could see the faces of the three or four when we pass the Sambro Island Lighthouse."

Valentine nodded heartily. He was always of the opinion that everyone making a tiny contribution would create a tsunami that not even the Kurian Order could stop.

The captain showed them some marks near his

boat's steering wheel. It was in the traditional wood, though without spokes. The wood-panel console beneath had dozens of little hash marks running just out of sight from a man standing at the wheel.

"Every time I bring human cargo in through the narrows, I kneel down, thank God, and make a mark."

"Will you make one for us?"

"You're not escaping anything. But it's nice to have celebrities on board."

"We're celebrities?"

"I don't have the faintest idea of what you've done, but you must be somebody important if you're headed over to the Baltic League. Glad to do my bit in the other direction."

The net boats they followed out of the harbor turned north. Behind them, a larger vessel Ableyard identified as a crab boat rolled more gently on the waves owing to its deeper keel. Its centerline had a sort of rack-catwalk running back from the prow to the bridge, filled with blue plastic barrels that served as markers for the crab traps. It was a big, powerful-looking boat, and rolled less than the *Out for Lunch*.

Duvalier wished she was on a boat that was rolling a little less. The motion gave her a headache and left her feeling nauseous. Ahn-Kha spied out her condition and stuck one ear out and one ear up; in the semaphore parlance of Golden One ears she knew that to be a good-humored reassurance. The sea didn't seem to bother him.

She didn't have time to decide between the ship's

rail and a toilet. An alarmed shout sounded almost as soon as they were in the Atlantic swell.

"A patrol boat! Christ, we're goners," one of the sailors called.

The boat was sleek and speedy-looking, closer in size to the crab boat now almost lost in the mist than to the *Out for Lunch*. It had a single turret with a cannon up front, probably a 30 mm or 40 mm, capable of tearing the fishing boat to pieces as easily as a twelve-gauge used on a bag of marshmallows.

"They can just stop and board you anytime?" Sime asked.

"There's no law out here," Ableyard said. "We fishermen have our own ways to keep order, of course, and there's our little Coast Guard, not that they're where you need 'em."

"First day out! This makes no sense at all."

"It makes perfect sense if the Kurians know you're carrying us," Valentine said.

"We were too visible in Halifax; that's the problem," Sime said. "I'm sure they have spies there."

Yeah, I'm sure news of me shopping with Stamp was all over Washington DC in minutes, Duvalier thought.

"It's quick action," she said. "The spy has to report to his superiors, who have to relay the information to someone who can make a decision about what to do about it, and then these sailors have to move their ship into a likely position to intercept. I think it's probably bad luck."

"Do you have weapons, explosives, anything?" Valentine asked.

"We have a shark stick," Ableyard said. "It can put a twelve-gauge round into something. You have to be touching, pretty much, and it takes forever to reload."

"There's the charges," an older fisherman said.

"I have a scuttling charge," Ableyard said. "If my boat's ever seized. It's large enough to blow it into matchwood."

"I have a bag with a few grenades," Pistols said.

"Best just to hide. Maybe it's a routine search," the old fisherman said.

"Nothing routine about searching an outbound fishing boat," Ableyard said. "If they're going to steal some catch for 'analysis,' that is. Not like there's anyone I can complain to. Law of the sea is whatever the person with the biggest boat and the biggest cannon says it is."

"Get me that scuttling charge," Valentine said.

Ableyard took them down to the smuggling compartments in the fish hold. The smell, though faint, made her seasickness worse. Stamp had it even worse; she was quietly vomiting into a wash bucket.

They hid, two to a compartment. The "false fish" would be laughable to anyone who would know they left that morning, and they hadn't had time to try to catch anything to add verisimilitude to them. No, any way you looked at it, they were screwed.

Pistols hid with Sime, Stamp and Alexander took another, Val and Duvalier hid in the third, and Ahn-Kha crammed himself into the fourth.

"I don't care what they say. I'm not getting taken like a rat in a hole," Duvalier said.

"So what are we doing?" Valentine said.

"Surprising them?"

Valentine whispered through the hole to Ahn-Kha's chamber and the Golden One growled something back.

"They're expecting diplomats, not you, me, and Ahn-Kha. It's not a destroyer; it's not all that much larger than this thing. Running down smugglers and whatnot is more their style. The chances of a couple Reapers being on board are pretty slim, especially in these waters. No Kurian's going to like the idea of swimming in the North Atlantic; it would kill them more quickly than us."

Ahn-Kha relayed another message: "Pistols says he's in. Sime says to shut up and not do anything unless they discover us."

They couldn't see the boarding party, but Duvalier counted footsteps.

The boarder with the machine gun fired in the direction his gun was pointing—right into the compartment holding Stamp and Alexander.

Duvalier leapt out and used her claws low, hooking one boarder behind the knee to take him off his feet and raking another one along the inner thigh, causing a gush of blood from the femoral artery.

Ahn-Kha was a hairy boulder rolling through, sending men flying this way and that. Using the enormous range of his arms, he reached up onto the bow of the patrol boat and swung on board. He jammed the scuttling charge under the gun turret and flicked the switch that closed the circuit on the fuse.

Pistols, meanwhile, had thrown an open jerry can of gasoline for the fish-preserving ice machine onto the rear deck of the patrol boat. He followed it with a grenade.

It was a mess in the compartment. Stamp was dead, her North Atlantic crossing cut short. The blood that had soaked through her carefully chosen outfit added an extra note of pathos, running across those neat nautical lines.

"Shit," Duvalier said. Stamp was a little silly, annoying even, but her heart was big, strong, and in the right place. What a loss.

Alexander was badly wounded. He had a tourniquet on his right arm and left leg. Sime and another man were up to their elbows in blood.

"Valentine, you bloody, bloody clown. I would have bribed us out of this. You risked all our lives and lost Stamp. She's a personal friend of the president," Sime said.

Duvalier didn't like Valentine taking the fall for her decision.

"Sime, it was me, not Valentine. I told him I was fighting no matter what."

"How did you know your bribe would have worked?" Valentine asked.

"Everyone has a price. You just have to figure out which currency works." He took a peek at his thigh. "Jesus. We have to get to a doctor."

"You're just grazed," Duvalier said. "I have some superglue. That'll close that up no problem."

"Superglue?" Sime gasped.

"We can't turn around now, in any case," Valentine said. "The Kurian Order's going to be visiting Halifax, investigating the loss of their boat."

"My days as captain of this boat are over," Ableyard said sadly.

"I'll buy you a new damn boat," Sime said. "I can't believe this tub's worth the paint flaking off it."

Sime clearly wasn't used to dealing with pain, Duvalier thought with satisfaction. It was nice to see him sweat and cuss out the inoffensive Captain Ableyard.

"Maybe I'll relocate to Iceland," Ableyard said. "I hear the women are incredible. They're a key link on the Northern Network."

The wind dispersed what little smoke the burning wreck of the patrol boat produced.

Most everyone instinctively made for the control room. Captain Ableyard did a quick head count and had his informal ship's medic—he'd spent two years driving a hospital ambulance before seeking refuge at sea—attend to the wounded from the fight.

Duvalier had come up on deck. She needed air before dealing with the bodies of the Kurian boarding party. One of the crew suggested putting them on fish-ice for now, so they could at least be buried on land.

They had company. The crab boat that had come out of the harbor with them had turned their way and put on speed, digging its weighed-down nose into the Atlantic rollers, dumping the water that came on board in streams of spittle running from each side of the grinlike rail. It had obviously seen the explosion and moved to render assistance. A searchlight above her control room turned on.

From the opposite direction, another low gray shape powered toward the direction of the explosion, heeling as it made a swift turn. It had a swept-back superstructure that was similar to that of the burning patrol boat, but details were indistinct in the morning fog. Its color was that of a wet greyhound.

It made sense that the Kurians would want to cover several points of the compass out of sight of Halifax. One boat couldn't do the job.

"This may be bad," Ableyard said, unlocking a wooden case near the wheel. He extracted a pair of large naval binoculars and gently rocked his hips as he examined the new mystery boat.

Bet those are worth a bit, Duvalier thought. When she was operating in the KZ, she took every opportunity she could to steal binoculars or telescopes.

Ableyard's big binoculars were so battered and worn that the black coating that had once covered the metal had all but rubbed off of the casing, leaving stainless steel shiny with the oil from various pairs of hands.

"Do you have another pair?" asked Valentine.

"Optics are family heirlooms in these parts," Ableyard said. "I've a telescope; it's a relic, not much better than a kid's toy. It's just above the chart table behind you."

With that he fell silent, observing the boat running toward them. It would beat the crab boat, easily. "No," Ableyard said, putting the silver binoculars to his face. "*No!* It's definitely a patrol boat. New England Fleet. They're burning a blue flare. That means we're to slow the engine to just enough to hold a course, and assemble on deck, hands above heads."

"We won't be able to try the same trick twice," Valentine said.

"If they even bother boarding us before sinking this pig," Ableyard said. "That turret is manned. It's aimed right at us. They're probably just waiting for an order to fire." His cheek twitched nervously.

"They might not know for sure what happened," Ahn-Kha said. "The boat behind is now nearer the debris."

"They must have our description," Ableyard said. "A big crab boat, mistaken for us? Not likely."

"Should we abandon ship?" Valentine asked.

Ableyard shook his head. "No point. We're in range. We'll be blown away before we can get the raft manned. I'd rather let the shells get me than freeze in that water."

"We can take some solace in the thought that the crabs that eat up the bits will be pulled up by your fellow fishermen," Ahn-Kha said.

"Hell of a thing to be thinking about, old horse," Valentine said.

"Our friend behind comes up fast," Ahn-Kha said. "The crab boat. I wonder why."

The crab boat showed a surprising turn of speed, but it wasn't making an escape; it was overtaking them, setting an intercept course between them and the other patrol boat.

"Damn if I know the name of that crabber," Ableyard said. "The captain must be insane. What does he think he's doing?"

As if in response, the blue trap-marker barrels fell away, revealing two crewed cannons hidden behind the false wall of plastic. Duvalier wasn't anything like an expert on naval weapons, but one looked like it might be a 30 mm. The barrels dropped quickly as the gunners aimed using foot pedals, and loaders stood at the ready with shells in racks like magazines.

"It's a Q-ship!" Ableyard exclaimed. "Damn if the Halifax Coast Guard wasn't shadowing us!"

"I'm glad the good guys found out about us, too," Duvalier said.

"I might have mentioned it unofficially to a couple of friends serving in the Coasties," Ableyard said. "They took the hint. We're going to have a no-shit naval engagement in about five seconds."

Duvalier found the spyglass in its bracket above the chart table and undid the little hook holding it to the wall. She left the control room to get a better view.

The patrol boat's gun shifted from their own boat to the converted crab boat. It fired. A yellow tongue of flame flashed briefly from the cannon muzzle and a second later Duvalier heard the report.

The shell splashed close behind the crab boat.

She felt a presence, and glanced down to see Valentine watching the action from the deck next to the control room, too.

Her seasickness forgotten in the excitement, Duvalier jumped up onto an emergency raft box bolted to the side of the control room and hung on with the aid of the overhang that shielded the front and side windows. Using the spyglass, she could now see both participants in the battle.

Naval cannon fire cracked across the distance between the two ships. The crabber, which she could now see was named the *Skylark* according to the white letters on her bow, returned the fire. Stabbing tongues of flame spat out of the cannon mouths each time one of the quick-firing guns sent a shell toward the Quisling patrol boat. The smaller of the two cannons turned out to be the deadlier, firing with a distinct sound, half spitting and half buzzing, peppering the water all around the patrol craft with splashes and sending torn pieces of hull and superstructure flying in all directions. Two secondary explosions ripped through the Kurian patrol boat, and the sleek little boat was transformed into a burning wreck in an instant.

The dead boat still came on for another thirty or forty yards thanks to momentum, before rolling on its side like a dying whale.

"Poor bastards," Valentine said.

Duvalier had learned her first lesson about naval actions: once the shells started flying, matters were decided very quickly. She and Valentine returned to the warmth of the control cabin. Ableyard was putting on speed to leave the area of the fight in case another boat—or worse, a plane—showed up.

"That'll teach the damn pirates to board in these waters," Ableyard said.

The crab boat dropped an inflatable with a power motor and a cowling to keep out the spray. It shot toward the sinking wreck, bouncing across the waves.

"Men won't last long in these waters. Let's hope a few made it off," Ableyard said.

"A moment ago you were damning them," Ahn-Kha said. His powerful breaths were fogging up on the front windshield of the control cabin.

Ableyard's fingers tightened on the wheel. His eyes didn't leave the little boat zipping to the wreck. "They're enemies right up until they drop into the sea. Then they're fellow sailors in distress. Heck, if they pull anyone out, they'll probably want to settle down in free land."

"If they pick up any officers, would there be a chance to question them?" Valentine asked.

"They'll be in the hands of the Coast Guard. They won't turn them over to anyone, except provincial authorities."

"Of course," Valentine said. "They probably wouldn't know anything after all."

Ableyard shrugged off the supposition that the Kurians had been informed of the name of his boat and its secret purpose. "I still don't understand it. There has to be twenty or thirty guys who think like I do for every one that wants to keep the Kurian regime propped up. Yet they still manage to find men to go do their fighting for them. At sea, yet. All they'd have to do is sail into Halifax and jump ship."

Valentine borrowed the binoculars and watched the *Skylark*'s rescue efforts. "Typically they have hostages left behind. They're comfortable, but they're hostages nonetheless." He handed the binoculars back to the captain.

Valentine looked over at Duvalier, and they shared a smile and a memory. For a moment, she felt a ghostly presence on her ring finger that had once held a fake wedding ring for almost a year.

The fishing ship followed a chain of islands leading northeast, navigating by getting radio bearings on stations that transmitted canned music or a tone. According to Ableyard, there were some unenviable Coast Guard duty stations on some of the little islands that were the first land ships crossing the North Atlantic hit in the northern latitudes.

Valentine, Duvalier, and Ahn-Kha offered to clean up the blood spilled on the deck. They talked as they worked.

"What's interesting is the failure point in the chain. Southern Command was responsible for the travel arrangements to Halifax. From there, it's the Refugee Network. Makes sense—they're used to moving people in secret, know how to do it better than anyone across the Atlantic and Northern Europe. So either the Kurians know a lot about their doings, which seems unlikely because they're otherwise successful, or someone from Southern Command tipped them, giving the day and endpoint of our journey that they knew about."

"You're being paranoid, Valentine," Duvalier said. "Things were sloppy in Halifax. I shouldn't have wandered around town with Stamp. We should have stayed in tight."

By the second night out, Ableyard judged them safe from the Kurian net. They were in the wide-open Atlantic and rolling in the waves, though the weather had turned a little warmer. Sun and warm air from the south brightened everyone's spirits. He, his old and weather-beaten boat chief, O'Neill, Valentine, and Sime chatted over beers in the crew galley.

Duvalier sort of joined in, half listening and wishing for oblivion. O'Neill said that she'd get her sea legs soon; he'd seen plenty go to sea and get sick. Since she'd kept her preboarding breakfast down, he predicted that by the end of day two of the trip she'd be able to eat a little soup, and by day three the symptoms would be gone.

"There have been three Battles of Halifax. I guess four now, if this little encounter counts," O'Neill said. As there was plenty of time for stories, he relayed the history of the Kurian gambits against Halifax.

A Kurian and his Reapers arrived at the town to help "organize" in the wake of the 2022 ravies plague and other disasters. Nova Scotia hadn't suffered greatly from ravies. The population was just too spread out and with too few roads, letting the locals set up checkpoints and choke points where a few military weapons and some tough volunteers made all the difference. "They had to be . . . ruthless," O'Neill said, summing up worlds of agony in one little word. Duvalier understood it to mean that they shot down anyone with the slightest sign of the plague like mad dogs.

The Kurian was evicted as soon as he started demanding that a new list of offenses should be enforced and criminals moved out to a special compound on the other side of the island from Halifax.

The locals, while suffering from some shortages, didn't much care for his ideas about how to organize themselves, and he lacked the muscle to ram his demands down their throats. They turned against the Kurian and sent him on a lobster boat back to Maine.

A few months later, pieces of the U.S. Navy led by a frigate now in Kurian control powered up into the harbor and shelled the town. The frigate's helicopter dropped flyers over the town, assuring the people that whatever idiotic rumors they might have heard, the Kurians were here to help, not harm.

The Canadians replied that they had some privation, but were making do. If anyone wanted to press the matter further, they could take it up with the government. In Quebec City.

The second time, in 2024, they tried to take Nova Scotia. A combination of human "militia" and Grogs landed under the guns of four destroyers and a rocket-battery support ship in order to "suppress the flow of weapons" moving south. The people of Halifax and the smaller towns knew that next to nothing was flowing south, except a few boats shuffling refugees.

While there wasn't much they could do about the guns of the ships in the harbor, at least initially, they did make life difficult for the occupying troops. Their equipment was sabotaged, and when that led to a few hangings, men and Grogs started finding themselves the target of everything from snipers to hidden bear traps. A preserved Grog-leg and the trap that crushed it (severing a vital artery) sits in the Resistance Museum in Halifax to this day.

The Kurians shelled some government buildings in return.

The Nova Scotians, showing tremendous courage, carried out, on one night of rain so heavy it was difficult to see more than a dozen meters, a small boat raid on the ships in the harbor, planting improvised limpet mines on the hulls. They sank three of the four destroyers—the crew was a far cry from the trained USN crews that had once operated the destroyers, and when the bombs went off they panicked and jumped overboard—and the rocket-battery ship managed to blow itself up in a spectacular explosion while firing a reprisal attack into the heart of the city.

The surviving destroyer hurried south, never to return. The garrison in town decided to give up and handed over all light and heavy weapons, and a good deal of valuable material was salvaged from the wrecks of the destroyers and the rocket ship.

The third "battle" took place a year later, when long-range planes bombed the harbor, mostly ineffectively, over a course of weeks. The Nova Scotians had nothing to fight aircraft with other than a few old cannons. They noted that every raid consisted of fewer aircraft. The Kurians were losing some due to mechanical failure and not a few defections with each wave, and while there was a good deal of loss of life on the ground, the Kurians finally decided that Halifax could be left on its own.

Which may have been a mistake. Over the decades, the Free Canadians built up a small but powerful Coast Guard, mostly small boats that waged seagoing guerilla warfare against the Kurian Order from the Maine and Massachusetts coasts to the Great Lakes. The Kurians produced a few seagoing surprises of their own, including amphibian Grogs, which Valentine identified as "Big Mouths," having had some experience with them on the Great Lakes and in the Pacific Northwest. Big Mouths could be trained to be adept at the sort of raids that had sunk the three destroyers at the Second Battle of Halifax. The Free Canadians now offered a bounty on Big Mouth heads, and there were a few tough crews who maintained a very nice, but sometimes short-lived, lifestyle as Grog hunters on the bounty system.

"Big Mouths are vicious bastards. Anyone who goes after them deserves their money," Valentine said. "If you can find the bases and get their trainers, they'll cause just as much trouble for the Kurians." Valentine told a few stories of his own experiences with them in the Pacific Northwest. Some of them Duvalier hadn't heard in full before.

"Maybe on your return trip, you could spend a few months as a technical adviser," Ableyard said. "The Coast Guard would love to pick your brain."

"We'll see how things are going back home," Valentine said.

He was still worried about the summer's campaigning in Kentucky. But Duvalier couldn't think of a way to take his mind off his worries, with nothing to do on a fishing boat rolling west. She had her own troubles— she was more and more nauseous with each mile into the open ocean.

She was seasick for a good part of the rest of the voyage and remembered very little of the first leg, save for not really caring whether the *Out for Lunch* sank or not in the rough spring seas.

According to Ableyard, the weather was "about average" for this time of year. Rolling around in the boat's lower forward cabin like a pea in a can, she would have hated to experience a bad spell.

Just about the time she was able to digest something other than crackers it was time to say good-bye to Ableyard and his "marked boat."

"It won't be so bad. A new radio mast, a couple of changes to the cabin and railing and you won't recognize her."

They were handed off to a German fishing boat somewhere halfway between Iceland and Ireland. That in itself was a tricky process in the spring seas. The boats threw over every fender they had and swung them across in a canvas sling with a safety line looped about the chest at the end of a yardarm.

The *Schöne Anna* out of Cuxhaven was somewhat larger, but had a similar arrangement to the *Out for Lunch*. It had a false wall in two of the fish holds. The

Germans had engineered a better ventilation system, so fresh air could be brought in through a vent—it even had a small heater. With luck, they'd need it only for the final run into the Frisian Coast.

Obviously, the conference wasn't taking place up one of Norway's fjords, or they could have just turned east. Kind of a shame. Duvalier had seen pictures of the fjords while paging through old books and magazines, and the stark contrast of mountain and sea appealed to her.

No, they were heading for Germany's North Sea coast. She'd set foot in Europe in an area not famous for much of anything she'd ever heard of. No Eiffel Tower or Amsterdam dens of iniquity for her.

Duvalier made friends with one of the crewmen, a young sandy-haired fellow who knew just enough English to offer obscene suggestions. He called her "tiny thing" and gave her his heavy wool coat—well, traded. He was interested in her duster and it was oversized enough to fit him—"*sehr wunderbar*," he called it. The seaman's coat was of the type Sime called a "duffel" and worked superbly in the wind and wet.

The captain's English was somewhat better.

"Ach, ve have little trouble. Kurians don't care about one or two. Most of those escapers, to a Kur, is better off without, yes? Keep him where he is, he so unhappy he make trouble. Maybe start resistance. So why not let the restless go?"

✗

It was a puzzle. Duvalier didn't care for mental house-of-mirrors games, where everywhere you turned all you saw was your own back, open and inviting to the enemy's knife. She liked to think about what she was going to do to them, rather than what they might do to her.

Still, someone tipped off the Kurians. They knew where they were leaving from and what day, but they didn't know that it was the *Out for Lunch* that bore them. That made a leak in the Refugee Network and its connections to the Baltic League less likely, as their passage had clearly been planned in advance.

So, a couple of gunboats had been lurking just over the horizon. Valentine had a point: the Kurian Order had plenty of advance warning of their departure.

Nothing made sense, however. It wasn't like their presence at the conference held some key to humanity's future. Sime was going on the trip to tell the rest of the freeholds, in no uncertain terms, that Southern Command was taking a breather. Who needed that message squelched, and why?

Or perhaps it wasn't the message, but the messenger. She, Valentine, and Ahn-Kha had given the Kurian Order plenty of reasons to wish them dead—perhaps Ahn-Kha most of all, since the Coal Country, where Ahn-Kha had fought with the central Appalachian guerillas, was still a mess and electricity was being rationed on the East Coast. Perhaps someone wanted Sime out of the way for reasons of high politics. She idly wished she'd read the newspapers that irregularly arrived by mail at Fort Seng.

Of course, for all she knew, Stamp might have been the target; in that case the entity that set them up had lucked out. She'd hinted that she was deep in UFR politics. If they were as cutthroat as some of the Quislings she'd known, it wasn't out of the realm of possibility.

CHAPTER FIVE

*T*he Frisian Coast: Alessa Duvalier may have wished for fjords, but she landed on a sunny coast as flat as if it had been rolled out on a baker's table, full of treacherously shifting sandbars and deceptive shallows. The sandbars form little islands guarding the coast, often reachable by the locals, who can wade out at low tide to some or row out through reeds to others. The sandbars are popular with clam diggers, individual fishermen who smoke their catch before taking it inland, teenagers looking for a private place to enjoy a bonfire and some beer, couples seeking some sun for a private thrill, or those who just enjoy a solitary walk next to the sea.

Smugglers also make use of the tricky waters of this coast. The sandbars are a perfect place for deep-sea craft or shore-hugging flat-bottomed barges to meet smaller boats, exchanging negotiable valuables for luxury items unavailable to everyone but top-ranking Quislings. Then there is just a good deal of everyday trade between fishermen; the English and Germans and Danes often meet in these waters to swap tea for schnapps, cider for cigarettes, and news for news, very little of which is good.

On the true shoreline, patches of the coast still serve as a resort area, with different grades of recreation. The best beachfront and most picturesque towns tend to be frequented by Mitteleuropean Quislings and their entourages escaping late summer heat. They bring enough money for there to be some of the traditional tourist-industry businesses: fine dining, boat charters, small, exclusive hotels, and of course health spa-resorts dedicated to the one common concern of the Quislings—keeping an energetic and youthful appearance.

Others further down the food chain still go to this coast, but stay at cheaper lodgings with smaller, muddier beaches, or go to campgrounds in the wilder and reclaimed areas of the coast.

There is a good deal of "reclaimed" coastline. Dredging and other shore management improvements have been ignored for decades, as the Kurians don't see much need for intercoastal trade—the more Balkanized and isolated their subject peoples, the better. The very few birdwatchers are pleased that coastal flocks are thriving in the newly wild areas, but for others in dying, cut-off towns in the border areas, the wilder parts can mean danger.

The fishing boat made use of one of only two channels kept open to this part of the coast, running a gauntlet of broken-down sea windmills. The thin windmills gave Duvalier a bit of a chill, since from a distance in the predawn they looked like a line of crucified Grogs she'd once passed through near Kansas City, Missouri.

The *Schöne Anna* paused at a sandbar on its way

back into Cuxhaven. It passed into German territorial waters with only the most cursory of searches. A pair of sailors came on board, swapped Turkish cigarettes for Scottish whiskey and a couple of Norwegian gold coins, and that was the end of the search. The Scotch was provided by the captain, the gold supplied by the Refugee Network.

The sailor who had traded coats with Duvalier gave her a little piece of knotted line fashioned into a bracelet as a souvenir. "Schöne Alessa," he called her. Then said something that began with *Vielleicht*, which Duvalier understood meant "perhaps," but she didn't understand any of the words that followed.

They spent no time at all in the little seaside village; they were under orders to get inland as quickly as possible, as the coasts were more closely watched than the interior areas, which were largely peaceful under the Kurians. This was accomplished by one of the wives of a hand of the *Schöne Anna*, who bundled them into a high-sided horse-drawn wagon with potatoes, a live pig, and some chickens as camouflage. Sime's dark skin and Valentine's Amerind features drew a few curious glances from the Germans, but the coast was frequented by tourists, so there could be a number of explanations, including a breakdown of transportation and a ride from a friendly local.

They rode for three hours, going northwest and therefore inland. Wind-farm graveyards turned into cow pasture, and they enjoyed a picnic dinner of cheese and bread and dried fish before she handed them over to Zloty.

Zloty was a Pole who'd lived in Germany most of his life. Duvalier liked his big, sad eyes. There was something of the tragic clown in him. He was a roofer by profession and had a permanent cough from the chemicals they used, though Duvalier also noticed that he smoked frequently, dreadful hand-rolled cigarettes that had only a hint of tobacco amid all the noxious chaff. How he was involved with the Resistance he did not say and no one asked. His English was quite good.

"I am to drop you off on a stretch of road. You will be picked up before dawn. A single man must stand with this torch," he said, handing them a flashlight. "Shine it on the old sign like you are trying to read it."

"Who is picking us up?"

"I do not know. Better that way. They try to have it so we are at most three people, and one outside our cell. Better if we are taken, you know?"

It was cool at night this close to the sea.

He led them, by dark, through cow pastures fragrant with what you expect to find in a cow pasture.

It was slow and tiresome, skirting fields and climbing fences in single file, but apparently it was safe. A few dogs barked, but no one investigated.

"The Reapers don't prowl around at night?" Valentine asked.

"Them? No, there are not that many, and it would be a waste of time. They wait for their blood at the hospitals and police stations. It is bad to be a vagrant in Germany. It is worse to be convicted of a crime of violence. Those sorts of troublemakers are never heard from again."

"That's not sufficient in the United States to keep a Kurian going. They need hundreds of lives every year."

Their guide shrugged. "We probably have more things against the law here. Just to live fully in these times is to be a criminal."

A mass of forest stood west of them. An old road simply disappeared into the woods—trees had broken up the pavement and grown up through the cracks; what was left of the asphalt was hidden by shadow.

Zloty inspected it closely before they moved on.

"Why the caution, then?"

"This can be a bad area. Few live here, many abandoned farms. The ones that remain are more watchful but less talkative, you know?"

"Will we be resting anytime tonight?" Sime asked, looking at the mud and cow filth on his hiking shoes.

Zloty replied, "We cannot stay at a hotel. The registrations, you know? There is a farmhouse; the farmer is friendly. We can stay above the cows and be cozy. Sorry to take you across the cow paths, but we are sure to be questioned if police see us on the road."

Later, when reflecting on it, Duvalier thought the ambush was like something out of *Robin Hood*. Dozens of young men dropped out of the trees in front of them, and a few behind. Some hopped over the wall they had been paralleling as they crossed the field.

They were mostly lanky teenage boys with a few young men. Duvalier thought she spotted a flash of hair and earring that might indicate a female, but you never knew.

It was a good-sized gang, certainly more than twenty.

They wore a mix of cast-off military gear, fancy dress (one character sporting a monocle wore a battered silk hat with erotic postcards shoved into the band, making him look like a cross between the Mad Hatter and a doorman for a classier strip joint), peacoats and wool knit hats, and trench coats. One thing all had in common was scarves, mostly long, wound several times around the neck, giving their heads a turtlelike appearance. Their hair was either messily hanging all about the face or tied back in a rough braid. Nobody went for the skinhead look. Maybe it was out of style.

They formed two small bands, one in front on the cow path and one behind. Now that she was alerted, Duvalier's ears picked up what were probably a few more of them creeping along the wall and moving through that deeply black forest to the east.

She'd been right about the girls. There were a few too-young-to-be-travelling-with-this-crowd girls with them. Duvalier thought they should have been at the dinner table doing their math homework at this time, not casting about the overgrown countryside looking for trouble.

"Is this the neighborhood watch?" Sime asked.

"We call them 'the Black Youth,'" their guide said in a low voice, talking toward the ground and spitting out the words quickly. "They live rough, hiding from the labor conscription and civic indoctrination. Just ignore them. If they want something, let them have it. A jacket or a timepiece is not worth your life, you know?"

Top Hat gabbled something, and Zloty nodded and responded, holding out his hands as they talked as if to caution him against coming any closer.

"Stay still," Zloty said. "He says we came too close to his forest. They wish an accommodation."

They look thin, Duvalier thought. Of course, they were mostly teenagers. Teenagers could thrive on about anything, and tended to be lean.

She hoped it wouldn't come to fighting. It would be like killing the Lost Boys from *Peter Pan*.

Top Hat walked up and down the line of "prisoners." He was careful to stay out of Ahn-Kha's reach—not knowing, of course, that she'd seen Ahn-Kha leap eight feet from a relaxed crouch like the one he was currently maintaining. Top Hat would have his head messily popped off like a shaken soda bottle being opened.

He paused in front of her and openly looked her body up and down.

Why was I born a woman?

Top Hat reached out and groped her through leather gloves. First he tried a breast. That must have disappointed him, because he switched from overhand to underhand and shoved it underneath the front of her jacket and between her legs.

"Is that all?" she asked. "Kid, I've been fingered by men with artificial arms that did a better job."

He didn't understand the English, but he took the tone as a challenge. He pulled up his hand, stuck the middle finger of his glove between his teeth, pulled it off, leaving the glove hanging there giving her the finger, and wormed his hand into her waistband.

A swirl of motion to the right caught her eye.

"Enough of that," Valentine said. He'd drawn his

old .45, the backup pistol he carried everywhere, and now held it leveled at Top Hat boy's head. "Let's not get piggy." His line of fire was well clear of her, but not the rest of the gang, and a few of them shifted.

The Black Youth produced weapons of their own. Mostly they were edged weapons, and a couple of short, sharp fishing gaffs that were probably more threatening-looking in theory than practice. But one boy had a double-barreled shotgun with a few inches sawn off the end that could take out half their party if it had buckshot in it.

Most of them were eyeing Ahn-Kha. And keeping out of his reach. So they had a certain amount of street smarts.

"Translate for me," Sime said to their guide.

"Let's all settle down," Sime said, stepping forward and holding his arms out in each direction, one toward Valentine and the other toward the boy with the shotgun. He gave the translator time to catch up. "If anyone shoots, there'll be bodies in somebody's cow pasture. The authorities can't ignore that. They'll call out soldiers to sweep the woods. No matter how good your hideout is, they'll find it.

"I have here two gold coins. Maybe I have more, but you'd have to kill all of us to get them, and we have powerful friends. I'm willing to pay to stay the night in this area; that's one coin. Your silence has a price, too. That's the second coin. So, what is it going to be? An exchange of gold, or an exchange of lead and blood?"

She was tired of the hand gripping at her pants. She briefly considered using her claws, but instead reached her own hand across, and found the trouser leg with his testicles. She pressed hard and he gave a little yelp and what she recognized was a German profanity. What a fool. Even a backcountry cop in Kansas knew to wear a cup in case of any rough stuff.

"Best take the offer," Duvalier advised. "Unless you want to be a featured singer with your Youth Vanguard Boys Choir."

The translator did not bother with that, but the kid got the message. The deadly embrace released, they stepped away from each other.

The leader of the mob took the coins and kissed them before pocketing them deep in his jacket. Then he laughed in Sime's face.

"A most friendly gesture," he said through the translator. "Be on your way with our permission."

A couple of the youths spat as they moved off. Not on anyone, of course, but the general intent was clear.

"See, Valentine," Sime said. "We still have all our limbs. It doesn't always have to end in blood."

Valentine shot Sime an angry look. Valentine evidently wanted to treat the mob like a mob and shoot one or two, which would no doubt disperse the rest.

"Ja. Yes," the leader said. He waved his gang back and then did a strange little flourish that involved his hand and forehead being directed at Sime, wincing a little as he bent slightly at the waist in pain.

"If you give every two-bit thug gold to leave us alone, we'll be broke in forty-eight hours," Duvalier said.

Sime shrugged. "I was told in my briefing that this

would be the only difficult part of the journey, getting inland on the German coast. There are experts helping us with the rest."

"Expertise like that almost got us killed outside of Halifax," Valentine said.

"I suppose we could strike out on our own," Sime responded smoothly. "Except we don't know where we're going. What do you say, Valentine? Warsaw? Oslo?"

"Everyone is getting raw," Ahn-Kha said. "We need some food and a hot drink."

"You feeling okay?" Valentine asked her.

"It's just my crotch. I've had plenty of scumbags cop a quick feel. At least this one was young and reasonably good-looking. Body odor like a summer swamp, but good-looking. Now we're out Sime's bribe."

"They would have run," Valentine said.

"What about the shotgun?"

"If it even was loaded, I wouldn't have given him a chance to use it. He would have taken my first bullet. He wasn't watching me so closely, because I had my gun on someone else."

"You didn't like seeing someone touching me like that," she said.

"Of course not. It's disgusting."

She shrugged. "One man's disgusting is another's champagne. I've learned that much in my years roaming around the zones."

"You okay?" Pistols asked, as he checked his guns before putting them back in their holsters.

Why is everyone worried about my condition? I'm not a

pregnant fifteen-year-old. I'm a goddamn Cat with over a decade in the KZs.

"Better than ever," she said. It was nice of him to ask and not make a big scene about it. She shouldn't have been so quick to judge. He seemed to like playing cards with Sime. Maybe they could switch from pinochle to poker one of these evenings and bury the hatchet. Valentine might even join in. She'd heard from sources in the Wolves that he was a pretty good cardplayer, too.

Their guide got them back in line and they struck out between the fields.

"We're being followed," Ahn-Kha said. "Some of the kids, I think."

"Tell the guide to stop," Sime said. Pistols loosened his weapon in its holster.

It turned out to be a couple, both in their early teens, a boy and a girl. They had a brief conversation through the translator.

"We want to travel with you. Just far enough to get out of the state. We've had enough of that gutter-pack."

"We'll be no trouble. We want to try to make it to the North. The Arctic."

Sime shook his head. "No, our arrangements—"

"Were for two more than we actually have with us," Valentine said.

"It's too dangerous."

"To whom? I doubt the Kurian Order took two kids out of Youth Vanguard training, or whatever they call it here, and inserted them into a gang of starving hooligans in the hope they'd be able to penetrate one of the

Refugee Network's lines. They don't waste their agents hanging out with kids."

"I'm in charge of this delegation."

"You are in charge of Southern Command's delegation," Ahn-Kha said. "The Kentucky Alliance is willing to have these kids with us. For a little way."

"You'll have to forgive him, Sime," Duvalier said. "He's always picking up strays. It's easier this way—believe me. Otherwise he'll bitch all the way to the Baltic."

In the end, they let "the kids" follow along. They shared their simple provisions with them. The kids produced some chocolate of their own, disgusting stuff that Duvalier recognized as KZ ration chocolate. If anything, it was worse than the American brand. She was a little surprised at that; she'd thought Europeans were connoisseurs of luxury goods.

They were passed over to a bike gang for transport to the Baltic, the Funkrad.

They were willing to take the kids along as well. They'd been expecting seven travellers from the North American delegation.

The phrase "bike gang" brings to mind leather, boots, and roaring motorcycles. This gang had the leathers, certainly, but they were leaner-lined, almost like sporting wear. The motorcycles were all electric jobs, slower but infinitely quieter. There were a few true bicycles in the group as well, pedaled by Germans with thighs like tree trunks. Along with the two-wheeled vehicles, there was a subcompact car and a van with cargo containers strapped to the roof and a rear hatch that held spare bike equipment, a camp stove, and other necessities for life on the road.

Most of Germany was well organized, by Kurian standards. Every person carried an identity card with home city and state. You needed no special authorization to move about your town or city, and within the state itself a pass was fairly easy to obtain. To leave your state, however, required approval from one of the regional security centers.

There were special exemptions, of course, and one of them was sporting teams and sports trainers. The Funkrad competed five or six times a year in Pan-European contests; the rest of their time was spent "training." The men and women on the bicycles were "supported" by "coaches and trainers," all riding the electric motorcycles, thirty all told, a group large enough to raise a cheer from sporting fans in the towns they passed through, but not so large it required much notice from city police or security forces.

Sometimes sports photographers rode along with the team, or journalists, or athletic candidates for membership on the team. Young fans who won entry into contests by participating in scrap metal or rubber drives could spend a week with their bicycling heroes as well. And sometimes they shuttled a handful of refugees from the northern foothills of the Alps to the North Sea.

Their pair of young lovers was dropped off at a junkyard near Itzehoe. One of the coaches knew the owner; the owner saved bike spares for the team, and they were always looking for help on their pickup routes. Even if the kids didn't like Itzehoe, they might discover a new location while searching through scrap piles and demolished homes.

The only tricky part was finding an out-of-sight spot for Ahn-Kha, who was sure to excite comment.

"Perhaps we could be trying out a mascot?" one of the cyclists asked Doktor Lauter, the head coach and manager of the Funkrad.

"No, make a space for him in the van. Throw some sleeping mats down. We can put him just behind the seats. We will simply take precautions, many precautions, every time we stop to have a piss."

That sort of earthy practicality marked their week with the Funkrad. They quietly buzzed through village after village on back roads as they headed east. Ahn-Kha suffered, having to stay in hiding, but the rest of the group relaxed and regained the camaraderie that had been lost with the death of Stamp and the wounding of Alexander.

The only one who seemed ill at ease during their time with the Funkrad was Pistols. Where the Germans were all sleek and graceful, he was awkward and waddling, a cowboy among ballerinas. They joked, she suspected, about the number of guns he carried (she knew the German word for gun: *pistole*, not that different from its English pronunciation). Pistols might be a tough enough man, but he was no cyclist or athlete, and he made no friends among the Germans.

Duvalier was no hand holder by nature, but at night she made an effort to socialize with Pistols. Sometimes she played cards with Ahn-Kha and him, or they patched their clothing. They fell asleep together in the back of the van, Ahn-Kha's bulk warming them like a hot stove, talking quietly about whatever drifted across their minds.

She'd made many journeys in her life, but she remembered the trip with the bike team as one of the best.

It was even fun. Fun was a stranger to her, or at best an acquaintance of limited contact.

Once in open country, flat and a mixture of woods, pasture, and field so that it resembled, to her, some parts of the Midwest, they began to really make time. The team's management knew which towns held one or more Kurians, which had tougher Quislings and which didn't, and they zigzagged through, heading mostly west, with little turns to the north.

One of the professional cyclists, a shaven-bald German named Horst who had leg muscles like oak roots wound around a boulder, took her out on a few trips on one of the coaches' road bikes.

She'd been watching him practice, quietly enjoying the view. Before she knew him, she'd just mentally named him Fritz; he reminded her a little of a German shepherd she'd known by that name.

She was comfortable on bicycles, and they were a simple, inconspicuous way to get around a Kurian Zone. But she'd never ridden to race, just to get from point A to point B or to disappear quickly.

Of course she couldn't match Horst's power. So when they rode, she took off cross-country or through the woods, where her reflexes gave her an edge against those legs of his. She led Fritz on a merry chase, turning frequently so he couldn't take advantage of his muscles to overtake her.

About the time she decided he was just lagging behind because he liked the view of her bottom bouncing above the bike saddle, she skidded to a halt.

"I'm lost," she said. "I hope you can find your way back to the rest of the team."

"They are south of us, heading for the Kiel Canal," said Horst. "We will follow it to the Baltic." Then he took a step closer and went on with "I would like to explore your canal."

Yeesh. Leave it to a German to put it like that. Much of the fun went out of the day. She'd have to deal with either hurt feelings or anger. And who knew how much of it would transfer to the rest of the team?

"Down, Fritz," she said, then realized with horror that she'd said it aloud.

"Excuse me?"

"I'm sorry, Horst. Horst. I'm not in the mood for that right now. You know? Wrong time of the month," she lied, but it would be a lie that wouldn't hurt his ego.

He shrugged. "I am not bothered by such matters."

"Well, I am. Red rain check, okay?"

"As you like."

They came to the Kiel Canal, a shipping lane that allowed the great former naval base access to the North Atlantic rather than the Baltic. It looked like a very well-maintained river, wide enough for large ships, with even banks and working locks and dams that allowed the flow to be controlled.

The wind blew relentlessly in this part of Germany and there were windmills for power generation everywhere. Only about a third of them seemed to be working, which struck her as strange for the efficiency-driven Germans. Some even had anti-Kurian graffiti written on them, but you could make out the letters only by getting off the roads and really close to the windmills, or by using binoculars, of course.

There were excellent paths and roads bordering the canal. And a heavy police presence, but they just applauded or cheered the Funkrad, or made obscene gestures, depending on the affiliation of the particular officer. Some of the barges on the water recognized them as well and honked their horns in appreciation.

Valentine joined her in cycling with the Germans, tucking his hair up into the little helmets they wore, in brief training runs, riding in the middle of the pack of Germans where they wouldn't be noticed and others could speak for them just in case. As they ran along the canal, it felt more and more like the pleasure jaunt they'd been promised, especially as the weather grew less foggy and more summery.

They dined on good hard bread, ham, and bacon. The people in this part of Germany ate very little flesh that wasn't pork. Even chickens didn't seem to thrive on this rain- and windswept coast.

✗

They said good-bye to the team on the salty shore of the Baltic.

It was a foggy morning, and the bike team built two bonfires and had a good old-fashioned Germanic cook-out. They purchased a year-old pig from one of the market towns and spit-roasted it with honey, produced huge green bottles of beer, and relaxed on the beach. Some of the braver souls swam in the chilly water. During breaks in the fog, they could just see barrier islands that sheltered the coastal shipping channel, but there seemed to be precious little shipping to be protected.

A small boat with two men in it rowed toward their fire. The oarsman and steersman hung on their oars for a moment, then pulled hard for the beach.

Sime and the coach of the Funkrad had a conversation with the steersman.

"Our boat is just beyond the sandbar," Sime said. "The dinghy will take us out to it."

The oarsman barked something. For a moment the mists parted and she caught a glimpse of a mast in the fog and something darker near the water.

"Two trips, it will take," said the coach of the Funkrad. "It's a tiny dinghy."

Duvalier went in the first run with Valentine and Sime. She noticed that both the sailors had identical white pants and sockless shoes. From the waist up they were differentiated, however, one in a sweater, the other in a canvas shirt and insulating vest.

"Seems like an odd choice, to get on another ship after being on land," Duvalier said. "Would have been a good deal easier to just take a ship the whole way."

"The Baltic Straits might be patrolled," Valentine said. "I think you can see land-to-land at some of the points. Or island-to-land, anyway. Easy to choke off traffic and do inspections."

They had to get out of their rowboat at the sandbar and tote it, oars, and luggage over the grassy sand and back into the water. Duvalier tripped in the surf and got wet, but otherwise it was an interesting exercise.

They soon reached the ship. It didn't draw much water, so it was able to anchor close to the sandbar.

It appeared that a sleek sailing ship would convey them on the next leg of the voyage to the mystery conference. Duvalier didn't know much about sails; until this trip her boating experience had been confined to river craft and barges, and those were all motorized. This ship had two masts and a sharp bowsprit holding the forestay. A few portholes lined the side, light glimmering in some. A little tent of glass ran down its center; she presumed there was some kind of cabin beneath.

Duvalier didn't like the look of it at first. All the other boats were built for sailors and their work at sea. This boat, though longer and far sleeker than the *Out for Lunch*, had a bathtub-toy shine to it.

A man with reddish-blond hair, wearing blue jeans, boat shoes, and a thick fleece with a Windbreaker shell, gave them a friendly wave. He handed her up on board. His hands were like Sime's, as sleek and polished as his boat.

"My name is Von Krebs," the man said, tapping his chest with an unlit pipe. "Lorherr Von Krebs. I am the owner of the *Windkraft*." He had more of an English accent than German when speaking their tongue, at least to Duvalier's inexperienced ear. "The Baltic League tells me you are from the middle of the former United States, yes?"

"Yes," Valentine said.

He had a good smile, and Duvalier felt somewhat better. Smiles usually told the truth about a person. "I am pleased, very pleased. One rarely meets Americans in these bad times." He shook hands all around.

Duvalier admired his shave. He didn't have so much as a shadow or a nick. Even Sime looked a bit ragged around the edges when compared to Von Krebs's standard. He must be very professional with a razor.

"Welcome aboard," Von Krebs continued. "Would anyone like some tea? I have milk, lemon, or sugar, all fresh, not from bottles or cans. We are great tea drinkers here in the Baltic. Even more so than our friends across the Channel."

Valentine and Sime nodded, and a sailor appeared with a tray of steaming mugs. Duvalier noted there was a small brown bottle of rum with a picture of a thatch-roofed hut on a beach, if anyone wanted to strengthen the tea into a more warming libation.

"I anticipate a journey of a few days, depending on wind and weather. I hope you will find the trip comfortable. I am afraid you are all to sleep dormitory-style forward, but I imagine I can make private room for the lady."

"No need," Duvalier said.

"Our destination?" Sime asked.

Von Krebs pointed north, out into the sea. "I just found that out this morning. They keep secrets even from me, sixteen years with the Refugee Network. We are bound for the Finnish coast on the Gulf of Bothnia—a town called Kokkola. Trade port with rail service, lively year-round. It is a delightful little place, at least at this time of year. I believe you will enjoy yourselves."

The second dinghy load arrived. Ahn-Kha heaved himself and his gear on board thanks to his apelike arms. The crew openly gaped at him, and Duvalier would have sworn that the deck rolled over a little as he stood at the ship's side. Perhaps they'd have to lash him to the center, like cargo.

They met the crew, who all had white pants, save for the captain, a tall, hawk-faced woman who wore clam-digger jeans that showed off her legs.

Valentine did a little halt step as he moved up to shake her hand, and it set Duvalier's antenna twitching.

The blond captain in the clam-diggers dropped Valentine's hand. "Wait, you are Indian Man from Lake Michigan Wisconsin You Ess Ayy! We have met before—I know certain!"

"Pleased you remember." Valentine smiled. "Yes, you were with the White Banner Fleet when I was a courier. I'm sorry, I've forgotten your name."

"Stepanek. Captain now," she said. "You have changed. Scars, I see. When we met before you had still the complexion of a boy fresh off the mother's teat."

"Yes," Valentine said. "We're both a little weather-beaten. Still hunting for art?"

"It is one of the reasons I sail the *Windkraft*. When Herr Von Krebs does not need her, she is mine to sail at will. As long as I am careful. I am very careful."

"One of the best sailors on the Baltic," Von Krebs replied in agreement. "I am glad you are acquainted with my captain. It is all the confirmation I need that you are who you represent yourselves to be. I was not expecting such an intriguing party. Though I should not be surprised, being Americans. You never can tell with Americans. And our large hairy ally who carries the bags."

"He's the representative of the Kentucky Alliance." Valentine flared. "You've probably heard of him. He was involved in the Coal Country revolt. I believe the international newscasts from the Baltic League mentioned him more than once."

Leave it to Valentine, Duvalier thought. *I've heard of a girl in every port, but one in every ocean? That's a little hard to swallow.*

"We must have drinks tonight to celebrate this reunion. I did not think you American soldiers lasted like this. I am very pleased."

"Good God, Valentine!" Duvalier sputtered. "How far do we have to travel to run into a woman you haven't been with?"

"Is she yours?" Stepanek asked. "You misunderstand our brief acquaintance, my girlfriend."

"She's not 'mine' in that sense, Captain," Valentine said. "She's my partner—comrade. We've worked together many times." He gave her the *what the hell are you doing?* look, which further infuriated her.

Emotions she couldn't quite control needed an outlet. "You'd think a few thousand miles and we'd be in uncharted territory for the legendary cocksmanship of David Valentine, but you'd be wrong, wouldn't you? Where do we have to go to meet someone you haven't penetrated? Beyond the Great Wall of China? Pitcairn Island?"

She regretted the words almost instantly. It was one thing to joke with Valentine in private, another to lose her temper in front of the delegation and a group of Baltic sailors. "Redhead crazy woman," they were probably muttering under their breath. Even those who couldn't speak a word of English must have known something about Stepanek and Valentine aggravated her.

"Calm down, Ali. We met once, on Lake Michigan. No joke, she was on a ship that had to take Southern Command dispatches to other freeholds."

"I was there to try to track down some art from the museum in Chicago," Stepanek put in. "We were not lovers; there was no time."

Really, neither of them owed her an explanation for anything. She'd made Val angry and the rest of the party from both freeholds was staring. Except for Ahn-Kha, of course, who'd suddenly taken an interest in how the dinghy was being stored on a sturdy davit at the stern.

"I'm sorry. Cooped up too long."

✗

The food on the *Windkraft* was some of the best she'd ever eaten, though the cook favored dishes that could be prepared in a big stockpot or roasting pan. The first night out they had a sort of very tender beef stew served over an exotic rice. The flavorful meat and potato and vegetables needed only the slightest touch of the edge of a fork to part. Von Krebs apologized for not having fresh bread to go with it; they "made do" with wonderful buttery crackers and pieces of biscuit with garlic butter. And wines, beers, and spirits. While Sime spoke about the wine with Von Krebs and recommended a selection, Valentine stuck with the milk they'd been offered with the tea, Ahn-Kha had apple cider, and she sampled the "Baltic tea." While she had drunk tea and coffee often enough in the past, usually it was just to get the warm heat-calories inside her. The bracing tea Von Krebs had acquired was a real pleasure to enjoy, especially in the manner he recommended, with a little German honey and lemon ("All the way from Greece," Von Krebs boasted).

"Do you always live this well here?" Sime asked their host.

"I keep myself well stocked with luxury items. It greases the machinery of the ports, both Kurian and of the free Baltic League. Would anyone care for a cigar? They are Spanish, but I'm told they are very good."

She spent the first night out of Kiel, a glorious evening in the mid-Baltic, chatting with Postle. The after-dinner habit that had begun with the cycling team continued in compact folding deck chairs made out of canvas and wood, and they put their feet up on the taffrail and watched the wake of the ship fade into the calm summer water.

He talked a little about his boyhood in Missouri. He'd grown up near Grog country, in the midst of the raiding and counterraiding of each other's homes and livestock. He lost his father on a "hut burn" and two uncles defending their own barns against Grog warriors out to make names for themselves. Like Valentine, he'd sought solace in books. He loved westerns, with their simple heroes who tried to stay out of conflicts until pushed one too many times just a little too far. Unlike Valentine, he'd been raised among throngs of family, mostly women, with several widows like his mother.

He extracted a silver cigar case from his "duty vest," which held a little bit of this and that a bodyguard might need. It had some simple filigree around the edges.

"Belonged to the Earp brothers. Wyatt Earp—ever heard of him?"

"Most folks brought up in Kansas have," she said.

"This belonged to him and came down through his family, according to the guy I bought it from."

"Do you really believe that?"

"It came with a certificate, but about all the certificate proves for certain is that I paid three hundred dollars for it. Still, it's old, it's nice-looking, and it makes a good story."

"You must like cigars. Do you keep a few expensive ones for special occasions? I don't remember seeing you smoke a cigar."

"Nah." He opened it up and extracted a little sheaf of pictures and a news clipping kept in a waterproof plastic bag. There was a little bag like a sugar packet that said DO NOT EAT.

"Poison in case of capture?" she asked.

"Ach, no. That's just a little sand to suck up moisture, just in case."

They spent a few minutes perusing his family photos. She made appropriately appreciative noises at the grainy, bent images. He wasn't much better as a child than as an adult, but ugly on the outside meant just as little as handsome.

He cautiously questioned her about her childhood. She mostly talked about her mom's struggles. He probed a little on her service as a Cat. "If it's okay for you to talk about it. I'm curious."

"What rumors have you heard?" she asked.

"That you can see in the dark. Disappear at will. You can be silent when you wish. Reflexes that make you a blur."

"The disappear one is false. Stage magician tricks aren't our style," she said. "I can be inconspicuous. You've seen me in action—was I a blur?"

"Hard for someone as beautiful as you to be inconspicuous," he said. "In the fight last month, I've no memory of seeing you at all while it was going on—I don't mean that as an accusation. I was focused on my gun sights. Watching you would have been a distraction."

He'd been avoiding flirting with her since they landed in Halifax until this instance. But this was the nicest kind of flirting.

She let it lie.

He rose, wobbled for a moment as his legs got used to the deck again. "Want a hot drink from the galley?"

"Not just now," she said. She had a lot to sort out about him. Parts of him she admired, but there was another half of him she didn't quite trust. He was reasonably safe on a trip with plenty to eat and drink, so his penis was moving up the to-do list. Overly attentive men were usually this way right until they were sexually satisfied, but then they lost interest until the juices built up again.

"You and David have a past; am I right?" he asked.

"We've been partners on three big jobs and two campaigns. That doesn't count the Rising in Ozarks a few years back, either. We're like any couple of partners who've served in a high-stress, high-risk job."

"Meaning?"

"It's kind of like a marriage with no sex."

"Kind of like a marriage, in other words." He chuckled at his own joke. She always found that annoying.

"Wouldn't know. I haven't been married," she said. "Doubt I ever will be. I think I'll have that drink after all."

They went down to the galley for more punch. Ahn-Kha was asleep, stretched out on the forward cabin floor like a bearskin rug. Valentine was reading one of the English books in the little ship's library, and Sime was shaving his head in a basin, checking his reflection in a mirror.

"It's getting cool up on deck," she said, grabbing her scarf.

Valentine looked up from his book—she couldn't see the title, but it was thick—and the others ignored her.

Back on deck, they tried to get the talk going again, but the camaraderie was gone and everything was awkward. They settled for watching the wake. Duvalier spoke a little of the seasickness, now vanished in the calmer summer Baltic.

Valentine's Polish gal at the wheel had been replaced by another crew member. The Polish sailing master, or whatever her title was, had a blanket around her shoulders and dozed in a hammock chair as she waited to be called by a nudge of the helmsman's foot. The fishing boats had autopilots that could maintain course for a while; perhaps with sailcraft the wind had to be taken into account in ways a machine couldn't handle.

Von Krebs came up on deck. He avoided them, lighted a cigar and politely smoked it downwind from them. He leaned against the rail, watching them with hands in his pockets except for the moments when he flicked cigar ash overboard.

The steady stare made her nervous. He looked like he was sizing them up to determine worth in trade. Would he hand them over to seagoing bounty hunters? No, if he was a resource with the Baltic League, he must possess a trustworthy enough background.

She didn't care for being stared at. She watched the ship's wake, so different from the churned water left by a propeller-driven vessel. The mild Baltic night and small waves meant that the *Windkraft* left a long, hairpinlike wake under her sails.

Something blacker than the night water appeared in

the far wake briefly, disrupting the wave pattern. All she could make of it was that it was dark and shiny. Water ran off its back in little sheets and rivers in all directions. It disappeared at the same one-two-three pace that it appeared, leaving a flat circle of water.

Something about it sent anxious pins up her spine. Maybe in daylight it would have been less ominous. . . .

"What was that?" she asked, pointing.

No one else had seen it. A couple of the sailors searched astern, exchanging quiet words in their own language. The helmsman glanced over his shoulder and Von Krebs came back to the rail.

"What did you see?" he asked.

"A black something breaking the water. It came up and went down again, maybe five seconds in all."

"Hmmm. Could you say anything about its size?" Von Krebs asked.

Some sensor in Stepanek alerted, and she opened her eyes and rose. She blinked at the wake.

"As big as a rowboat, maybe," Duvalier said.

"Was there a fin?" Stepanek asked. "Did it blow water into the air?"

"No, I don't think so. I didn't hear a noise, but it was some ways off. Something broke water, but it wasn't a fin."

Von Krebs scanned the water. "It could have been a whale. There are many whales in the Baltic year-round."

"Was it just one creature, or several close together?" Stepanek asked.

"It could have been several, I suppose. It didn't rise out of the water by more than a foot."

"Big—," Stepanek started to say.

"Foot? Oh, yes, a foot," Von Krebs said. "Twelve inches. I forget you Americans still use old English measures. Well, keep watching. Whales will sometimes come up and say 'hello.' Porpoises, too, for we will drive fish and create a bow wave they can ride."

She watched the water for fifteen more minutes, trying to look out on both sides as well as to the rear, but then gave up. Perhaps the whale, if it was a whale, had been travelling in a southerly direction while they headed northeast. Still, she doubted it was a whale; didn't they expel a lot of water with the air in their lungs? She didn't know much about it beyond "thar she blows" from childhood reading.

Stepanek didn't settle back down into her napping chair, either; instead she swept the stern regularly with her gaze. Maybe it was just paranoia on her part. She just wasn't used to travelling this far this easily.

CHAPTER SIX

$\text{\Large Y}$

Kokkola on the Gulf of Bothnia, Finland: The city of Kokkola is an ancient gateway between Sweden and Finland, roughly halfway up the serrated Finnish coast on the Gulf of Bothnia. The "old" town is old indeed, dating to the fifteenth century, with tidy little homes representing traditional Finnish wooden architecture.

In 2022 it was considered a small Scandinavian hub in a good location for meetings and conferences. Hotels and meeting space, built in the clean-lined, open style of the region, filled every summer with organizations looking to take advantage of the glorious far-north summer weather and long, idyllic nights—in July the sun rises around three thirty in the morning and doesn't set until eleven thirty or so in the evening.

Since the arrival of the Kurians, the population that was once roughly fifty thousand Finns has swelled to roughly one hundred fifty thousand people, in the form of émigrés from all over the Baltic. They brought with them their determination not to end up under the heel of the Kurians. Finland, now militarized to a greater extent than at any time since the "Winter War" when the Soviet Union invaded on the eve of the Second World War, maintains a small naval base, an army garrison, and a two-plane and two-helicopter military airfield for keeping an eye on the coastline. The forces assembled there are neither so great that it is considered an important military center in the great strategy rooms of Europe nor so small that independent headhunters or Kurian warships dare raid that section of the coast.

Ease of access by sea or air, conference space, and a few local amenities made the Baltic League select Kokkola as the location for the Ninth All-Freehold Conference. Seven hundred delegates (and their translators) from fifty-one freeholds or remote, unorganized territories made the trip, not even knowing their final destination until they arrived at the jump-off point designated by the Baltic League for the last leg of their voyages. The largest and most far-reaching short-wave news network set up a special broadcast center, though to hide the location of the conference a little longer, the broadcast aerial went across and by undersea cable to Sweden before being transmitted out to the world from an old military base north of Stockholm. All their broadcasts had a thirty-second delay, allowing censors to squelch any inadvertent information that might reveal the location of the conference.

The conference was expected to last two weeks. As events turned out, it became a near–record breaker, running to the very last day of that fateful July. The conferences usually made history in the form of long-range planning for picking off weaker Kurian Zones and helping to better establish new freeholds. No one, least of all the delegates from Southern Command and Kentucky, could have guessed just how much history would be made at this meeting.

X

The light hardly ever stopped this far north. It went full dark only as the clock approached midnight, and dawn came again before three. Even with all that sunlight, the summer heat never felt oppressive; there was a golden quality to the shine rather than the midsummer hot hammer she had grown used to beating down on her neck. Duvalier felt like a plant; the sun of the northern latitudes seemed to energize her.

They passed a pretty little island with a lighthouse set above some abandoned-looking buildings, and as that receded into the summery morning mists they entered Kokkola waters, guided by freshly painted buoys.

"Someone has been at work here for your meetings," Stepanek said. "The last time I was here, two rusty old buoys were all I had to go on. Good thing it is not a difficult harbor in these days."

"In these days," Duvalier had learned, was a common expression among Balts, or whatever you called the mélange of Scandinavians, Finns, Russians, Germans, and so on who used these waters.

Duvalier was enough of a deepwater sailor by now to sense the change in the air and current as they glided into the glassy Bothnian Bay waters under a brilliant blue sky.

"The waters are like the Caribbean," Valentine said, as he stood at the rail with her. Stepanek was busy navigating the *Windkraft* into the harbor, using a little motor that she learned existed on their second day out. Valentine had neither sought nor avoided Stepanek's company, though she'd heard them after a meal on the middle night of the passage discussing her art acquisitions. He did relish a chance to have a conversation unconnected with the Kurian Order.

They passed a single ship on patrol, a tough-looking armed tug with a cannon up front and some kind of antiaircraft set of machine guns to the rear. It even had a spinning radar antenna.

"Monitor," Von Krebs called to Stepanek as they approached. "Use the confirmation signal."

Stepanek signaled them with a small searchlight, clacking out some sort of code. The tugboat flashed a brief acknowledgment.

After that, Von Krebs helped out with the rigging forward, following Stepanek's commands. They made one more turn and found enough wind to bring them the rest of the way into the harbor under sail.

"Did you ever see that creature in our wake again?" Valentine asked.

She hadn't, and said so.

"I talked to Stepanek. The real danger in the Baltic when you're at sea are Big Mouths. They've found torn-up boats with the crews missing. They just climb on board and eat everyone. It's bad enough that there's a permanent bounty on them, payable with jawbones brought into any Baltic League–controlled port."

She shrugged. "It looked like one big creature to me, not a school, but then I only saw it for a second. Doesn't seem to matter now that we've made it."

The harbor side of Kokkola was festooned with the flags of all the freeholds, attending or otherwise. It was quite a display. Duvalier didn't recognize a third of the flags.

Some men in an inflatable motorboat roared out to them and threw a line. Their little boat then gently pulled and nudged the *Windkraft* up against the quay.

A greeter, a milk-skinned woman in a powder blue suit with a yellow scarf, met them wharfside, calling first in Swedish—for the name of the ship and the language, according to the answer provided by Von Krebs.

"*Windkraft*. English," returned Von Krebs.

"Thank you," the woman answered. "What area do you represent, and how many are you?"

"Five total, from the United Free Republics and the Kentucky Alliance. Two voting delegates. The rest are attending."

"Welcome to Finland and the Baltic League, allies," she said, showing a brilliant and presumably genuine smile. The *Windkraft* bumped up against the wharf, and some dockhands in what looked like brand-new clothes tied her up and secured the gangplank.

Duvalier had a moment's disquiet at the newness of everyone's apparel. That was the sort of thing that could mean a trap. Or it could just mean the Finns were putting on a show to impress their international guests.

They had to say their good-byes and thank-yous to the crew of the *Windkraft*.

"What will you do now?" Valentine asked Stepanek and Von Krebs.

"We will return you at the end of July, when the conference is over," Stepanek said. "I am not sure of the exact route yet, but I know it is to the north, across the Gulf of Bothnia. I believe they mean to take advantage of the summer and keep you far from any Kurian areas for the journey home."

Valentine nodded. "During the conference, what will you be doing?"

Stepanek shrugged. "Rest. Enjoy the summer weather. I will take a little trip to Helsinki. It is too bad you have these meetings. You could see the private collection."

"What about you, Krebs?" Valentine asked.

"Von Krebs. The *Windkraft* will go for a refit. I know some people a little way south on the coast, among the islands. They are wanderers like myself, refugees given the house by the Finns with the understanding that they would restore it. A very beautiful spot. I will have a holiday. Meetings do not interest me. Perhaps do some kayaking if the weather remains favorable. Finnish summers, spirits, and saunas are not to be missed."

"I'm jealous," Duvalier said.

"You may perhaps wish to spend a weekend? It is a large home, at least by Finnish standards. I do not think my hosts will mind."

"Will you be attending any of the sessions?" she asked Von Krebs.

"Ha! No, not my sort of thing at all. I do understand there will be some fine dinners and parties at night. You may expect me at some of them. If you wish to visit, or explore this forest coast in the *Windkraft* once the maintenance is done, simply leave me a message at the conference center."

That let Von Krebs out as the agent, then, unless he

intended to chitchat his way to information about what had transpired that day.

"Aren't you part of the Refugee Network?" Valentine asked Von Krebs.

"Yes, I have certain connections that let me smuggle more-prominent individuals out of central Europe. But even so, I am a small fish. They do not need me to do much more than ensure that attendees such as yourself arrive and depart in safety. I would rather enjoy the summer weather outside, you see. And the social atmosphere. This is a very 'big deal' as you Americans say for this coast. Influential people will be coming from Helsinki, Oslo, Stockholm, St. Petersburg, even Copenhagen, though the Kurians control that even more than they do Oslo or Stockholm."

She didn't much like Von Krebs, but he'd improved, like Pistols, over the days they'd been together. She might take him up on it at that. Save her from having to watch Valentine snuffle around his Polish sailor's well-muscled crotch like a hound on a hot scent.

At the bottom of the gangplank they were directed to the Ostrobothnian Center. A rattly old blue and white school bus waited for them, or they could walk a few kilometers, following a simple map provided by the woman at the quayside. There were also a few "city bikes," in the same blue and white, available for borrowing.

They decided to walk to the hotel together. Ahn-Kha carried far more than his fair share, and stayed at the back of the line, with Valentine falling in at the front. Maybe she wasn't the only one put off by the fresh paint on everything and the new clothes on everyone.

It was a tidy little city and Duvalier found herself admiring the well-organized Finns. They had many of the same difficulties as the Canadians in Halifax, but you wouldn't know that the town had burst its seams thanks to a flow of refugees. Maybe the town fathers or whoever was running the joint ordered the residents to haul in the laundry and tie up the dogs.

Ahn-Kha attracted a good deal of attention. She'd seen some Big Mouth jaws hanging in the windows of sea outfitters near the wharf, but she doubted if they'd ever seen Gray or Golden Ones up here. The children, as usual, dashed out into the street to touch his fur or point at his ears, twisting this way and that at sounds of the city. Ahn-Kha bore the circus-sideshow attention with his usual good humor, and began to sing what she guessed was a bluegrass song he'd picked up in Kentucky. Soon he had a throng of kids dancing about him, the girls in little impromptu ring-around-the-rosy circles and the boys doing stomping dance moves that she couldn't quite place in her experience.

There wasn't much traffic to endanger the kids, luckily. The sparse vehicular traffic was powered by either natural gas or muscle, though there were a few larger trucks parked in the alleys that seemed to be fitted out for diesel. She'd heard there was still plenty of oil up around the Arctic Circle, and they were near enough.

They passed a couple of parks, some theaters, and a lively strip with cafés and restaurants. German seemed to be the unofficial second language according to the menus in the cheaper eatery windows, French in the tonier ones, but there were a couple of cards in English as well.

The hotel was one of the taller buildings away from the city center, and once out of the denser blocks and in the park ring they were able to follow its roofline to the entrance even without the map.

The hotel reminded Duvalier a little of a ski jump; it had that same triangular shape with an upswept curve. On the curve side there were many little terraces, so each floor had a nice patio looking out on the Gulf of Bothnia. The sunset views would probably be spectacular.

"This is it," Valentine said unnecessarily as they crossed the street toward the hotel. He might be nervous; he sometimes grew talkative when worried.

There was a revolving door in good condition. The hotel had a double layer of glass at the lobby entrance, probably to keep out the winter weather.

Inside, the decor was sleek, mostly done in muted whites and pale greens. There were dozens of uniformed staff waiting to assist them. Near the front desk, they were met by a large notice board standing on an easel explaining in six languages that the hotel restoration was a two-year project funded by the Baltic League, and when the conference was over it would be converted into temporary housing for refugees awaiting more permanent placement.

Opposite the hotel was the conference center. It ran two levels, with huge glass panels letting in light from the south onto what looked like concourses. If Duvalier hadn't known better, she would have thought from the exterior it was some sort of art museum or perhaps a music hall. It had a steel arch with cabling that created an interesting, suspension bridge–like network above the door.

There were smiling, friendly-looking blond police officers in pairs wandering around the plaza between the hotel and conference center. They were unarmed save for radios and what she guessed was pepper spray, but they wore tactical backpacks. She suspected the backpacks held more substantial weapons. The roofs of both the hotel and the conference center had two observation points each—two that the casual observer could see, anyway. There was also a checkpoint for vehicles entering the hotel or conference center parking and dock areas, with dogs doing the searches. There were three armored cars of the sort used in the KZ to transport valuables and prisoners to the Reapers parked discreetly around the buildings; they probably held backup forces. Security seemed to be adequate against a single madman or a small unit attempting to shoot up the conference. Hopefully, anything company-sized or larger would be spotted long before it arrived within a few kilometers of the conference.

They had a series of large notice boards in the lobby, each titled with a language or languages. While Valentine went to the desk and took care of getting them checked in to their reserved rooms, she found the English board and read the two sheets of paper tacked there. They had scheduling and information about the conference, a short list of rules, and some notes on translation procedures.

The room situation was odd. Ahn-Kha and Sime, the official delegates, each had a room. "Everyone else" from the United Free Republics and the Kentucky Alliance was crowded into a smaller room with two double beds. Ahn-Kha and Sime unofficially rearranged matters for the comfort of the team. Duvalier warmed to him when he made the offer of his own room to her. She declined, after amusing herself for a moment with the thought of games she could play with hidden microphones if the Kurians had managed to bug the hotel. Then she enjoyed the chance to get a shower with unlimited hot water, something she hadn't had the opportunity to do since before Halifax. It was glorious.

When she was done with that, she found an unofficial meeting going on between Ahn-Kha and Sime.

As voting delegates, Ahn-Kha and Sime had a special orientation to attend. Ahn-Kha had become all business since their arrival. He'd put on a long, sleeveless robe that Duvalier had never seen before. It was some kind of Golden One formal wear, like a Nehru jacket for musclemen.

The voting delegates also had to designate alternates in case of illness or an emergency that would render them unable to fulfill their duties. Both Sime and Ahn-Kha chose Valentine. Ahn-Kha was at least polite enough to ask her if she was interested in being an alternate. She smiled and declined. Sime didn't even give her a moment's consideration.

X

She wandered around the town a little while the others registered them into the hotel and the conference. It was strange to walk along a street with doorways and shop windows beckoning, but not understand a single word spoken or printed. She recognized address numbers, and the letters were familiar but decorated with accent marks and what she'd learned in Germany were called umlauts.

There was a very old patch of town with tiny wooden buildings laid out more haphazardly. Most were unpainted but in very good repair. She finally came across a permanent metal sign that also looked like a pre-2022 relic and explained that the old town was an example of traditional Finnish wooden architecture.

Off the main streets, there were individual homes, often square and steep-roofed, and small, more-recent apartment buildings. Most of the homes had little patches of garden, some watched over by decorative gnomes or trolls.

There was still a disturbing doubt. Perhaps the Kurians were planning something like their raid on the hotel. Or what if a shadow organization posing as the Baltic League selected this town and had forces positioned already? That seemed ridiculously unlikely, especially among these diligent, spic-and-span Finns.

She borrowed one of the public bikes from a rack in town and took a training ride around the outskirts of town. She went a couple of miles up the roads leading north, east, southeast—the best maintained—and south. At each minor intersection she slowed and hopped off her bike and examined the roadway and the shoulders.

She checked wheel tracks in dried mud puddles and such. It looked like most of the traffic this time of year was on bicycles. There were hoofprints, too, and some footprints.

The one difficulty she had was at the Finnish garrison, right at the edge of town between the bayside and the airport. As she passed the gate, slowing to take a look through the fence at the brick dormitories, a couple of wolf whistles pursued her.

Her mistake was thinking they were compliments. She ended up being pursued by a small silver car with a police bar running all around the roof. Lights zipped around the roof bar like photo flashes.

She was questioned by a sergeant who spoke rough-and-ready English. She explained that she was part of the conference, gave her name and delegation so they could check her out, and waited.

They cleared her and the sergeant told her to "enjoy us exercise air, Kentucky woman!" as he gave her bike—not her butt—a push down the road. These Finns were well behaved.

The Kurians weren't in the neighborhood, unless there was a very small advance party. If that was the case, they'd probably be Finns, hiding in town with the locals. They'd spot her as a stranger long before she recognized them.

It should be night. Her body told her so, but the sun was still at a height she was used to thinking of as mid-afternoon. Weary, she turned the bike back toward town.

She decided to relax, at least for her first night. The

way things looked, she'd have plenty of time to pedal around checking out back roads. It never hurt to learn the local territory.

They decided that Ahn-Kha and Valentine would acquaint the Finnish security with the intelligence they'd discovered. Ahn-Kha, as a voting delegate, might get more attention from whoever was running the show, and Valentine felt it was his duty to go along and see that the information was treated seriously.

The sleeping arrangements weren't ideal, but she'd fared worse many, many times. Ahn-Kha gallantly offered to give up his private room to her, but she refused. She suspected that was a relief to Valentine and Pistols. Ahn-Kha had many fine qualities, but his digestion still hadn't adjusted to the fish-heavy Scandinavian cuisine. On the diet of salty fish, he produced gas that was probably a violation of some international convention on chemical weapons.

The hotel suite was smaller than ones she'd known in the United States. It had one compact bedroom and a second sitting room with a folding sofa bed, plus a toilet and a shower. There were cots in the closet—the Finns had been expecting a larger delegation from the United Free Republics and Kentucky.

Valentine and Pistols offered to take the sitting room.

"I don't see how you'll manage that without sleeping on top of each other. The couch is fine by me," she said.

The little side tables were pressed into duty for gun cleaning and maintenance. Pistols spent some time with Valentine talking about the advantages of color-coding the bottom of his magazines with mildly luminous paint of the sort used for dots on gun sights, and they went to work on the magazines for Valentine's old .45 Colt automatic, using colored tape for now.

The conference had its "soft opening" the next day. There were no meetings or votes, just a lot of open meetings for the delegates to get to know one another.

She was registered at the conference as well, a "non-voting associate" from the Kentucky Alliance. A helpful man at the door with a cross-draw pistol somewhat hidden under a sport jacket directed her to the credentialing desk.

The big open hallway between the glass wall and the individual conference rooms was almost empty. There was a circular desk near the doors with a few Scandinavian types (she was getting used to everyone being blond, tall, and in possession of magnificent teeth) and she opened with the universal line.

"I'm sorry, does anyone speak English?"

It turned out they all did.

Even though the conference had not officially opened yet, there was still business taking place at the center in some of the smaller rooms, and the credentialing and security desk in the main lobby was busy. When she gave her name and freehold they retrieved a file for Kentucky—she noted it looked new and was nearly empty, whereas many of the others were dog-eared and filled—and opened it. The security man stepped over and looked at two photographs with the conference assistant, one that was faint and assembled line by line via some form of transmission, and a second, much better and more recent, of her leaning on the railing of Von Krebs's yacht looking out to sea. She remembered Von Krebs fiddling with a modern-looking camera, but she hadn't seen him take the snap of her.

Effective little shit. Was he part of the security staff? Or were the transport people just supposed to take a picture of everyone they'd been assigned to convey?

A uniformed security man took her over to a beige wall outside one of the conference rooms and had her stand on a little piece of tape. He moved to a second piece of tape and took her picture with a camera that spat out an instant color photograph. Back at the desk one of the workers stuck it in a device and centered it on her head, punched it out of its surroundings, and placed it on a badge with her name, then ran it through a laminating machine. Then they photocopied it—those machines were rare!—and put it back in the Kentucky file before handing her the conference identity card and the lanyard. The back had some simple safety instructions. She noted that all firearms had to be turned in at the security desk, but it said nothing about knives—or sword-sticks.

"You must wear identification in this building, or for group activities at your hotel. The ninth floor is the conference area there."

"Thank you."

"May I help you with anything else?"

It was worth a try. "Have the Lifeweavers arrived yet?" she asked. She wondered what she'd have to do to get an audience with one to request more Lifeweaver aid for Kentucky.

The staff exchanged a couple of words and she recognized "Lifeweavers" repeated.

The woman who'd made her ID smiled sympathetically. "No one can say. They always attend, though they take little part. Since the disaster in the South Atlantic only one or two are expected. They are here already; I am sure. I know the White Ravens are here."

"White Ravens?"

She bit her lip in thought. "Do you call it something else? Those humans who communicate with them for us and guard them. They are connected in some manner, you know? Do you have such people in America?"

"Oh, I see. I'm not sure if I'm supposed to talk about that," she said.

She'd heard rumors about humans who joined up with the Lifeweavers to serve them, like priests attending to a living god. She'd be tempted to take an offer like that. She felt a strange sort of comfort in their alien presence. They were so wise and remote. It would be fascinating to see the cosmos through their eyes, even secondhand.

She attached the little alligator clip and took a walk around the concourse on both levels. It was nearly empty, with just a few attendees like her vacantly wandering, or little groups of Baltic League organizers hurrying about with carts filled with plastic storage bins. She had a few curious looks from the sleek attendees.

Well, she'd have an opportunity to talk with one sooner or later. A Lifeweaver or two would make all the difference in Kentucky.

As she walked away, she heard more Finnish behind her, and a stifled giggle. Sometimes she cursed her enhanced hearing. Sometimes you didn't want to hear everything that transpired behind your back.

She wondered what the joke was, but felt certain it was about her. There was just something about Europeans that made her feel awkward. Back home, everyone was ragged.

To be honest with herself, she felt a bit of a ragamuffin. It was one thing to shrug and say "screw that noise; I'm just here for the food" and another to be among them—these people were clearly taking the conference very seriously and putting on their best. And here she was, your basic Midwestern farmyard scarecrow. Her pants were thin at the knees and the collar of her shirt was frayed and wrinkled. And these were her presentable clothes.

No wonder the late Thérèse Stamp had nudged her about buying new clothes.

Curiosity satisfied, she wandered around the grounds of the conference center. At the sunken fountain plaza there were garbage bins and several sand-filled basins for tobacco. There were some extinguished matches and butts in the sand, but not many. As for the ground and the fountain itself, both were immaculate. Wait—there were a few silvery coins in the fountain, thank God. These Finns were starting to turn into civic-minded robots in her imagination. That, or there were a lot of make-work jobs cleaning public spaces for the refugees who'd come up the Gulf of Bothnia.

She went into town and looked in shop windows. Finally, she found a store crowded with racks of women's clothing, with more stacked in disorganized bins. All used or patched stuff, by the look of it. It smelled of industrial-strength detergent and critter killer. Hopefully it would be cheap.

The shop had only a few staff, and all those seemed to chat with one another in a polyglot tongue that was discernible to her only through a couple of brief English phrases ("okay," she'd learned, was virtually universal).

A nice pencil skirt, some tights, and a new blouse and jacket later, she felt like a new woman. The clean, simple lines of the women's fashions popular up here suited her thin frame. She could almost admire herself in the mirror in the neat, severe lines. Almost.

As it turned out, her purchases were very cheap. The clothing became less expensive the more you had to buy. Rough work clothes and boots, along with winter layers, were the pricier, sought-after items up here. People had fewer occasions to dress in formal business attire, and it would hardly stand up to field use to be worth the purchase price.

They didn't even offer bags, but they showed her

how to roll up the jacket and skirt and then bundle everything into the shirt for transport. She left the store ready for the conference, or whatever other social occasions the stay in Kokkola might bring.

She wasn't the only one who'd polished up a little, with the start of the conference looming.

Ahn-Kha had found a barber to trim his silky arm and leg hair and whiskers. His facial hair all ended on a neat plane now, slightly longer at the point of his jaw, going up in a nice edge getting shorter and shorter as it approached his jawline. He looked almost dashing. She would have liked to see that scene, giving instructions to a local barber who probably couldn't speak more than a few words of the various Scandinavian languages.

Pistols had gone "Euro." He'd changed his hair completely, right down to the color. It was now white, with perhaps the tiniest bit of ice blue tint. He'd also acquired a black leather jacket, cut like a classic old navy peacoat. It hid his pistols admirably and looked good on his stocky frame. The nautical attire made his face seem more the product of wind and weather than childhood disease.

Valentine had gotten a haircut, but otherwise hadn't changed much. His eyebrows had been trimmed, too, and someone had put a clean edge on his nails. He'd had all his clothes cleaned and pressed, but he hadn't made any purchases. Valentine being Valentine, he'd probably bought some pathetic-looking family a hearty meal and new clothes.

Sime, of course, didn't need any buffing. He was always as polished as a jade statue. He had a slightly different smell to him, though; perhaps he'd been trying French soaps again.

CHAPTER SEVEN

*T*he Pan-Freehold Conference of 2078: Each Pan-Freehold Conference has made history, in its way. The first, in 2048, was memorable just because it occurred. It meant the Resistance had enough of a structure that they could coordinate their efforts to meet somewhere in safety. It took place outside of Helsinki, which at that point was under disputable Kurian control, moving each day and meeting each night. The practice spawned the phrase "Helsinki White Night Shuffle," still in use to describe a fly-by-night organization. Only five freeholds, four from the northern parts of Eurasia and Canada representing all of North America, attended, with others participating via shortwave. The only major achievement of the conference was setting up a system for communicating between freeholds, a system that remained one of the Resistance's most deeply held secrets for generations.

Another meeting wasn't held for six years. The Pan-Freehold Conference of 2054 took place in the Australian Outback, starting the tradition of switching between the Northern and Southern hemispheres. While it was better attended than the first, it was considered something of a failure because the freeholds failed to come to a decision about the objectives for the next few years. It was also the first conference that had Lifeweaver observers attending—in this case five who were aiding the Australian/New Zealand/New Guinea/Indonesian freeholds.

Four years later, the conference was held in Canada. It was successful but not memorable, except perhaps for the quality and quantity of the beer. The Black Year of 2062 was a disastrous affair held off the coast of Argentina. The Kurian Order managed to attack it with low-level precision bombers, creating chaos, and then seeded the entire island with air-dropped "wild" and very hungry Reapers. The 2066 meeting never really got off the ground because of security concerns; it took place mostly over phone lines and short-wave radios as they looked for security solutions for the next one. Security was a major concern of the next conference, held in 2070. The conference was dispersed among many safe houses in a remote district in the Akita prefecture of Japan, an area in the Dewa mountain chain where the people live quietly and strangers are marked. While the communications gear worked, and there were no raids, the camaraderie of previous conferences was missing—just as much was worked out during the nightlife, it seemed, as at the daytime meetings. The 2074 meeting, hosted by the South Africans deep in the bush, marked more than twenty-five years since the first Pan-Freehold Conference, and news from around the world was largely positive. Gains had been made nearly everywhere, and even formerly quiet Kurian Zones had seen an uptick of Resistance activity. For the first time, the Kurian Order seemed vulnerable. But again, the conference broke *down over disputes about where the next blow should fall heaviest. The Chinese, North Americans, and Andean multifreehold associations each thought a good part of a continent could be reclaimed if supported properly by the others, and the conference ended in acrimony.*

By 2078 no one was expecting much. The past two meetings had been tumultuous and everyone was expecting a quiet, businesslike affair among the quiet, businesslike Scandinavians. Perhaps returning it to Finland would evoke old, romantic memories of revolutionaries scuttling from basement to basement, living on boiled potatoes, coffee, and rounds of head-blasting vodka mixed with aquavit and gin.

Indeed, very little was agreed upon at the conference beyond the quality of the cuisine. The delegations all asserted what became known as the "after you, Alphonse" protocol for major cooperative efforts against the Kurians. There were the usual lower-level exchanges of technology and information, selection of books that could be used for coding messages, arrangements for liaisons to return home with different delegations—the inaction that Sime had promised had apparently become a reality.

Duvalier had very little to do at the conference. On the rare occasions that required a vote by the delegates, Ahn-Kha was the only one of their party who was at all involved, though they showed the votes and delegates on large view screens. Ninety percent of these were ceremonial, according to Ahn-Kha, mostly devoted to voting posthumous thanks to some hero of the Resistance. Supposedly there were also secret votes, but Ahn-Kha said they probably wouldn't be happening until the end of the conference, once the issues had been wrangled out.

The United Free Republics and the Kentucky Alliance had arranged, through Sime, for a small per diem, which provided them with just enough Finnish currency to get a decent meal and toiletries. It turned out that Ahn-Kha and Valentine had also had the sense to bring a few bottles of real Kentucky bourbon as trade goods, and they commanded a very handsome profit for the pair at the nicest of the local bar/restaurants, as well as their hotel lounge. They shared their profits with her ("I used a little of your baggage allowance anyway, since you always travel so light," Val explained), so between that and saving on her per diem by eating at the conference's buffets, she had pocket money for indulgences. After a splurge on chocolate, she saved the rest for items that would last longer or perhaps a nice souvenir.

She watched Ahn-Kha vote a couple times out of interest. He had an identification card that carried a magnetic strip, and when it came time for a vote, he stood in a short line in front of one of the electronic vote recorders placed on conveniently located podiums at the edges of the aisles of the plenary conference room. Ahn-Kha inserted his card, and a screen brought up his designated language (English) giving him Yes, No, or Abstain options. Each voting delegate's choice was displayed on a movie-theater screen. A few of the very large, multinational freeholds, such as Canada, Mongolia, and the Andes Chain and the Indo-Pacific Territories (which included

Queensland and the Australian Outback), had more than one vote.

For those needing translation, they'd either brought their own translators or they could access a network with instantaneous translation given in a dozen languages over a local network. Most of the seats had plug-ins for headphones—you just pushed buttons on a "dial" to go to the channel for the language you wanted.

Then there were smaller meetings in other rooms. The meetings had subjects such as "Refuting and Using Kurian Propaganda" and "The Home Farm: Four Ways to Improve Production" and "An Examination of the Debriefings of Six High-Level Defectors."

The conference had a daily "newspaper" that mostly covered corrections and changes to the schedule, though there was, oddly, a humorous, dialogue-free cartoon at the bottom of the back page every morning. Just the thing to put a smile on your face before the "How Many Lives per Year to Support a Kurian?: Latest Analysis" session at nine a.m.

As for the food and drink, it was very good. Every delegate received plastic tokens: red for food, white for entertainment and personal necessities, and black for alcohol, tobacco, or indulgence foods such as chocolates and quail egg–type delicacies. The only problem was that the tokens were useless in town; they could be used only at the hotel and conference center. Vodka, schnapps, and a Danish liquor called aquavit were the cheapest liquors (beer, oddly enough, could be bought with any colored token, thanks to local sources and a patriotic gesture by a Polish brewery that had managed to get a large supply of beer across the Baltic to aid in the fight for freedom), and wine tended to be the most expensive source of alcohol.

There were exhibits on the concourse, mostly by weapons and communication-gear manufacturers. "Micromanufacturing" and "anysourcing" seemed to be popular buzzwords, according to the flyers she picked up. There were live fire demonstrations of guns that allegedly had only three moving parts and could be manufactured with the simplest of metal-stamping technology, ways to create explosives that looked like attic insulation, cinder blocks, bricks, or conduit, and to Ahn-Kha's delight there was a special heartroot booth that showed all the different ways to grow the Golden One staple and turn it into dishes for human consumption or animal feed. They had heartroot with honey, thick heartroot stews, even heartroot smoothies mixed with dried fruits that claimed to supply a full day's protein and carbs in a single shake.

There were also a few weirdos, or "Moonrakers," as Valentine called them. There were people in the alleys of town who set up displays selling crystals that allegedly interfered with a Reaper's sense of your lifesign, lucky charms handed down through families that supposedly kept children safe, even brass rings "guaranteed to fool anyone and pass all detection tests."

Duvalier looked in on a room devoted to "War Games." For games, they were carried out in deadly seriousness, with military staff officers from the vari-

ous freeholds testing operational alliances and theo-
retical attacks on various Kurian Zones. From what
she could gather, your freehold had "resource points"
of population, raw materials, and technology that
closely matched real-world numbers, and you could
allocate your resource points to building up your
economy, or military, or some combination of the two,
the classic "guns or butter" choice, in other words.
You could also spend resource points in Kurian Zones
to slow them down or cause distractions.

Duvalier, who'd served her whole life more or less
as one of those resources raising havoc in the KZs,
knew it wasn't quite so simple as that. Why the population of Kentucky would fight the Kurians tooth and
nail when the population of Kansas wouldn't was a
more complex question than could be quantified in the
war games tables and charts. She was just a fraction of
a "resource point" in game terms, but if she got lucky
she could kill a Kurian or take out an entire Quisling
brigade headquarters. You couldn't just spend a certain amount of money to shift the allegiance of a population; if you could, the Kurians probably would have
bought out Southern Command decades ago.

Or perhaps they had. Unsettling thought. She some-
times wondered if there was something rotten high up.
Since that wild summer after Solon's collapse, when
Southern Command seemed to be on a roll, toppling
Kurian Zones almost as fast as they reached the borders,
the advance had ground to a permanent halt at the Rio
Grande and the Mississippi. Guys like Val suddenly
brought up on dubious charges . . . with smooth talkers

like Sime running the show now. "Show" wasn't even the right word; it was more like one long intermission.

While waiting in line at the bakery, she ran into the sergeant with the nearly unintelligible English who'd questioned her outside the garrison. After exchanging a few forced comments about the weather and how she was liking seeing the sun set at eleven thirty in the evening, he made a rather ham-fisted attempt to arrange a dinner date. "Food, huh? Eat? Both?" he said, waggling his forefingers at her and then at himself.

She couldn't imagine the conversation and she didn't want to have sex with him, so she shook her head no and said "boyfriend" a few times.

They chatted some more as the line moved forward. He had a holstered pistol she admired. He extracted it for her. It was a Glock 17, looked like, with an extra-thick handgrip—the sergeant had large hands. She admired it.

"You get one, gun basement," he said. " 'Stand?"

She didn't 'stand, so she shrugged.

"I take you. I take you."

He did take her, all the way to the center of town. Down a little alley off the main plaza in front of the sulfur-colored town hall and civic center, he showed her a gun shop. She spent an hour perusing the stock while he chatted with the owner and leisurely ate a breakfast quiche he'd purchased at the bakery.

She selected a Glock 17 similar to his save for the factory grip. Through the sergeant, she negotiated a deal with the owner. He arranged to swap out its current handle for a rubberized diamondback grip. The owner also put new luminous dots into the sights of the pistol—free of charge.

He let her onto the garrison gun range and she put fifty rounds through the gun, familiarizing herself with it. Her sergeant—Ruddi was his name, apparently—must have sensed something about her, since he quit trying to get her out on a date and instead wanted to hear Duvalier talk about ways to kill a Reaper, or a Big Mouth (they were a serious problem in the Baltic and in the waters of the Danish straits).

They cleaned their weapons together. She learned two Finnish expressions. *Varo!* meant "watch out" and *anteeksi* was a common way to say "excuse me."

One of the garrison soldiers brought them a tray of fresh*ish*—meaning dried and salted—fish, potatoes, and vegetables of the summer harvest. They had beer out of a cask as well, with a label burned into the side of the cask with a branding iron. Some popular local brew, a very decent lager, she thought.

"See. We dinner, after it all," Ruddi said.

She laughed and agreed.

The gun had set her back the majority of her expense money. She'd have to live very cheaply on the free stuff for the delegates and their associates, perhaps step up her attempts to get invitations to the nicer dinners and receptions.

✗

The town had an old-fashioned public bathhouse and sauna. There were also numerous private ones that were "welcome to the delegates" so everyone could enjoy the Finnish tradition of sauna, even though it wasn't midwinter and they'd miss the full effect of running into the snow to cool off.

The Baltic League had come to some arrangement with the owners, and attendees of the conference were free to use the bath part, though you still needed a little money to tip the staff. Massages, pumicing, and individual lathering with a sponge was extra, of course.

She visited the larger baths out of some mixture of curiosity and boredom.

There were one or two curious delegates like her there for the experience. Most of the attendees seemed to be older locals, who bought monthly passes at reduced rates. From what she could see, it was as much social ritual as personal hygiene. The Finns came to the baths to chat over tea, exchange canned or preserved items from their gardens, read, even play chess.

The bath part was fascinating. After soaping and rinsing in a little stall with a wood slat chair to sit on, you stepped on through to the men's or women's (or mixed, for the daring, and she wasn't that daring, more because she was embarrassed by her dreadful feet than modesty) soaking pool. In a true nod to the Old World, the water was heated by hot rocks dropped into a little cistern at the bottom of the pool. A grate was put over the rock bed to add a measure of safety. The heated water circulated through the natural tendency of the hot water to rise, as far as she could tell. The cooled rocks were extracted regularly and returned to the fireplace by cheerful attendants who joked with the old men in Finnish.

She loved it. Except for the part where the old ladies beat each other all over the skin with leafy birch branches. Supposedly it kept the skin young and supple (according to an English information sheet they handed her). She'd engaged in conversation with the Finns mostly through pantomime, though the oldest ones knew a few polite words of English that had been taught in the schools of their youth.

On her third time she brought Valentine, and a little pair of canvas slippers so they could go to the common room together. They both wrapped thin towels around their waists, like most of the Finns. The women were unconcerned with exposing their breasts in a bathhouse, or at least those who were concerned about it stuck to the women-only side. When she emerged from the bath to move to the sauna—still enjoyable in the cool, bright summer of the north—she felt deliciously sexy with the wet wrap clinging about her waist and buttocks. That was an unusual feeling for her. Valentine's maleness brought it out, she supposed, though everything above her waist counted him just as an old friend. Well, the reproductive organs did have their own separate consciousness. Between odd moments of arousal and her monthly cycle, it sometimes felt as though her ovaries were running the show.

Val's wet towel didn't leave much to the imagination, either. Most of the other attendees were staring at his scars, the big exit wound in his leg and the burn marks on his back in particular. One, who'd heard them speaking English, asked, "You have in wreck?"

"Boiler room accident," Valentine said. He'd told Duvalier about being scalded by steam while pursuing a Kurian through the bowels of a Kurian tower in Little Rock.

"Ooch," the Finn said sympathetically. He pulled at his bottom lip, as if trying to extract English vocabulary. "You are. . . lucky . . . for being alive."

Valentine smiled and shrugged.

He'd endured more physical pain than she had fighting the Kurians. She liked to disappear when the bullets started flying; Cats just weren't of much use in mass slaughter. He'd suffered emotionally, too. She'd been brought up in a Kurian Zone. She sometimes thought most of her emotional responses were like burned circuitry from that. The wiring was there; it just had no power. Most of the time.

"Been meaning to tell you, this weekend I'm going away," Valentine said. "Three days at most—trip to Helsinki."

"With Eva Stepanek?" Duvalier asked. The pleasant sexiness boiled up and disappeared like water on one of the rocks fresh from the fireplace.

"Yes. I'm curious about her art collection. She's really proud of it. It's all in storage, but when she's no longer sailing, she plans to open a little gallery or museum. She hasn't decided which. She wanted to show me some of the finds. I'm no expert, of course. Maybe when we met years ago I was too skeptical of her plans—I honestly can't remember. She seems to want to prove something to me."

That she can suck a cock with the best of them, I imagine, Duvalier thought.

"Helsinki is the biggest city in Finland, right?"

"Yes, it's ten times the size of this, easy. Bigger than New Orleans, I think."

"You think that's wise?" Duvalier asked. "You're supposed to be at this conference."

"The conference is interesting in its way. I think if the Kurians were going to try something, they would have done so already. In any case, it's a weekend. Half the delegates will be at the coast and the rest will be preparing for their next week's presentations."

"If the Kurians only found out the location after the conference started, they might still be staging a force strong enough to make it into the harbor," Duvalier said.

"The Lifeweavers haven't shown up yet. Unless they're disguised. If I were the Kurians, I'd wait until I thought I could bag them. Sime told me they weren't expected until the end of the month."

"You'd think they'd have arrived while the location was still secret. Maybe the Kurians are out hunting for them."

Valentine pulled at his chin. "If so, that's something for the Finns to worry about. I don't see how we can make a difference. If I could point to some tangible dangers, I'd just alert the Finns anyway and be ready to help. But you're right—it is odd that they aren't here from the start.

Maybe the Baltic League doesn't trust the Lifeweavers any more than the other delegates do. There's always talk that the Lifeweavers are just Kurians pretending to aid us. Fighting both sides of the same war, as it were."

Duvalier had heard that theory proposed from barstools by veteran soldiers and scraggly-bearded kids more than once over the years. It was the sort of idea you'd come up with after an evening's drinking and bullshitting.

"The New Universal Church came up with that one," she said with a laugh she hoped didn't sound too forced.

Valentine let it drop. He knew she felt closer to the Lifeweavers than most.

"Could be," Valentine said. "Still, there's not much scheduled for the weekend. Some demonstrations in the field. Oh, Ahn-Kha will like the heartroot part. The Finns have a lot of mossy bogs around all these lakes. It's doing very well there. It just freezes up in the winter—you can chip it out if you get real hungry and defrost it—then it goes right back to growing in the spring. I had a heartroot omelet for breakfast, as a matter of fact. It wasn't bad, especially since they used a good cheese. It's a little tasteless without support."

"Heartroot? Great. Unless he gets it just like Mom used to cook, it gives him terrible cabbage farts," Duvalier said.

Valentine smiled. "Still another reason to be in Helsinki this weekend."

"Have you actually done anything at the conference?"

"Once we passed on the warning, I've just been doing what suits my fancy. There was a discussion about Xeno products. I was in the audience, but they had me talk a little about the legworm ranchers. They didn't even know where to find the meat on a legworm or that the leather came from egg casings. I was able to straighten them out on a few things. Some delegates from Russia claimed there were a lot of legworms in the tagia up near the permafrost line. In the winter they go into the usual hibernation nest-pile, get snowed over, and sometimes people get curious about the heap, climb it, fall in, and are never heard from again. They're terrified of the damn things, to tell the truth. They can believe the Kentuckians have built what amounts to a society handling them. What about you?"

She shrugged. To tell the truth, she was a little bored with it all. She never followed the grand strategy of the fronts beyond information about where the enemy was operating. Her vague feelings of unease probably came out of the boredom. She was so used to being ready to deal with death jumping out of the trees that she couldn't relax—even with the aid of a sauna. "I sat in on a few talks. You have the headphones on and it's like watching a foreign film, only there's no film. As to finding a Kurian infiltrator, the security people are making sure there's nobody wandering around re-cording stuff. The thing is, note taking isn't against the rules; everyone's jotting down notes all the time. If there is a spy—or spies—he's got to be bored."

"The voting delegates get special meetings. Ahn-Kha has said there might be something in the works for In-dia. There's been a lot of talk about it. To hear them talk, the Kurians there are worse than the ones back home; they fight with each other more than with the Resistance. They're trying to get Australia and Russia to commit to getting enough arms to Mumbai for a rising. Those guys with the turbans, the Sikhs, that's what they're here for, to get more weapons out of the other freeholds."

"If only Southern Command could have knocked over Georgia. We could arm the whole world."

"The Atlanta Gunworks, you mean?" Valentine asked. "They make good stuff, better than we do. If we took it over—"

"Suddenly they'd be making crap guns like most of the stuff Southern Command stamps out."

"I wasn't going to put it quite like that, but yes. Funny how everyone hangs on to vintage firearms if they can get them."

"Maybe she's just after your bourbon."

"It's true. I have one bottle left. Thing is, she's not really a drinker. Odd, because all of the other Poles here toss it down like iced tea. This is the hardest-drinking meeting I've ever been to."

"You're just used to Southern Command." While Southern Command made her crazy at regular intervals, she did admire it. You're not supposed to drink in uniform, and they didn't think too much of you if you drank much out of uniform, either.

They split up and returned to the areas for their respective genders to dress. Her skin felt lovely thanks to all the steam, even without a thrashing by birch branches. She was in the mood for some really good food and maybe a little wine, and she didn't have the money for a weekend at the expensive joints with the menus translated into French.

Ahn-Kha would be eating heartroot all weekend, which would give him gas, which would make the hotel untenable.

She decided to send a message to Von Krebs.

CHAPTER EIGHT

*T*he Bothnian Coast, July: *Long stretches of the heavily for-*
ested Finnish coast are almost uninhabited. Few have the re-
sources to live in a remote home through the long, dark
winter, so most of the vacation and year-round homes of the
pre-Kurian era are empty of everything but bears, red foxes,
and other wildlife.

Still, there are a few fine homes left on the coast, mostly near
towns of year-round activity such as Kokkola, as well as smaller,
more humble dwellings around villages devoted to fishing and
sealing on the coast. The Gulf of Bothnia has its charms for
some, including the fact that the low-salinity water freezes over
for several months out of the year, making it one of the largest
expanses of ice outside of the Arctic and Antarctic regions—an
ice fisherman's paradise, if you have the ability to cross the
sometimes treacherous sheets and drill your way through to wa-
ter. In the summer, the small, isolated beaches see a rush of
campers and fishermen taking advantage of the mild weather
and long sunlit dawns and dusks. Through the other seasons
one might consider it an ideal climate for a philosopher or writer,
with opportunities to spend weeks on end quietly and warmly

indoors, if you have the resources, though the market for writing and philosophy is much lessened in the dark days of the Kurian Order.

She dropped a message for Von Krebs at the conference center first thing the next morning, before she lost her resolve to do so.

Wandering briefly through the conference center, overhearing conversations she couldn't understand, she wished in vain to be on her way home. Even Pistols seemed to be enjoying the conference. He called the atmosphere "stimulating," a word she doubted he had used often before their trip.

Not that the trip wasn't good for her. She'd put on weight. The Finns used a lot of sour cream in their soups and dressings, and after an initial bout of indigestion, she was thriving on regular meals with plenty of fresh veggies. There wasn't much of what she considered fruit at these latitudes, but the berries made up for it.

She wasn't mentally stimulated, either. To be honest, she was bored.

It wasn't for the lack of characters attending. There were a few big, burly, savage-looking Scandinavian guerillas who were either Bears or such beasts personally that they could have given the Bears a tougher time than they'd seen outside of a Reaper conclave.

One in particular caught her eye. He was a blond giant, like some hero out of an epic who was just waiting for a Valkyrie to carry him off from the field of the slain. He'd been partially—well, there was no other word for it but "scalped" in some encounter or other, and it left him with a huge pink patch where his hair should have been on the left side. As if to compensate, he'd let the right side grow into a long fall, giving his head an asymmetrical but strangely appealing look. He wore a thick fur jacket and what looked like wolf-skin boots; he'd left the wolf faces atop the shoes, as a matter of fact. She quietly inquired about him at the security desk.

"Rolf, that one is. A Norwegian. The last survivor of an entire company of Bears. You know Bears?"

"I know Bears."

"All died but him at Trondheim. A terrible fight, but Trondheim now, no more Kurians. Oslo and Bergen and the south coast of Norway is all they have."

"And they're welcome to it," the security woman at the desk said. "Damn stupid Norwegians."

The activity woke her appetite. She went back to the hotel, wondering what she'd do with herself until the afternoon. She expected Von Krebs to get the message by noon. It was in her nature and her training to observe people's routines. She'd seen Von Krebs most days around lunchtime in the hotel, having drinks with friends. He usually hit the convention center first.

She decided to use the hotel buffet.

Meals came in two varieties—free buffets for the attendees, and personally funded meals that could be delivered to your home or eaten at an elegant table near a romantic fire.

The only head-scratcher for her was the monitors. The hotel lobby set up six big, brilliant electronic screens that produced pictures and video so sharp that they were hard to distinguish from real life. One of the hotel workers said they were Finnish-made; there was a substantial electronics remanufacturing industry closer to Helsinki and Turku.

So, with all that amazing technology, what did they do? Ran conference updates about schedule and speaker changes in between reruns of *Noonside Passions*, the ubiquitous Kurian Zone daytime drama. Duvalier couldn't stand it, but Valentine would sit quite happily, drink coffee or tea, and soak up plot points about infertile women and black market scoundrels, leavened with plenty of New Universal Church sermonizing.

It was popular around the world, so they could get broadcasts of the day's show in several languages. Moreover, since it was propaganda masquerading as entertainment, it was broadcast everywhere. Valentine liked to pick the story lines apart sometimes, trying to pick up hints about what the Kurian Order was worried about this particular month. They would do a series about energy rationing and conservation, or add a subplot about why it's important to keep your teeth clean, or to report privately owned transmitters.

Still, every day there were little groups of men and women watching one of the several broadcasts and rebroadcasts. Some worked on notes held in their laps, others grabbed a hasty meal and watched, and still more talked and chuckled as the show proceeded.

As Duvalier idled and wondered whether she

should go to the pharmacy in town for more stomach powder (her cranky gut was improving with the ample dairy and fiber), she sipped some watery fruit punch and watched the watchers. One German woman grew so excited at a *Passions* plot point that she hopped up and ran to one of the lobby phones to call over to the conference center. All Duvalier could get of the conversation was a character's Germanicized name mentioned a couple of times.

People get worked up about strange things. She'd known Bears who would read Jane Austen novels to one another, crying openly at the little heartbreaks of the books' heroines.

She'd rather spend her time sleeping. Dreams were better than anything a television writer could create. Now that she'd been eating well for a few weeks, her dreams had quit being about banquets and switched over to sunny fields, music, and sex.

Then she'd get up in the middle of the night to use the toilet, pass through the front room of their suite on the way to the toilet, holding her breath against the funk swirling around Valentine and Pistols (did they secretly hold farting competitions?), and return to her bed to drop into a deep and dreamless sleep.

Von Krebs broke his usual routine. She didn't see him around the hotel for lunch, and when she checked back in with the message center, she found that he hadn't come in for his notes yet.

With nothing better to do, she saw Valentine off at

the train station. There was a Finnish holiday of some sort on Friday and a few of the conference attendees were taking advantage of the light schedule to see Helsinki. The Helsinki train, on turnaround, was having a twenty-minute break and crew change. The sailor rather pointedly looked at a map and timetable in a display window.

Down the straight-shooting line, the tracks vanished into the pine forest. Duvalier thought Finland could supply much of the world's population with wood if it had to; everywhere she looked in this country there were beautifully tall pines, as straight as if they were designed with an architect's T square.

"I'm getting out for a long weekend, too," she said. "I'm taking Von Krebs up on his offer to see the coast from his friend's house."

Valentine had just a small canvas bag, the one he used for his pistol, ammunition, holster, knives, and the cleaning kit for his weapon. He made a show of adjusting the strap. "Glad to hear it. Get a little sea air and sun."

"What's with the gun? You're not really taking a train across the country for art," Duvalier said.

"My gun's in there, yes. The rest is shaving kit and a change of underwear."

"A Southern Command packet of weekend-leave condoms, too, I hope," she said. "Remember the daughter you left on Jamaica."

"I do. Too bad she doesn't remember me. Why do you bring that up?"

"Thought I'd remind you to keep your weapon on

safety this weekend," she said, but there was a laugh in her voice as she did so.

"Not that it's really your business, but I really am going there to see her art collection," Valentine insisted. "It's a day there, two days around Helsinki, and a day back. I can't get in that much trouble. I'm not interested in her beyond the paintings. I don't know that she has a physical interest in me. You have sensitive antennae— would you say she's into women?"

"I left my lesbian-detection kit in the stable at Seng. Sorry."

"She knows her art."

"I've seen better 'art' beckoning from a New Orleans balcony," Duvalier said.

Valentine ignored the jibe. "Just think. People used to spend their whole lives involved with . . . art. You'd study it at school, tour museums, get to know artists and gallery owners. Write books about it. Isn't it incredible?"

"If you go in for that sort of thing, yeah. A frog in a frying pan doesn't give a squirt about who owns how many Renoirs, and we're frogs in frying pans. That's easy to forget up here."

Valentine looked down the tracks. The train had arrived and the conductors were helping people find their cars. "Wonder if we'll ever get to a world again where people can build a life out of art."

"When did you get this art bug? Usually you're going on about some book or other that's interesting you."

"We'll have to cut this short, Ali. Train's boarding.

You have fun, too. I'm a little surprised. Von Krebs doesn't seem—"

"He's not. I just want to be on the ocean."

"It's a gulf of a sea, technically."

"Well, whatever. Saltwater shoreline. Never had much of a chance for it since our trip to the gulf waters. Be careful, Val."

"You, too."

He gave her a nudge with his elbow as he picked up his bag and joined his fellow passengers in going up onto the train. Duvalier saw Eva Stepanek waiting for him by one of the cars.

That evening a messenger tapped on their door as she was brushing her teeth. She was alone. Pistols was out on the town; he'd also made local friends. A couple of the Finnish police working security in the area around the hotel and conference center had found a fellow marksmanship enthusiast and Pistols had gone to the range with them. They were having a boys' night in one of the bars, trying the local vodkas.

The conference center messenger handed her an envelope made of thick, expensive-looking paper. Her name was written on it in a rather bold, all-capital hand.

She opened it and read the contents.

Wednesday, 7 p.m.—So pleased you decided to come. Boat has been refitted, just finished giving it a test in the open sea. Arrive whenever you like tomorrow.

He included a map and an address. The house was on the coast south of town. Apparently the home even had a name: Summerset House. She assumed Von Krebs had translated the name from Finnish for her.

She'd kept up with her laundry, so she had plenty of clean clothes. She spent an extra half hour in the tub, enjoying having the hotel room to herself.

The next day she took one of the city bikes out to the house. It was only a dozen kilometers outside of town, and her legs enjoyed the exercise.

The houses on this part of the coast road were discreetly hidden by trees at the end of long driveways. A few of the driveways were closed by new growth or gates.

Summerset House on the gulf was low and lean, architecturally fashioned like a glass sandwich between thin roof and foundation. She recognized the style by now as exaggeratedly Scandinavian.

Apart from a few walls and a white brick fireplace, you could see right through most of the house on the ground floor. The angle didn't reveal whether the same was true on the small second floor, sitting like a pillbox atop the house, with its own rooftop garden.

It was surrounded by a sort of patio made of smoothed river stones. The well-tended look to the house and grounds whispered discreet wealth.

She'd been kind of hoping for a cute little A-frame lodge. She'd seen a few along the coast that looked cozy, the perfect place to return to after enjoying a day in the gloriously invigorating summer sun of the far north. This house looked more like it was waiting for the photographer from *Architectural Digest*—yes, she'd glanced through old copies a few times in her travels, though the super-glossy pages made for unsanitary wiping.

Of course, she didn't know what she'd get with Von Krebs. There was a kind of phoniness about him. He put on lordly airs, as if he were a colossus astride the world, when he actually was just a good Baltic sailor who knew a lot of people on the various old Hanseatic coasts. She'd been half expecting a shack with old bedding stuffed in the holes to keep out the wind, half expecting a towering manor house made of dark volcanic rock. Either seemed to be possible with him.

Instead, the clean-lined, sprawling little house exhibited a refined sensibility. There wouldn't be any silly little brightly colored gnome or troll statues of the style she'd seen decorating the doorsteps and lawns of the ordinary people of this part of the coast. Which was too bad; she'd have been much more at home with those sorts of people.

She was met by the owner, a man who spoke only a little English, but he made the point that Von Krebs was out with his wife and daughter on his yacht and was expected back soon. He mostly communicated with "the" plus "noun" constructions. When he gestured out the vast windows looking toward the gulf, he said, "The sea." When he took her into the kitchen, where he was puttering around with a knife and some vegetables, he said, "The cooking."

He called himself "Harald," but whether that was a first or last name Duvalier could only guess. Finnish names, especially surnames, were brutal, so she believed it to be his first name.

In the living room there was a stereo in a heavy wooden cabinet. An old-fashioned phonograph for playing vinyl records and a device that played large tapes interested her for a half hour or so while he rattled around in the kitchen. The open interior of the house let them share the space in such a way that he still was able to act the host while making dinner. Every now and then he held up a glass—the first for water, the second for wine—making pantomime inquiries if he should pour her a drink. She smiled and declined.

The bathroom and toilet were in a deep red with white accents that reminded her of fresh beef. She used the toilet and briefly luxuriated in the waterfall-style fixture for the sink, using liquid soap that filled the room with a summery aroma she couldn't quite identify.

The house was set well back from the shore, perhaps two hundred yards or so, and the ground sloped down sharply (she assumed, she didn't make the walk right away) to the actual shore. The stretch of plain, unbroken grass between the two lines of trees reminded her a little of a bowling alley or some kind of sports arena. Whoever had built the house must also have had the grounds leveled.

Someone kept the lawn intact—it looked like it was

mowed at least weekly. Again, that bespoke wealth. Nobody these days kept more than little patches of grass; grounds tended to be put to use growing vegetables or keeping turkeys or pigs.

Feeling oddly like a character in a Swedish film about upper-middle-class ennui, she paged through a book on art, wondering how Valentine was getting on with Stepanek's paintings in Helsinki. She wondered if he was enjoying the nightlife in the big city, if "nightlife" was the right word for a place where the sun didn't set until it was approaching midnight.

Every now and then Harald wandered through the room, inquiring about her needs in a labored fashion, as though he'd just been in another room consulting an English phrasebook. Finally, she saved him the trouble by curling up in a comfortable chair and pretending to sleep. The pretense turned into reality.

She woke when Von Krebs returned with the wife and daughter, typical Finnish blond specimens of skin and hair that made her feel like a thin, freckly mess.

They smelled like wind and sea. They'd been checking out the post-refit *Windkraft*.

They ate a nice dinner of just-caught lobster, with some kind of cream-based sauce. It was delicious, but a rather awkward party since the family refrained from all but necessities in Finnish out of well-mannered regard for their guest, not wishing to exclude her from the talk. Von Krebs was the only one capable of speaking fluently to both sides. They asked polite questions about

America and the suffering of the areas under Kurian control.

She wasn't sure how to answer *that*. Drawing any kind of an honest picture would ruin everyone's dinner.

The conversation moved on to the loveliness of the coast and the health of the Finns living on it, with the mixture of fresh seafood and a land diet. It appeared that Harald's family chose to live here for his health. She mentioned her frequently sour stomach.

"You need a night on the water," Von Krebs said. "Salt water cures everything; did you not know this?"

"Seems like it's tough on the skin, but I'll take your word for it," Duvalier said.

"Do you remember the little lighthouse we passed on our way into the harbor?"

"Yes."

"It is a lovely spot. We can take the *Windkraft* and visit it tomorrow, if you like. It has a small garrison of the Finnish defense forces. But they do not mind visitors. We can make an outing of it. The sunsets are spectacular from there. Shall we go?"

That sea-hardened face of his was hiding something. He might just want to spread her out on a lonely beach and use her just to see what sex with an American was like—she'd heard a joke once about a Frenchman making love to a corpse on a beach thinking she was an American—or perhaps he was seeking an in with Sime, though what good either could do the other was beyond her.

"We'll make you a hamper," Harald said. "Some wine, too."

"You are all so very kind. Honestly, this is the big surprise of the trip."

They set out the next day, early, with her as the only passenger. Thanks to a few delays with the *Windkraft*, they didn't actually leave for the lighthouse until it was after ten in the morning.

Only two of his white-pants crew remained on the *Windkraft*. They were sufficient to handle the boat under Von Krebs's direction. He let her take the wheel while they adjusted the sails.

He seemed strangely alive. Maybe it was the influence of being at the wheel of his own boat; but if so, why did he employ someone like Stepanek?

They arrived at the island, wooded like the rest of Finland's Bothnian coast, after an hour's sailing, thanks to fluky winds. Docks with skewed, weatherbeaten planks led up to the edge of the little island settlement like a fun-house path.

The lighthouse island had a steepish, rocky slope up from the beach and the tiny marina. But the navigational tower wasn't the only sign of habitation. She could just make out some big, barnlike roofs above the trees and weather-beaten old houses. The lighthouse itself was nonfunctional, according to Von Krebs, but still served as a landmark for Kokkola harbor. It was painted in red and white stripes. They had faded over the years, but the contrast was still striking enough that they were the first colors you could distinguish from the blue of the sky and the green of the island.

She'd learned to trust her intuition over the years. The fishy smell on the island unsettled her.

"Wow. I was in an agricultural fertilizer plant once. They used ground-up bits of fish. It's the same smell."

"I suspect someone had a catch go bad in the summer warmth. This is a mostly unvisited anchorage. The Kokkola harbormaster would go mad if you dumped your load of rotting fish to bob around in his harbor."

They skirted the depressingly abandoned buildings and made for the lighthouse. Von Krebs said there were animals living in the abandoned buildings and he feared rabies and hantavirus. So they took a more picturesque path through the trees, climbing the lighthouse hill.

Other than a little more wind than she liked, it was a perfect day, with not a cloud in the sky.

They found a few tables and benches of a design common the world over beneath the striped lighthouse. It had a marvelous view of the bay.

"Here's a nice spot for our picnic."

"You're unhappy here. Homesick?" Von Krebs asked.

"I'd like to head home, to tell the truth. There's nothing for me to do here, at least nothing more important than what I could be doing back home."

He looked up, nodded.

Nets, heavy and wet, fell all across her. She struggled, and the more she fought, the heavier and more entangled she became.

They rolled her up in the nets like a rug, with a few kicks for good measure, and she felt herself being hoisted across two men's shoulders.

Three strong men helped secure her. They had that same horribly fishy smell she'd noticed earlier. They put her in handcuffs before unwrapping her from the nets. She was put into a cheap tube-steel chair, with her arms around one of the metal supports for the wooden back brace.

"What the fuck is this?" she asked.

They were inside the lighthouse, at the bottom. The stairs up reminded her a little of a nautilus with its natural ascending spiral. It reeked of decay, overlain by a fresher, fishier smell, as though someone had just shoveled the day's catch out the door.

Von Krebs stood as though posing for a photograph with one leg up on a sea chest, leaning forward across his thigh with arms casually crossed at the wrists.

"Are you just an ordinary bastard, or the traitorous kind?" she asked.

He smiled, and the room got a little colder. "You know, I have a great interest in pain. Just how much pain an individual can take before they vomit, void their bladder and bowels, pass out, even die. Yes, you can die from pain, even though the injuries providing the source for the pain are themselves nonlethal. Let me tell you another way I am beyond the sadists of old. I can savor it in ways they could not imagine. I will feed off your aura as it slowly, agonizingly, leaves your body."

"I gave myself up for dead years ago. I feel like I've

lost this aura your kind finds so precious. I'll probably disappoint you."

He opened the chest, unrolled a small chamois sheet, and began to extract what looked like medical instruments, laying them on the chamois. There were scalpels, probes, clamps, scissors. The stainless steel took on an unnatural shine in the darkness.

He also had rope and surgical tubing. Perhaps he was a vivisectionist.

She noticed her sword-stick was in the corner. No one had investigated it closely, so they hadn't found the switch that unlocked grip from sheath.

"You three, out. Wait outside the door. You may hear her screaming."

The fishy-smelling men retreated.

"Meet Chien," Von Krebs said.

The small nude Asian woman, who had what looked like a barbed octopus with long folds of skin between its limbs riding across her back, descended the stairs from the shadow above. Its limbs engulfed her neck, breasts, and waist, offering a sort of obscene modesty.

One dreadful tentacle reached out and tapped Duvalier, once, twice, three times.

Chien shimmered for a moment, then Duvalier found herself looking into an exact duplicate of herself, down to the smallest freckle and chipped tooth.

"Chien speaks good Midwestern English. Her Spanish is also excellent, but I do not believe she will need that. It's one of the reasons we selected her when we found out you were coming."

"When did you learn that?"

"Ah, I never reveal sources. Even to those with but five minutes left to live. Chien, how do you do?"

"Very good," Chien said.

"See? She does not say 'very well.'"

"Well, maybe I do," Duvalier said tightly.

"A risk few will notice."

"Security won't let her get much done, unless she's got a backpack nuke along with that Kurian."

"Oh, you think the disguise is to work a nasty mass murder of delegates? You could not be more wrong. This disguise is just a temporary one, in order to get in close enough contact to—well, it is best if that stays a secret as well.

"We don't need the original anymore," Von Krebs said. "I intend to mix pleasure and pain with you from here until your death. It will only help me evolve into the higher form the Kurian Order has put me on the stairs of becoming."

He was insane.

She tested the cuffs. He'd put them on too tightly for her to wriggle out. Once an Oklahoma police reservist had taken her into custody and put her in cuffs. When she whined that they were too tight, he loosened them—after all, she was in the back of his car and there was a steel grate between them. . . .

He was dead within two minutes of loosening the cuffs. She'd straightened the wire necklace she'd been wearing—it was an old coat hanger—and stabbed him in the eye when he turned around to check on her after she faked a bloody nose.

They'd made a mistake. The handcuffs were sound

enough, but the chair they'd put her in was a relic. She kicked herself backward, and as she hit the ground the backrest splintered.

She bent her spine, wriggled through the cuffs, a difficult feat for anyone but a young gymnast or a Cat. She got her foot against the chain and pushed hard. A hand came out, bloody.

The pain would only help.

The Kurian doppelgänger backed away. It was odd to see herself look panicked.

Von Krebs stepped forward, a long-bladed Liston knife in his hand. She picked up the broken chair and hurled it at him. He ducked just long enough for her to get to the Other Duvalier.

She got nails and teeth into the bitch and the disguise vanished. Instead she was wrestling with a living umbrella of muscle.

Von Krebs came, blade held high, and she rolled, putting the Kurian between herself and the Mitteleuropean. He altered his slash, but still took a chunk out of the Kurian's back.

That sent a shock through the Asian girl and her face writhed in pain. *Well, dance with the devil and he'll step all over your toes.* Von Krebs himself recoiled in horror that he'd injured a Kurian.

No time to let up. She drove stiffened fingers into Chien's throat and the girl coughed blood like she'd been given the Heimlich.

The Kurian released its grip on the naked girl and humped across the floor. Duvalier stomped hard on its back and it folded up around her leg, clawing. She drove the heel of her foot in hard, dragging it across the floor as she went after Von Krebs, leaving a trail of bloody bluish slime that was the Kurian's juice. The grip began to relax, but it still had the hook-tipped tentacles in her flesh.

"Stay back," Von Krebs said, waving the long knife.

"Fuck you. Traitor."

He probably saw the hate in her eyes. He came at her while the Kurian was still fighting. She dropped and he overshot, tripping over her and dropping the knife.

They both reached for it and she got the handle before he did; his fingers closed on the blade in what turned into bloody agony. She relished the feel of pulling the blade out of his grip, knowing she was severing flesh and blood. She threw herself across him and opened his throat, cutting off his scream with a wet, blubbering cry.

Throwing on her coat, she hurried away from the lighthouse. No telling what kind of alarm had been sounded. Of course, they were expecting a version of her to be returning to the conference. . . .

Risking a trip through the dilapidated little village that they'd avoided on the way up, she saw a small house under guard. Boards were nailed across the windows and the door had a chain on it. Perhaps the small Finnish garrison was being held prisoner inside.

Why not just kill them and free up the manpower? she wondered.

Perhaps the Reapers needed feeding.

She hurried down to the dock that held the *Windkraft*.

"Ist das—"

"I'm Chien, you idiots," Duvalier said tightly.

"Where to?" the one who spoke English asked.

"To Kokkola harbor—where else?" she said.

They looked at each other uncertainly. "Where is Herr Von Krebs?"

"There is a problem with the Finns. He is smoothing things out. Hurry, I haven't all night!"

They raised anchor and used the pilot motor to move away from the island. Once into a better breeze, they worked the sheets and caught a favorable wind for the harbor. The sleek white vessel kicked up a wake.

Speaking of the wake . . .

The black thing she'd seen returned, this time multiplied a hundred times over, rising and falling in the bay waters.

"Christ on his cross," Duvalier said.

The crewmen expressed alarm in German, variants of "what the hell," it seemed to her.

"Faster!" she cried. "Surprise is essential!"

One of them stood still, looking from her to the pursuers as though trying to figure out the connection.

The lights of the harbor side were distinct now. She could make out details on the dock and wharf.

The black backs of the Big Mouths were gaining. Did this thing have a siren? Fireworks? Anything?

"Have you a flare gun?" She mimicked the firing and sputtering of a flare.

One of the men nodded and pointed to a small box strapped just below the wheel. She took it from its bracket and opened it. It was similar to the ones she'd seen in Southern Command's arsenal, perhaps a little larger. She aimed it over the pursuers and fired.

Dazzling white light shone in the harbor. She saw, briefly, the details of the Big Mouths, eyes and teeth breaking the water briefly as they pursued.

The sailors moved, trying to shorten sail.

"Don't," she said, pointing the empty flare pistol.

Now they could hear shouts over the water.

The crew had had enough. They moved toward her. She drew her sword and struck first, cutting down and across, opening up the first from shoulder to groin. The second saw what had happened to his mate and he turned to run, perhaps for a weapon, perhaps to hide belowdecks. She leaped after him, slashing at his legs, and opened the tendons behind his knee. Wanting no delay, she slashed again across the buttocks.

She left him flopping there in a growing pool of his blood.

They were almost at the wharf when she made it back to the wheel.

At the last second she threw the *Windkraft* hard over. The sails flapped and sagged, fighting to do their duty. The stern came up hard against the wharf, just missing a fender and crushing and splintering woodwork.

She left the wounded crewman to the mercies of the Big Mouths and cat-jumped to the dock. Soldiers, police, and a few Finnish men in civilian clothes were gaping out at the bay. Dozens, if not hundreds of the

Big Mouths were rising out of the water and climbing onto the wharf and docks.

"*Varo! Varo! Varo!*" she shouted, as loudly as her small frame could manage, jumping and pointing out into the bay.

CHAPTER NINE

That same day, just a few kilometers away, Ahn-Kha had his first secret voting session.

As usual, he sat near Sime. Sime was almost Golden One–like in his ability to control his temper in social situations, hide his thoughts so that even his eyes revealed nothing, and moderate his words. If he ever gave up his role as the United Free Republic's political fixer, he would be welcome among the Golden Ones in Western Kentucky.

The full sessions of the conference had a president presiding over them, though she (in this case) had no powers other than to call votes and announce results. By tradition, the president was the delegate from the host freehold, in this case Finland's representative of the Baltic League. The president was also the last to cast her vote. With thirty-seven voting delegates, the ability to break ties was her privilege, at least in theory. The votes tended to be massive majorities in favor or against—for example, the first vote of any session was always an all-delegate ceremonial vote to continue the war against the Kurian Order. It passed 37–0.

Treachery Thursday, as it would later be known, began quietly enough. Friday was an official free day for the conference, giving everyone an extra day in the middle of the conference's three-week official schedule to tour or go on excursions that would take more time. Ten voting delegates were not in attendance that Thursday, having started their breaks early, catching special trains for Helsinki or the ferry to Sundsvall across the gulf, now considered "Little Stockholm" and the capital of Free Sweden.

The president, after a short delay, stepped to the podium and asked for a quorum vote, to make the following votes legal, and a vote to make the proceedings secret. There were a couple of holdouts on both because so many delegates were absent (as the "no" votes explained on the record before voting). Both passed easily.

With the secrecy vote in place, the outside monitors were turned off and security guards moved to the other side of the doors to secure them, two men to a door.

The president read a few dry lines about their duties to keep the debate and, if voted, the outcome of the secret session confidential beyond the official summary that would be issued to the governments they represented. Ahn-Kha approved of the expedient; it allowed the delegates to vote their consciences based on the debate and their own instincts without having their individual votes reported back to the home governments. Though in general he found secrecy ineffective. Enemies usually had the tools and talent to discover what was trying to be kept secret; all the classification did was keep the home population from finding out about the matter.

Which led to another problem with the conference, when you came right down to the wheat and chaff of these votes. The Freehold Conference could vote resolutions left, right, and center, but the home government had no obligation beyond technicalities to obey.

Ahn-Kha returned to the president at the podium. She was weary-faced this morning.

"Now, I'd like to introduce a special delegation from the Lifeweavers," the translator said in his earpiece. "They wish to address the conference about an important development."

The Lifeweavers entered in single file from a side door just beyond a grand piano that stood opposite the president's lectern.

Lifeweavers could look like anything they wanted. They could have paraded into the plenary session in the form of giant praying mantises if they chose. In this instance, they looked like an international trade delegation. They all wore blue pants and gray jackets with open-collar shirts of various colors. Their countenances serene, they glided across the dais.

The conference murmured. "So many," said Sime. "Something must be coming."

Some of the delegates bowed; a handful even fell to their knees. In any case, all eyes watched the sixteen Lifeweavers move to the center stage.

The audience hushed, not sure what to expect.

"There has been a startling development in our joint war against the Kurian way of life and death," the Lifeweaver in the middle of the group said. Ahn-Kha discovered that he was speaking Golden One, and glanced around at his fellow delegates, expecting expressions of confusion. But each one was giving the Lifeweaver his undivided attention. Indeed, some had even removed their translating earpieces. Headphone or no, the Lifeweaver had them hanging on every word and gesture.

"There is no way to make this news any kinder with soft words or halting preambles. We have come to an agreement with the Kurians. There will be peace."

A smattering of applause broke out.

"The peace I speak of is settled between our kind and the Kurians. Whether you will enjoy the same peace is up to you. This is the one incontrovertible reality: The Interstellar Tree is being divided. Your world, I am afraid, is to be in the Kurian sphere. We must leave it. In turn, the Kurians will abandon all the old portals to any world save the one back to Kur."

Ahn-Kha had been told more than once that the "portals" were just legends. He knew better, of course; his whole tribe had marched through one of the portals well before he'd been born.

Ahn-Kha wondered if, underneath the psychic projection he was watching, the creatures were capable of blushing with shame. They certainly deserved to.

"We did not agree to the withdrawal without conditions attached to the territories that freed themselves from the Kurians. These are the broad outlines of the arrangement. All territories in rebellion that have attended two of these sessions or coordinated with the Baltic League over the course of the last ten years will be left free. Both sides will disarm to a level of police protection, with provision for 'national guard' type units to handle emergencies and limited special forces for operations against international pirates and other gangs operating beyond the reach of national police."

"That lets Kentucky out," Sime said, slamming his notebook shut. "It's like they wrote those restrictions to exclude it."

"I know which way I will vote, then," Ahn-Kha replied, surprised at the hard tone to Sime's voice. Ahn-Kha knew he was not as keyed in to human emotion as his companions, but the only emotional displays from Sime he could remember before this were outbursts of laughter in more relaxed settings.

On the podium, the central Lifeweaver continued. "Individual nonaggression pacts will be worked out between neighboring territories. Future hostile acts will end the agreement as far as that rebel territory is concerned; others will remain untouched so long as they do not materially, financially, or politically support the combatants. Anti-Kurian newspapers and radio programming will be stopped, and in turn the individual Kurian territories will not widen the fighting by taking aggressive action. The main military bodies will carry small arms and light artillery sufficient for police actions and nothing else."

"Seems to be a lot of wiggle room in that," Sime said. "If this is the pitch they're using to sell it, imagine what the unvarnished truth is like."

"You are probably wondering how it will be determined that the Kurian operating areas have also demilitarized. The Baltic League will organize an international group of inspectors to evaluate the disarmament on both sides."

That incited a buzz of conversation. Ahn-Kha distinctly heard heavily accented ejaculations of *"Impossible!"*

The Lifeweaver waited for the side talk to diminish. When he again had their attention he continued. "In time, it is hoped that trade will be established between the rebellious territories and the major regional-level Kurian Territories."

"Jesus, what'll they want as currency?" the delegate sitting behind, from Vancouver, Canada, said.

"I can't believe anyone's going to go for it," his seatmate muttered back.

"Look at friend Sime," Vancouver continued. "This must be a dream come true for the Free Republics. They've dropped out of the war."

How would the delegation vote? Ahn-Kha had observed that the voting delegates were divided into three factions, two major and one minor. None had enough votes just in and of themselves to pass anything, so passing any resolution that was not what Sime called a "no-brainer" required some cooperation between the factions. The minor faction consisted of delegates who were cranks. They tended to be from freeholds away from the fighting and did not much need the cooperation of other delegations.

The second-largest faction Ahn-Kha thought of as the "Guns" group. They were led by the scarred giant from Norway who'd survived Trondheim, the "Stalingrad of the Twenty-first Century." They generally were interested in whatever would bring the fight fastest and hardest to the Kurian Order.

The largest delegation was the "Butter" group. They'd dominated the conference, and were most interested in whatever would build up their freeholds to something approaching the capabilities of most twentieth-century nations, and mostly waging a defensive war against the Kurians. Ahn-Kha suspected that most of the Butter group would accept the offer, but it couldn't pass without a majority of the Guns group adding their votes.

The Guns group would be heavily influenced by the Norwegian. He was at this moment perhaps the most influential human in modern history. Ahn-Kha wondered if he knew how important he'd become, and craned around to try to get a look at him.

There he was, huddling with some other Scandinavians and the representatives from the Pacific Northwest and Vladivostok, all in the Guns camp. Sime had mostly voted Butter over the course of the conference. Ahn-Kha wondered if it was on instruction from the UFR government.

"We will give you forty-eight hours to consider this. Consult your home governments if you have the ability. The arrangement you are about to be offered is the best one we could get. In a very short time our bargaining power on Earth vanishes, for lifespans beyond guessing without a collapse of the Kurian Order."

The alarmed buzzing started up again. To him, it sounded like a beehive being poked by a stick.

The Finnish president returned to her podium. She was red-eyed from crying.

"We will have a thirty-minute break," she said through their earpieces.

"I am sorry, but we are leaving," another in the Lifeweaver party announced.

As he moved down the aisle, a little throng from the Butter group joined Sime. "Were you expecting anything this big?" a man with a slight Australian accent asked.

Ahn-Kha rounded on them, clearly angry.

"Sime, you knew about this?"

Sime's cool composure was breaking down. He had sweat on his upper lip.

"Of course not."

"But you knew something was in the wind," Ahn-Kha countered. "Is that why you gave leave to David and so on?"

"I will do you better," Sime said. "I'll tell you everything I know about the matter. There were whispers around the president's staff that some kind of 'accommodation' may be needed. It's one of the reasons Southern Command has played it so quietly since Javelin dropped in Kentucky rather than the Coal Country."

The delegates filed out, to find a small buffet laid out on the concourse outside the big meeting room with the piano. There was a good deal of talk about when the Lifeweavers would pull up stakes and whether the vote would go for or against making the freeholds permanent. Or at least permanent until the last Lifeweaver ship took off with a full cargo of leg-worm leather.

Ahn-Kha made a show of laying out his food for eating, but he actually hardly ate a bite of what he put on the plate.

A wild, blood-splattered redheaded creature threw open the glass doors to the concourse. "The Kurians are here!" Duvalier gasped.

She had blood caked all over one wrist and her clothes were stained. She stood there panting, more winded than Ahn-Kha had ever seen her. "We're about to be attacked. Call the army, air force, navy, whoever you can get!"

CHAPTER TEN

*T*he Defenestration of Kokkola: It proved to be the shot heard round the world. It also led to a good deal of historical inaccuracy. There were a few countries that mixed up players, participants, and notes. Most of the freeholds played up their own role in the affair—it was always the cowards on the other side of the world who were ready to hand over the keys to the planet to the Kurians.

As best as can be determined, the Kurian plan was to co-opt a few key players at the conference to ensure that the vote tilted their way, toward what's now called the "Terrible Truce." Of course there were a few ready to end the fighting and work something out that left their freehold intact. Then there was the legendary Rolf of Trondheim. The plan for him, it appeared, was to use a Kurian posing as Alessa Duvalier to either render him indisposed for the vote, or perhaps have the creature dispose of him in some manner and then switch over to his appearance and have the most renowned Resistance fighter in the Baltic League vote for peace and perhaps sway enough from the Guns group to allow it to pass.

None of the more serious reporting that followed gave any

credit to Alessa Duvalier, which was just the way she liked it. Rolf of Trondheim and, of course, the photogenic Ahn-Kha were given most of the credit for uncovering the plot and starting the Grand Offensive against the Kurians (within a year, it was possible to buy a stuffed Ahn-Kha in Helsinki to give to your children).

For once, a conference of humans settled on the right course of action. The Kokkola Resolve was short and to the point: immediate, all-out warfare from every freehold against the Kurians whenever and wherever they could be found was voted on and passed with just a few abstentions.

She needed food. How long since she'd eaten? Twenty-four hours, at least, since she'd had a meal. An incredible aroma permeated the buffet room and her mouth went soft and wet from the saliva that filled it so quickly that she had to swallow in surprise.

As she heaped a plate with food, she watched the security station work their phones, with increasingly worried faces and urgent switching of communication modes. Police and men in uniform began to appear and stand at the doors.

Duvalier fell upon the roast like a famished hound. As she ate, Ahn-Kha gave her the news.

It hit her hard.

When she was a little girl, she heard stories about angels who were secretly helping mankind. They'd come down to Earth to give mankind knowledge, weapons, and most important, the freedom from fear they needed to face the Reapers in battle.

She always wanted to meet the angels. Through a strange combination of circumstances involving a Quisling who'd been molesting her, she did. She'd murdered the evil rat, which seemed a strange gateway to an encounter with an angel, but that's how it happened.

Hard to imagine angels playing politics.

To say the abandonment was a blow was an understatement. It was like she was standing on an entirely different planet. Everything she had thought to be true had suddenly gone wrong. The people, entities, angels—whatever you wanted to call them—who had inspired her, trained her, that she'd fought for, were quitting the fight just when it seemed as though they were getting ahead in the struggle.

What utter and complete bastards.

At least the rumors that the Lifeweavers were actually Kurians running both sides of the war were laid to rest. If that were the case, they'd keep playing their roles as long as each side needed an "other" to keep the confusion and killing going.

All the risks she'd run . . . Maybe it would have been better if she'd died in some ditch in Nebraska, rather than live to see this. All this time she'd fought with hope—lately it had been turning into certainty, after seeing how easy the shambles of the Kurian Order states collapsed if you just kicked them hard enough—and now that certainty was gone and hope was picking up its coat and hat.

Her gut was doing flip-flops. She briefly wondered if she'd passed out from exhaustion and was dreaming all this. The line of Lifeweavers up on the stage, all roughly the same age and looking like their bodies had been designed rather than lived in, added a surreal quality. But no, her gut sometimes woke her up, but a sour belly had never made an appearance in a dream that she could remember. This was all too real.

She recognized one of the Lifeweavers in the party. His appearance now was exactly as it was then, when she and Valentine received the mission to go into the Midwest and assess the threat of the Twisted Cross. His robes were a little more formal, chosen for the occasion, no doubt.

Of course, everything with the Lifeweavers was for appearance's sake. She'd come to terms with their being master illusionists long ago. There was no reason they couldn't all be standing on the stage in the guise of old cereal box characters, if they so chose. They went with what worked, and tall, elegant, attractive, and stately individuals in prophet-hair and robes seemed to work with humans.

"My lord," she called. "Father Cat!"

One of the security detail interposed, but the Lifeweaver waved him away. And there she was, face-to-face with a living demigod.

"How could you abandon us?" she asked.

"I'm sorry?"

"We met years ago, in Arkansas, at the lodge for the Cats. I had a new aspirant with me, black hair—"

"Perhaps it was another using this guise," the Lifeweaver said. "We find it easier to work from templates.

Wait, you are Alessa Duvalier? Yes, we know you, the red wrath of the Midwest. Have you met Rolf of Trondheim? He is another great one of your vintage.

"Do you think we like this? We don't. The negotiations were handled by others, the decisions made by others. As it was explained to us, we get two planets, forever and absolutely, in exchange for Earth."

"I gave my life to you," Duvalier said.

The Lifeweaver nodded gravely. "No, you gave it to your kind. It's the oldest and best definition of heroism."

"How can you quit on us? We're winning this thing for you! Do you understand? Winning!"

"Precisely. You and those like you made this settlement possible. Had this planet been in the relative state it was thirty years ago, or even fifteen, we would never have had such an opportunity. You certainly deserve our thanks, and more."

"Thanks? No thanks," she said. "Why are we being given up? I know your kind have died here, too. Isn't there another—"

"Why do they want Earth? First, you humans are rich in aura, and you breed quickly under different levels of stress and deprivation. Second, they made a case that Earth, being one of the few direct portals to Kur, and yet also a portal to many other worlds, was an ideal route for invasion. Earth is their new castle gate. Holding Earth saves them a fight on other worlds."

She felt like she was flailing. What would Val say? Some cool, long-ranged argument, she supposed. She pretended to be him for a moment: "And once life here is consumed to the bedrock, what then? Don't you think they'll come across those gates, 'forever and absolutely' or no? When they come, won't they be stronger than ever?"

"We will be stronger, too," the Lifeweaver said. "If it is a matter of being left, there will be some population transfers allowed. You have little to hope for on the new Earth. Your emigration could be arranged to one of the worlds reserved for us. There is a plan to settle some humans on Eheru to ensure the survival of your species. Of course, the climate will not be that of your native Midwest."

"Leave my home, friends, the whole shooting match?"

"I do not say it will be easy, only that we can offer you a better future than you have if you remain on Earth."

"Leave—my planet?"

"We respire and take in water much as you. You would find one of our worlds peaceful. 'Idyllic' is not too strong a word. It would be easy to forget you are an exile among your fellows. No problem about leaving, as long as it is done quietly. The Kurians are only too glad to be rid of as many of our children among men as possible."

"You don't think much of humanity."

"I don't? You are from the United States, once a refuge for those who abandoned their cousins and fellow citizens in some land that had gone to devils incarnate. Look just a hundred years ago in your own history, at the Laotians after Vietnam, the Persians after the Shah, the Poles who fled their beloved land. They built better lives in peace. You might do the same."

She began to respond, but he held up a hand. "I am being told we are in no small amount of danger. If you'll excuse me, we must remove ourselves."

She ran to the windows of the second-floor concourse and looked out at the endless sunset of a Kokkola summer.

A sea of gray backs filled the street in front of the conference center. The bigger ones shoved the smaller out of the way to climb onto prominences like benches and the decorative border around the plaza fountain. They hooted and honked, making it sound like a traffic jam caused by a huge flock of Canada geese.

By instinct she joined Ahn-Kha, Pistols, and Sime.

"Are they dangerous on land?" Pistols asked.

"Very," Duvalier said. She'd seen a little of what Big Mouths could do when she was in the Delta country south of New Orleans. "They can shoot across short distances in a blur. They don't look like they can move any more quickly on land than a sea lion, right up to the point when they launch themselves like a missile."

"There must be thousands of them," Sime said in wonder.

Rolf, the Norwegian Bear, appeared with an old revolver in his hand. "The best I could get, at this point," he said.

"The garrison won't be able to do shit to them," Pistols said, handing Rolf the Judge. He looked big enough to handle it.

They seemed to be just milling about, waiting,

nudging one another, and squabbling over comfortable spots on the roads and verges and parkland about the conference center, rather than moving in for an assault.

"I hate those fucking things," Rolf said in slow, unsteady English. "Trondheim was full of them in the summers. They bred them, fed them bodies for the giving of the taste of human flesh a fondness. In the end, they turned them loose in Trondheim, too."

"How did you beat them?" Duvalier asked.

"Kill enough and they start eating each other. They are cannibals of the bad wounded and the fresh dead. Easier meal than chasing down men."

"They will not harm anyone," one of the security people was shouting. Others took turns yelling in different languages. "They are here as bodyguards for an emissary from Kur, a member of the Great Circle itself."

Sime was standing in a knot of shorter delegates from the Butter faction, trying to calm them down.

"What is the Great Circle?" Ahn-Kha asked.

"Like I'd know," Duvalier said.

"A Kurian is about to speak to the conference."

"So much for our trip to warn security," Ahn-Kha said. "I wish my David were here. Or perhaps not. He might go mad."

"I can go plenty mad for both of us," Duvalier said. "If one more person tries to tell me what great news this all is, I might turn into a one-woman mental asylum for manic-obsessive cockpunchers."

Most of the delegates returned to the main auditorium. The curiosity of what a Kurian might say to them impelled them, and it was as good a place to make a last stand as any. The security staff waited at the now bolted and barricaded doors. No one was getting out, and hopefully not in, until the matter was resolved.

Duvalier watched from one of the upper-level concourse doors with Ahn-Kha and Rolf. Sime returned to his usual spot, and Pistols sat next to him in the half-empty auditorium.

The Kurian drifted out onto the stage. Unlike the others, he did not make an effort to appear to walk naturally; his legs hung down as though he were a body hanging from a dry-cleaner's rack. While his form was human, his face was masked. Kurians, when they bothered to appear human, often hid behind some sort of helmet or mask. Perhaps trying to imitate human emotions was too taxing when what they really wanted to do was assess their surroundings.

He had four Reapers with him. Unlike the Four Horsemen of the Apocalypse, they appeared identical.

Still, it must be some kind of special Kurian, to go into a building full of potentially violent enemies. They were such a cowardly bunch that the only way even their trusted allies were usually able to speak to them was through a Reaper.

"I would like to thank the deputation for arranging our presence. I assure you, I mean no one here harm.

"We are not your enemies. The intelligent and resourceful have never had anything to fear from us. We appreciate the virtues of mankind just as much as your erstwhile allies do. I will not attempt to tell our side of the story, or take advantage of the fact that your so-called Lifeweavers are using you as pawns in their own game against us and disposing of you at need and to their advantage.

"The fact is, Earth is an important crossroads. I imagine many of you played a game called Risk at one time or another. As you recall, it is a game of dominating continents. There are only a few routes to move between continents, and if you remember, the old United Kingdom territories provided numerous ways to strike into continental Europe, as well as being a path to North America. Earth is like that piece of territory—it is a route to our home world and many others. We cannot be secure on Kur with your planet in the hands of our enemies. Therefore we have given up less important planets in exchange for this one.

"Once you come to terms with that unalterable fact, you can decide rationally how best to serve the people you are responsible for. While the Lifeweavers are still here you have some negotiating power. As they have told you, the best arrangement you can hope for can be achieved now, with their aid. After they depart, you lose your leverage, and offers will be less generous than this one. The longer this destructive insanity goes on, the worse your deal will be. Questions?"

"When do you need an answer?" a delegate asked, fortunately for Duvalier in English.

"We would like a vote tonight," the president said.

"They're necessary for our security."

"Time to choke a squid," Duvalier said. "I need to go to the bathroom. Coming, Ahn-Kha?"

The mighty Grog flexed and broke off a chair leg. He handed it to Rolf.

Rolf tested the break. The hollow tube made the improvised stabbing spear look like a huge cardiac needle. "Not sharp enough."

Duvalier took a little stiletto and shoved it into her tube-steel leg. "I think this'll work."

Ahn-Kha tried again with another chair. This time, he twisted the tube as he broke it. The break formed a sharp corkscrew.

"Much better," Rolf said.

"Can we kill four? With these?" Duvalier asked.

"We just need to distract that Kurian," Rolf said. "All we need are a few seconds of confusion."

"Confusion is my middle name," Duvalier said. "Give me a couple minutes, then come in like you're security stopping a disturbance."

She crept into the auditorium, discreetly, as though embarrassedly returning from a bathroom break, and found a seat next to Pistols and Sime.

"Don't suppose either of you can sing backup?" she asked.

Standing up, she decided on an old number from her chanteuse days at the Blue Dome. It was way vintage pre-2022, but it always got a good response:

One way, or another, I'm gonna find ya, I'm gonna getcha getcha getcha getcha . . .

The "Q&A with a Kurian" sputtered out like a candle hit by a fresh breeze. The president looked at her in shock as she did a little hip grind and pointed at the Kurian. She tried to work up the courage to take off her shirt, like a surprise stripper gone terribly wrong.

"I'll take care of her," Ahn-Kha said, moving leisurely across a nearly empty aisle toward her. He'd acquired a security vest somewhere. Rolf moved toward her going down the stairs.

She took a few steps toward the Kurian, still singing the golden oldie. Sure enough, the Reapers moved up to form a protective wall between her and their Kurian.

"What the hell do you think you're doing, girl?" Sime shouted.

There was pandemonium all across the audience, with some standing to object, others tentatively moving to help, and still more diving for cover between the rows of seats.

Ahn-Kha, with one gentle vault of a long arm, made it to the edge of the stage, shielded somewhat by the piano.

In midline, with hands on shimmying hips, she drew and threw the stiletto in one smooth motion. She struck the midstage Reaper full in the eye.

Ahn-Kha hefted the piano and hurled it at two of the Reapers. The polished black wood shattered into a thousand sad little notes, the last the piano would ever play. The local pianist would have to import another instrument for the next Kokkola music festival.

Rolf leaped, used a chair to vault, and was on the stage in an instant. A Reaper moved to intercept, and he stabbed it hard enough with the improvised spear that the point came out black on the mid-back. He pried the dead thing off as Duvalier made it to the stage, ready to bury her teeth in the Kurian if she had to.

Ahn-Kha and Rolf were fighting the Reapers knocked down by the piano.

The Kurian was a diffuse blur, fleeing toward the stage door opposite the wreckage of the piano. But she was faster, and snatched it up by what turned out to be the crotch between two of its longer legs.

"Gotcha," she said.

"You will all die," the Kurian squealed. "Those creatures out there will not leave so much as an earlobe uneaten. I've called for them. You will die if you don't release me."

"I will die," she said. "I'm mortal. You're not, but I'm prepared to put the issue to a vote. All in favor of turning you into octopus salad? Sorry, fucker, the vote's unanimous."

The image blurred and she was left holding a writhing octopus shape. Tentacles lashed at her face, leaving painful welts that brought tears to her eyes.

She ran for the window. The Kurian managed to get a limb around her neck and it tightened. In turn she clenched her neck, bending her jaw forward to put space around her voice box.

A black curtain rose across her vision and the lights began to twinkle behind the curtain.

The snake around her neck gave one final yank and then released, taking some hair on the back of her neck and leaving a raw burn.

Rolf, bellowing in Norwegian, held the Kurian aloft

above her, reminding her for a fleeting moment of a picture she'd seen in an old book of an ancient warrior with the head of Medusa. For a moment she thought he was going to make a Kurian kebab, but instead he burst out of the scrum and made for the lobby. She followed, knocking over a Lifeweaver who'd appeared out of nowhere blabbing something about diplomatic immunity.

Rolf went to the lobby windows and stabbed his chair-leg spear into a vast pane, breaking the glass out of the second-floor overlook on the courtyard. The Big Mouths, so tightly packed that their backs resembled a writhing, rock-covered beach, turned their toothy faces up at the noise. He tried to throw the Kurian, but it clung to his arm, chest, and face with a whipping mass of tentacles. Blood ran from the gory pulp of one of Rolf's eyes. He yelled something in Norwegian and threw himself through the glass.

The Kurian let out a gassy hoot as they fell together.

Rolf flailed back and forth with the chair leg, breaking jaws and turning great-fish eyes to pulp with his blows. He fended the Big Mouths off with the Kurian wrapped about his arm. It flailed in all directions with its tentacles, now fewer in number, some having been bitten off by the snapping jaws all around.

A fitting end for the Last Bear of Trondheim.

Still, the Big Mouths crashed through the feeble barriers and the glass of the lower level.

The Finns worked in layers. Teams of men with shotguns gave short-range cover to soldiers with big support machine guns in slings. The crackle of gun-fire was so intense it sounded like surf.

The machine gunners took Big Mouths down in rows. Then the shotgun men blew basketball-sized holes in the wounded with their open-choke riot mod-els until they gave only an occasional twitch.

Rifle fire from the handlers was returned by snipers on the roof of the conference center. The Finns were as methodical and efficient with their weapons as they were with street cleaners, and once a couple were shot down the rest fled.

The Big Mouths, caught in a feeding frenzy, either died gorging themselves or followed their handlers back to the waterfront. Duvalier had no way of know-ing it, but fast-moving "cavalry" on bicycles had al-ready stormed the wharf—they were retreating to a slaughter-yard.

"Glad that's over with," she rasped. The words came out like they had been dragged across sandpaper. She extracted a hook from her neck, a claw the Kurian had left there when he was ripped from her grasp by Rolf. It was blackish and translucent at the edges. She'd never been one to take souvenirs of the dead—explaining why you had a chain of Reaper teeth could cause difficulties for a Cat—but she decided she'd keep this one, at least through the voyage home.

Looking in the bathroom mirror back at what was left of the hotel, she saw that she had so many marks on her neck from the Kurian's suckers that it looked as though she'd been trying to win a hickey scavenger hunt.

What chance did humanity have, without the Lifeweavers? No Lifeweavers meant no Hunters, and no Hunters meant the Reapers had nothing to fear.

She'd known Christians who'd had a crisis of faith. Sometimes it was the little things that sent them into despair, a single death from disease rather than a trench full of corpses. The Lifeweavers, to her, always explained the inexplicable. They took the long view, saw temporary losses as just that. They never panicked at bad news or rejoiced in a victory.

If they had given up on Earth, what hope had anyone?

Maybe the delegates should have taken the deal.

Her stomach was killing her. She should never have had that roast. She should have kept her diet light, a little rice and soup would have done nicely.

A hot bath would relax her.

Her hair needed a little trim. The part where the Kurian had ripped out even her quite short hair had made everything uneven. Using her sharp skinning knife, she did her best to even things up a little. She accidentally cut her thumb in the process. It was a slice running perhaps a quarter inch deep at its deepest, and it bled profusely.

Sucking at the cut, she decided the pain wasn't so bad.

God, she was closer to forty than thirty. How had she lived so long? Sooner or later the odds would catch up with her; they always did.

She should have investigated Von Krebs more care-fully, gone to that house on the gulf better prepared. Were it not for fortune, the whole population of Kokkola might be working its way through those damn Big Mouth digestive tracts right now.

It was the easiest thing in the world to make a long cut in her arm, running parallel to the bones. She was used to creating wounds without the hesitation stabs of a novice. She admired the work, the brilliant red line as straight as a sure-handed surgeon would make.

As she settled into the bath, the water turned pink and then red. She felt more relaxed and peaceful than she had in years; even the pain in her stomach subsided.

She began to have the most dazzling, warm dreams, though she couldn't describe them, beyond the sense that there was music all around. Exalted, perhaps for the first time in her life, her whole body glowed in sat-isfaction that was better than any sex.

Something intruded on the wonderful dreams. Pain. The singing faded, and she heard a slapping sound. It took her forever to connect the noise with the pain she felt in her cheeks.

She came back to half consciousness. A bronze-skinned man with a scarred face looked down at her. He had the devil's eyes and they blazed with unholy fire. She tried to shut it out, but the devil kept calling her name.

No! The devil wouldn't get her. She would run, back toward the singing.

CHAPTER ELEVEN

*T*he Return: *While the repercussions of mankind's defiantly violent answer to the Kurian offer rippled across the globe, in Finland itself, and across the Baltic League, the average freeholder nodded in quiet satisfaction at the news that the Kurian diplomat had been torn to shreds by his own bodyguard. "Serves 'em right" in various Nordic idioms probably sums up the most popular reaction.*

Sensationalists got hold of the story first, and turned it into a tale of Kurian treachery unmasked by the unconquerable human spirit.

Only later were more serious researchers able to piece together the Kurian plot to force a vote in their favor, a vote that would be broadcast worldwide by the Baltic radio network. There is the philosophical idea that once a matter is introduced into words, it becomes something that can be imagined and eventually accepted. If the news went around the world that the conference had voted to accept the Kurian "peace" offer, the word "peace" would have been on everyone's lips. As it was, the Kurians proved too clever for their own good. Had they just made their offer and left it to the

delegates to decide, with the Lifeweavers advocating that
they accept this last, best chance, who is to say whether the
Butter faction would not have gathered enough Guns to
carry the vote?

She woke to the familiar rocking of the sea and the
steady growl of an engine. She sensed that they were
on a larger ship than any they'd used to this point. She
was in some kind of dormitory with two bunks and
just enough space for a little table that held a washba-
sin and tap.

She sensed a presence nearby. Valentine sat in a canvas chair, a book on his lap and another open on the
arm of the chair. He looked tired.

"Where am I?" she asked.

"Ferry to Sweden. Or I should say, up the Swedish
coast. We'll take a train across, then back to Halifax
and home. Your only worry at this point is eating."

"Christ, I can't even die right," she muttered.

Valentine tut-tutted. The man had ears like a bat.
Arrogant ass.

"When did you get back?" she asked.

"The night you had your bath. You've been uncon-
scious or sedated. One of the Canadians with us is sort
of a nurse-midwife-doctor, so you've had medical attention since we took you out of the Kokkola hospital.
They gave you blood and plasma there, but they
wouldn't release you without running a few tests.
They don't know how stingy you've been with your
nine lives."

"That's debatable."

"You're going to live, Ali. The war's over for you for a while."

"Is that an order, Major?"

"I think we had this discussion before we left. You outrank me. I can't give you orders."

She felt too tired to talk, so she didn't respond.

"You went a little mad and did a dumb thing," Valentine said. "I don't know exactly what it was, but I hope—"

"Nothing to do with you and your glorious cock, Val."

"I'm sorry I missed the mess at the conference."

"Hope you at least had fun in Helsinki," she managed.

"I learned a lot about art. Or rather, the value of art, or how our skipper friend decides what art she wants to buy. It's not that different from a used-car lot, as it turns out. She acquires what she thinks will be worth something if the world ever sorts itself out again. Quite a vision."

"She was a vision," Duvalier murmured.

"It wasn't an affair, Smoke. I just wanted a little glimpse of that world. It was that or fishing, and I've fished plenty of northern lakes in my time. Still, glad that you were there to take care of things. Why were you cutting yourself, when every Finn sergeant should have been buying you a Koskenkorva?"

She'd been running risks all her life. If, deep down, she wanted to die, wouldn't she have been less cautious, at least a few times? It is so easy to screw up in the Kurian Zone. Of course, being driven in a collection van to the Last Dance wasn't her idea of an easy death.

Funny, when you looked at his face, you mostly came away with the memory of the scar running vertically near his eyes. But he had a few other cuts and divots marring his beautiful skin. She knew plenty of women who would have spent fortunes for that skin. They were like two collections of scars talking to each other, the scars masking what lay beneath.

She wasn't sure she could even form an honest answer into words, so she put him off. "I'm not ready to talk about it yet. Give me some time."

Valentine's upper lip twitched as he patted her hand. "Sorry. I thought this trip would give both of us a rest. Let's talk more when you're up to it."

"Don't go," she said. How many times had she wanted to say those words to him? But to do so would make her sound vulnerable. Needy. "Nice to have you here. Don't mean to be a burden. Do you have somewhere you need to be?"

He sat. "Need? My need's in this room. I don't think you know how much I need you. How much the Cause needs you. Every time you've been at my side, we've had success. All my screwups seem to happen when you're not around to kick me in the butt and set me straight. Damn it, woman, you're my oldest and best friend."

"What about Ahn-Kha?"

"He's like a brother to me. We're bound up in this together, in some way I can't explain. Maybe he can, with his philosophies. He's family. You're the person I want to have around. You're the person whose absence leaves me, well, lonely. I can't ever pay back what you've given for me.

"You pulled me out of darkness once. I'd like to return the favor. If I have to, I'll attach tow chains to Ahn-Kha and have him haul you up back into the sun."

She had no doubt he cared for her. They were family; they'd been through too much together. She spent the rest of the day quietly in her cabin eating, mostly easy-to-digest soups. Potatoes and ham and summer vegetables. It wasn't great, but it was better than most travel food she'd eaten.

That night, she asked Valentine to bring her something to read.

She ambushed him right away so his defenses would be down.

"I want a real night with you. In my bed, in the biblical sense. It won't change anything between us," she said, and she hoped it would be true. She'd been able to turn off her emotions for sex in the past, out of necessity.

"Aren't we a little beyond that sort of thing?"

"I just want to feel good for one night. You know I don't get many guys. I don't like most of 'em, and the ones I do like get scared. You're not scared."

"I used to be, a little."

She'd thought so. This conversation was more interesting than anything that had happened since everything went to crap in Kokkola. "Well, it's been years since I scared you."

"True."

"Be mine, just for a few nights on this trip. I need to clear away the cobwebs."

"I don't think it's been that long for you. What about—"

"The cobwebs in my head, buster."

They'd come close a couple of times. When he first knew her, he made a few halfhearted, half-joking attempts to get into her pants. When they were posing as husband and wife on the Gulf Coast, at night he'd hang up his Quisling Coastal Marine uniform and give her a friendly kiss on the cheek.

She grew to like those kisses, look forward to them. She was actually a little sorry when he was posted to command the Coastal Marines on the gunboat *Thunderbolt* and the time came for the real operation to commence.

One hot night, bored and unable to sleep, rather than crawl out onto the roof of the neighbor's apartment and sleep, they'd stayed in on their sweat-soaked bed and rather groggily groped each other. It had started out as a few good-natured elbows thrown, and then matters escalated. They'd both satisfied each other enough to fall asleep, exhausted, but you couldn't say they'd been lovers—more like kids messing around.

Still, the night stayed with her for months after. She could still feel his youthful, hard cock in her imagination. It featured in a few of her fantasies.

He sat, staring at her.

"I know you're not afraid," she said. "I'm curious, and I can't believe you aren't."

"Once an old tent mate of mine tried to argue me into trying sex with him," Valentine said. "Strangely, this feels a little like that conversation. Not sure it would feel natural to me."

"I've always found unnatural a lot more exciting," she said. She leaned over and grabbed him, pulled him to her by the front of his shirt.

They found themselves kissing. Impossible to say who started it. As for the disrobing, he took the initiative, with increasing excitement as she explored him for the second time in their lives.

He shivered every time she touched him, twitching about like an overexcited horse. Perhaps he hadn't been fucking that Pole in Helsinki. He jerked like a teen with a girl's hand on his prick for the first time.

He proved an impatient and overeager lover. He spent himself rather sooner than she would have liked, though he was tenderer than most men afterward. If he had the impulse to slink out of her bed like a restless dog, he suppressed it admirably.

Giggling, she admitted to herself that he really wasn't that good. Maybe it was nervousness, or he was just uncomfortable with physical intimacy with her. Or maybe she really was "one of the guys" to him, and he'd just dipped his toe into emotional bisexuality.

Or perhaps it was the tiny bunk. There wasn't really room for two people on either the top or the bottom bunk. She couldn't even really open herself the way she wanted to. The ship's side got in her way on one side, and the high rails for the bunks made it difficult to get comfortable on the other. Only afterward did it occur to her that they could have just piled a couple of plastic-covered sea mattresses and all their bedding on the floor.

The journey home was more easily accomplished than the outbound leg.

They traveled with Sime and the Canadian and Greenland/Iceland representatives. Duvalier wasn't even aware that there were people in Greenland, but the post-2022 climate had created a thin strip of habitable earth on the southern coast of the huge, icy island, and the Scandinavians had returned with their fishing boats.

Valentine joked that now that the Resistance had committed to continuing the struggle, it did not matter so much if the delegates all were lost in the chill northern latitudes or not.

They were back by late August, sped on by rumors of action heating up in Texas and Kentucky and all along the Appalachians. Valentine spoke often of August and September being a forbidding time of year, historically.

They were met by a small delegation welcoming them back to the Kentucky Alliance. Ahn-Kha's name was cheered. His ears stuck out horizontally true, a sure sign of embarrassment. The summer heat and humidity of Southern Indiana felt dreadful after the Baltic cool.

Colonel Lambert was part of the official delegation, of course, along with Captain Patel.

"You arrived just in time," Patel said, speaking

mostly to Valentine. "All hell's breaking loose to the south. The Georgia Control is attacking on a wide front. They've got troops stretching from Nashville to the Daniel Boone National Forest."

"When did it start?"

"Day before yesterday."

They'd been travelling for ten days. Did it have anything to do with events in Kokkola? Were the ripples already spreading?

At least Valentine had made no more mention of getting her out of the fight.

"I guess we're alone in the fight. If there is going to be fighting."

"Southern Command will get back in it, if I have anything to do with it," Sime said. "I didn't realize until this neutrality proposal how weak they must be. Nobody makes an offer like that if they think they have a chance at winning. It's a bluff, and I intend that we should call it."

They said farewell to Sime at the Evansville airport. A little two-engine scout reconnaissance plane was waiting for him to speed him back to Texarkana. Ahn-Kha shook his hand, his hairy face grave.

"We might have done better to negotiate," Sime said. "Without the Lifeweavers—"

"Without the Lifeweavers we have a few more years of Bears, Cats, and Wolves," Valentine said. "They'll dwindle and die."

"We've attempted to breed them," Sime said. "That generation is at least a decade away from beginning to be useful."

"Ordinary people are going to win this," Valentine said. "Ordinary people in the Kurian Zone. Watch for it."

"I hope you're right, Valentine," Sime said. "Well, good luck."

He shook Duvalier's hand—she still thought his touch a trifle reptilian, and he still reminded her of a Kansas Quisling, through and through. He boarded his plane.

"Well, the dice are thrown," Colonel Lambert said.

They had a minute while the plane taxied and everyone moved out of the way.

Alessa Duvalier chuckled. "Valentine, you used to play chess. I sort of remember you got into it in Omaha with some bigwig there. What was it called when you move a few pieces at the opening to tempt your opponent into doing something stupid?"

"A gambit," Valentine said. "You sacrifice a pawn or two in order to get your opponent to open up his defenses."

"But whose gambit was it?" Ahn-Kha asked. "Ours or theirs?"

"Maybe we only took a pawn in Kokkola," Duvalier said. "And now we're alone in the fight. We have to live with that."

"See that you do," Valentine said. "But it always was our fight."

GLOSSARY

Bears—The toughest of the Hunter classes, Bears are famously ferocious and the shock troops of Southern Command, working themselves up into a berserk rage that allows them to take on even the Reapers at night. Also famous for surviving dreadful wounds that would kill an ordinary man, though how completely they heal varies slightly according to injury and individual.

Cats—The spies and saboteurs of the Hunter group, Cats are stealthy individuals with keen eyesight and superb reflexes. Women tend to predominate in this class, though whether this is due to their bodies' adapting better to the Lifeweaver changes, or to the fact that Cat activities require the ability to blend in and choose a time for acting rather than more aggressive action is a matter of opinion.

Golden Ones—A species of humanoid Grog related to the Gray Ones. Golden Ones are tall bipeds (though they will still sometimes go down on all fours in a sprint) mostly covered with short, butternut-colored fur that grows longer about the head-mane. Expressive batlike ears, a strong snout, and wide-set, calm eyes give them a somewhat ursine appearance, though the mouth is broader. They are considered by most to have a higher culture than their Gray relations. Their civilization is organized along more recognizable groups, with a loose caste system rather than the strictly tribal organizations of the Gray Ones.

Gray Ones—A species of humanoid Grog related to the Golden Ones. Their hair is shorter than that of their relatives, save for longer tufts that grow to warm the forearms and calves/ankles. Their bodies are covered in thick gray hide, which grows into armorlike slabs on some males. They are bipeds in the fashion of gorillas, with much heavier and more powerful forearms than their formidable Golden One relations, wide where their cousins are tall. Unless organized by humans otherwise, they tend to group into tribes of extended families, though in a few places (like St. Louis) there are multitribe paramountcies controlling other tribes in a feudal manner.

Grogs—An unspecific word for any kind of life-form imported or created by the Kurians, unknown to Earth pre-2022. Some say it's a version of "grok," since so many of the strange, and sometimes horrific, life-forms cooperate; others maintain that the term arises from the "graaaaawg!" cry of the Gray Ones when wounded or calling for assistance in a fight. In most cases among the military of Southern Command, when the word "Grog" is used it is commonly understood to be a Gray

One, as they will use other terms for different life-forms.

Heartroot—A Golden One staple, it is a fungoid like a very thick mushroom. Rich in proteins, carbohydrates, and fats, it is ground into animal feed. It is difficult to eat raw, but baked and coated in honey, it is reasonably tasty. It may also be braised or roasted and added to stews to provide more protein content when meat is short.

Hunters—A common term for those humans modified by the Lifeweavers for enhanced abilities of one sort or another. Up until 2070, the Hunters worked closely under the direction of the Lifeweavers in Southern Command, but after so many of them fled or were killed during Consul Solon's incursion, the Hunter castes were directly managed by Southern Command.

Kurians—A faction of the Lifeweavers from the planet Kur who learned how to extend their life span through the harvesting of vital aura. They invaded Earth once before in our prehistory and formed the basis for many legends of vampires. Although physically weak compared to their Reaper avatars, Kurians are masters of disguise, subterfuge, and manipulation. They tend to dwell in high, well-defended towers so as to better maintain mental links with their Reaper avatars. Face-to-face contact with one is rare except for their most trusted Quislings. Some have compared the Kurian need for vital aura with an addict's need for a drug, especially since the consumption of vital aura sometimes leaves the Kurian in a state of reduced sensibility. Most Kurians live life on simple terms—concerned with whether they are safe, do they have enough sources of vital aura, and how can they gather a large supply and keep it against their hungry and rapacious relatives.

Kurian Agents—The Kurian answer to the Hunter class, Kurian agents are very trusted humans, often trained from early childhood to utilize psychic powers similar to those of their Kurian masters. There are reports of Kurian agents able to assume the appearance of other races and genders, confuse the minds of their opponents, and even read minds to uncover traitors.

Legworms—Long, centipede-like creatures introduced to Earth in 2022 that reach lengths of more than forty feet and heights of eight feet or more. They are a useful but stupid creature, able to bear heavy loads, but can be urged to move at a pace above a walk only by a skilled rider and constant prodding. Their chewy flesh from around the hundreds of clawlike legs is high in protein and edible, barely, and the skin from their eggs makes a tough, breathable form of leather that is a valuable trade good if harvested before the newly hatched legworms consume it. They lay eggs in fall and become sluggish and torpid in winter, when they gather together in masses to shelter their eggs.

Lifesign—An invisible signature given off by all living organisms, in proportion to their vital aura. Reapers can detect it, especially at night, and are able to home in on humans from miles away. It is possible for a human to train him- or herself to reduce lifesign through mental exercises or meditation, and it is possible to camouflage lifesign by hiding in densely wooded areas or among large groups of livestock. Earth and metals do tend to block it. There are some who maintain that a sufficient quantity of simple aluminum foil can conceal lifesign, especially if one keeps one's head properly wrapped, but empirical evidence is lacking, since individuals who try to sneak past Reapers by relying on layers of foil rarely return.

Lifeweavers—A race thought to have populated some nine worlds, modifying or creating an unknown number of life-forms. They appear to be some form of octopus crossed with a bat, equally at home in the water or gliding between treetops. A faction of Lifeweaver scientists on a planet called Kur created a schism when they began to use the vital aura from other living creatures to extend their own life span. Soon open warfare broke out. The Lifeweavers were successful in keeping the Kurians confined to Kur for millennia, but the Kurians managed to break out and invaded Earth and an unknown number of other Lifeweaver-populated worlds in 2022, our time.

Logistics Commandos—A branch of Southern Command that concerns itself with acquiring difficult-to-obtain supplies, mostly medicines and technology. They do this by purchase, trade, and outright theft. It is common for veteran Hunters to go into the Logistics Commandos as a form of retirement from fighting.

Moondaggers—A religious military order that fights for the Kurians. They were created and closely directed by a branch of the New Universal Church that is more patriarchal and theocratic than the typical churchmen. Famous for their brutality, they were key in putting down the revolts in the Great Plains Gulag in 2072. They were nearly destroyed, however, when they resorted to similar tactics against the legworm ranchers in Kentucky in 2075–76.

New Universal Church—A religious order of trusted Quislings who help manage the spiritual and intellectual needs of the human subject populations in the Kurian Zone. Much of their time is spent rationalizing the deaths of those taken by the Reapers and keeping the human breeding stock quiescent. Higher-level churchmen are often trained by the Kurians in similar psychic skills as those used by Kurian Agents. The New Universal Church might justly be compared to the older Anglican one in that there is a "High Church" of important intellectuals and decision makers who provide executive-level direction to the Church's activities. They gather intelligence and carry out their operations through their agents and small but deadly Special Forces units. Then there is a "Low Church" of foot soldiers, so to speak, who provide day-to-day service to the human population in the form of hospitals, entertainment centers, and organizations such as the Youth Vanguard and the Women's Army Auxiliaries. The Low Church organs also act as one of the filters for selecting candidates for the Reapers, especially among the sick, unemployable, and troublesome. The New Universal Church, for all its talk of "redeeming mankind, and reclaiming our promise," is resolutely unforgiving of physical weakness and social misfits.

Quickwood—An olive tree–like plant that acts as a catalyst in a Reaper's bloodstream, freezing it in place and killing it quickly. The only drawback to Quickwood is its rarity, as the small supply that Southern Command managed to acquire was virtually destroyed by Solon's forces, though some seeds were saved and a few plants now thrive in both the wild and in controlled and defended environments. The Kurians are working on modifying their Reapers to be immune to Quickwood, but for now the Reapers deal with a Quickwood wound by a fast self-amputation, if practicable.

Quislings—Humans who work for the Kurian Order. There is a great deal of dispute as to what exactly constitutes a Quisling, but usually someone at the bottom rung of the social ladder who follows orders is not considered to be actively supporting the Kurians, even if he or she happens to drive a collection van for the Reapers. Quislings are more commonly held to be those actively working for their master Kurians in pursuit of immunity for themselves and their families. Quislings who do great service in the name of their Kurian lords are sometimes awarded a "brass ring" granting immunity from the Reapers to themselves and their immediate families.

Reapers—The avatars of the Kurian Order, Reapers are very powerful humanoids that form the basis of most of our vampire legends. With only a vestigial reproductive system and a simplified digestive process based on the consumption of blood and a small amount of flesh, Reapers are fast, strong, and deadly, particu-

larly at night when the connection with their Kurian
master is strongest. They are strong enough to tear
through metal doors and hatches, can jump to second-
or sometimes third-story windows, and can run as fast
as most cars can move on all but the best-maintained
roads. Hunters find Reapers most vulnerable during
daylight hours, when the Kurian connection is weaker,
especially directly after a feeding, when the Reaper is
sleepy from the blood intake and the Kurian is dis-
tracted by the absorption of aura.

Twisted Cross—A military faction of the Kurian Order, the members of the Twisted Cross use trained humans to operate fighting Reapers in a manner similar
to a Kurian lord's. The Twisted Cross activities in North
America were stillborn when the Golden Ones revolted
and destroyed their base in 2067. There are reports of
more-successful Twisted Cross military formations operating around the Black Sea and in Southeastern Europe and Asia Minor, the Asian subcontinent, and
Japan.

Vital Aura—The energy created by all living things,
but enriched and refined in sentient, emotionally developed creatures. Thus a human will have much more
vital aura than, say, a much heavier cow or pig. This
energy is what sustains Kurians over their extended,
and seemingly limitless, life span.

Wolves—The great guerilla fighters of the Hunter
class, Wolves are famous for their endurance, senses of
smell and hearing, and ability to operate without logistical support. They are the most numerous of the
Hunter classes, trained by the Lifeweavers to be a

match for the fearsome organs of the Kurian Order. They can cover long stretches of ground in their all-day runs, often evading even mechanized opponents. They often act as the eyes and ears of larger operations, or provide a communications link for Cats operating alone in the Kurian Zone and Bear teams needing support and guidance on their way to hit a key target.

Baltic League—A collection of Scandinavian and Baltic-shore countries composing the largest freehold in Europe. While the Kurians do control the major cities of the coasts, extending as far north as Trondheim, they rule with a very light hand and their position is precarious. Much of their vital aura comes through trade or headhunters who steal victims from farther south. While not militarily powerful in its own right, the Baltic League has what is perhaps the best information-gathering network in the world. It builds and distributes electronics that allow the freeholds to communicate, maintains a shortwave news network (often jammed locally by the New Universal Church or contra-programmed) and manufactures arms to be shipped to rebels elsewhere. While the Baltic League is probably strong enough to get rid of the Kurians entirely, it prefers the very weak hold of the present Kurians to whatever scorched-earth tactics might be used if it were to execute a coup to get rid of them entirely.

Freehold—Any area in active resistance to the Kurian

Order. Every man, woman, and child in a freehold tends to be familiar with the use of a variety of weapons to secure their homesteads, and highly motivated to keep out of the grasp of the Reapers.

Kentucky Alliance—Ranging over three states, the Kentucky Alliance at this time includes some of the mountainous coal-mining areas of West Virginia, much of Kentucky, with influence spreading to North-Central Tennessee all the way to the mountains north of Nashville, and of course the small industrial city of Evansville in Southern Indiana on the Ohio near the operating area of Colonel Lambert's Southern Command brigade assisting the new freehold. It is a mixture of legworm clans, who ranch their enormous mounts and smuggle goods from Missouri across the Appalachians to the Virginia tidewater, townsfolk, farmers, and miners, with a few bourbon-bottlers thrown in for flavor. It is unique among the freeholds in that it accepts Xeno species introduced by the Kurians as allies, making the first instance of Human/Grog cooperation in the history of the Resistance.

Kurian Zone—Any area controlled by the Kurians and their Quislings. Some are as small as a county, while others span an area that covers several states. The level of organization and militarization varies wildly. In much of the West, the New Universal Church is a common denominator, organizing social services and political propaganda for the subject people.

United Free Republics (and their military arm, Southern Command)—While not the largest of the freeholds in North America (that would be Alaska and the Yukon) or the best organized (that would be the flinty Green Mountain Boys with their town-hall system and county-by-county headquarters), they were, up until the 2070s, the fastest-growing and most aggressive of the freeholds in North America. The Free Republics have mini-territories in Missouri, the southeastern tip of Kansas, Arkansas, Eastern Oklahoma, and Texas save for a few spots on the coast, some of the Rio Grande valley, and a good deal of drier country bordering New Mexico. The political structure is very similar to that of the old United States, and it uses a slightly modified version of the Constitution to govern the "several states" that it includes. Self-sufficient in food and energy, and with a well-armed populace that is capable with even support weapons that are handy in most homes and garages, it lacks only advanced, high-tech manufacturing capability and air resources to control the Mississippi and the skies over the central portion of the old United States.

THE NOVELS OF THE VAMPIRE EARTH

by

E. E. Knight

Louisiana, 2065. A lot has changed in the 43rd year of the Kurian Order. Bloodthirsty Reapers have come to Earth to establish a New Order built on the harvesting of human souls. They rule the planet. And when night falls, as sure as darkness, they will come.

This is the Vampire Earth.

WAY OF THE WOLF
CHOICE OF THE CAT
TALE OF THE THUNDERBOLT
VALENTINE'S RISING
VALENTINE'S RESOLVE
VALENTINE'S EXILE
FALL WITH HONOR
WINTER DUTY
MARCH IN COUNTRY
APPALACHIAN OVERTHROW
BALTIC GAMBIT

Available wherever books are sold or at
penguin.com

R155